Rupert the Devil

by
Jeanne Montague

Dales Large Print Books
Long Preston, North Yorkshire,
England.

British Library Cataloguing in Publication Data.

Montague, Jeanne
 Rupert the devil.

A catalogue record for this book is
available from the British Library

ISBN 1-85389-575-X pbk

First published in Great Britain by Robert Hale Ltd., 1976

Published in Large Print September, 1995 by arrangement
with Jeanne Montague.

F
928410

Dales Large Print is an imprint of
Library Magna Books Ltd.
Printed and bound in Great Britain by
T.J. Press (Padstow) Ltd., Cornwall, PL28 8RW.

Place me as a signet upon thy heart, as a signet upon thine arm, for Love is as strong as death.

(Canticles, viii, 6.
The Secret Lore of Magic.
Idries Shah.)

ONE

As dawn slid under the curtains, rising like mist to creep across the panelled room, Venetia Denby awoke and could not sleep again.

She rolled over onto her back, aware of the unfamiliar mattress beneath, the alien pillow under her head, staring into the shadows of the tester, seeing the black solidity of the bulbous posts at the foot, the watery sheen of the silken drapes, finer than the serge ones on her own bed at home.

A shiver ran through her, but she stayed quiet, unwilling to rouse her sister Ella, who slept soundly beside her. In that still hour, when even the birds had not started to call, she wanted no harsh discord; happy to be alone with her thoughts to relish the delight of being in Oxford, at last.

For a while she hugged this tremendous fact to herself, then she slipped out of bed, padding across the polished wooden floor with its Turkey rugs resembling colourful islands on a brown sea. The casement was tightly shut against the night air, and Venetia flung it wide, inhaling the exhilarating dewy freshness, leaning far out and gazing enraptured, at the city spread below. Oxford, the Royalist headquarters from almost the beginning of the war, was the place which had become Venetia's lodestar—and now, she was really there.

Her mind was still dazed with the speed of events of the past days—the sudden flight from their home in the Cotswolds which had been threatened by advancing Roundhead troops. It had been a last minute rush; servants jostling each other as they ran, emerging from doorways carrying their own or their master's private possessions. In the courtyard had been a confusion of neighing horses, sweating grooms, carriages and wagons into which refugees and goods were hastily piled. Venetia's stepmother, youngest child in her arms, big-bellied with the next due at any time, had frantically tried to round up the toddlers, who were wilfully running about, getting in everyone's way, while their nurses distractedly attempted to control them.

Samuel Denby, big and floridly hand-some, looking much more the jovial country squire than a fighting man, had stamped about giving orders. Dogs had barked, while children cried, mingling this uproar with that of arguing, tearful female voices, but eventually the cavalcade had creaked into motion, beginning its journey to Oxford.

On arrival the previous night, it had been too late to do anything except pack the little ones off and fall, exhausted, into bed. But now it was a glorious sparkling morning and Venetia stretched her arms wide in a transport of joy. It was good to be alive on this day of 15th July, 1643—to be eighteen years old, and part of this bustling city, crowded with troops and Courtiers, noblemen and their ladies, instead of stuck in some dull backwater, missing all the excitement. Soon her betrothed, Michael Haywood, would be calling, and, in a matter of hours, her dearest ambition would be fulfilled when he took her to meet his commander, Prince Rupert.

Her heart thudded at the thought—chin cupped in her hand, she leaned on the window-ledge, dreaming. It was as if the Fates had conspired to bring about this war especially for her, answering her prayers and her longing, when she had spun that strong web of want, its threads reaching out over time and space to draw him towards her.

She had heard his name long before the war—back in 1636, when her father had returned from a rare visit to Whitehall Palace, and regaled his children with stories of the Court and news of the arrival of the King's nephews, two German Princes, Charles Louis and his brother, Rupert. It was their first time in England, the homeland of their mother—she was Elizabeth, only sister of Charles I, and had been married young to Frederick V, Elector Palatine and Duke of Bavaria.

Venetia's father had enthused about Rupert—an adventurous youngster, already an experienced soldier.

Rupert—it had appeared very strange to her English ears then, foreign, exotic, variant, so they told her, of 'Robert'. She was ten and impressionable, repeating it to herself—Rupert—Rupert. The sort of name to whisper into her pillow, tossing all night to the rhythm of it.

Locked away in the peaceful village, occupied with her studies, domestic duties and the perplexities of growing up, Venetia forgot the Prince, yet, somewhere at the back of consciousness, there remained the image built up by her father's words. Then, suddenly, the political seesaw tilted and he went home to help Charles Louis form an army to try and win back the Palatinate. Their father had lost it along with Bohemia, long ago when he had set himself up in opposition to the powerful Catholic, Ferdinand of Austria.

England raised money to back them. Young men seeking adventure offered their swords in the service of the widowed Queen Elizabeth and her gallant sons. In Venetia's own family, Mallory, her eldest brother and fledgling soldier, volunteered to go. She ached to be a boy, to fight beside him and for him! The Queen and her cause were but grey shapes, meaning little to her—it was Rupert who was real! Rupert whom she longed to serve!

Mallory marched away, full of high hopes and ambition, and Michael went with him. Weeks passed, and they arrived home unexpectedly full of stories of the battle of Vlotho in Westphalia, and how the Palatine army had been vastly outnumbered by the Austrians. Prince Rupert, a Colonel at eighteen, had led the cavalry with reckless bravery, but they were beaten and he was captured and shut up in the grim castle of Lintz.

The months flowed by, as smoothly as the Danube beyond his prison walls. Venetia performed the daily round learning the housewifely skills which it was appropriate that she should know in anticipation of being a bride. She was maturing quickly; there was a glow now in Michael's eyes when he came on his decorous visits. An answering response stirred her blood, filling her with unrest, making her wish that he was not quite so circumspect in his treatment of her.

But now, in England, trouble was brewing. There was strife in London between King Charles and his Parliament, its ripples spreading wide over the country. In their mellow Tudor manor on the borders of a snug village, the Denbys found their own lives disrupted. Venetia understood little of the principles involved, but she was upset by the loud dissenting voices of her father, backed up by his sons, Mallory and Jonathan, as they argued with friends who could not share their support of the King.

Their closest neighbours, Tobias Fletcher and his boy, Giles, questioned the concept of absolute monarchy, the tax demands and foreign policy, the management of the Irish affairs and, most of all, the behaviour of his French Queen. They shared the general alarm at her popish agents in Court, the freedom of priests and Jesuits, the virtual suspension of anti-Catholic laws.

The Fletchers visited the Denby house no more, and Venetia was forbidden to speak with them. The clouds were gathering ominously, and the storm broke while people were still trying to convince themselves that Civil War could never happen.

Although their father's face was serious, Mallory and Jonathan were unable to conceal their delight when, one morning in August, Michael came fresh from the courier, waving letters and shouting;

'Prince Rupert has landed at Tynemouth with his brother, Maurice. They have come to fight for King Charles!'

Venetia had been half way down the wide staircase when she heard him. The name broke like the blare of trumpets in her ears, as the men shouted it below. It swelled on a surge of sound—Rupert of the Rhine!

That stormy petrel had been released at the pleas of his Uncle Charles, who needed him by his side in the coming conflict and nothing could stop Venetia's brothers from riding to Nottingham to join him.

The village settled back into its usual somnolence after the flurry of departure, but now its serenity was ruffled by the backwash of events shattering the world beyond the softly rolling hills which sheltered the valley. A post-boy bearing news, a sudden influx of troops moving through the area, and Squire Denby's lads coming home on leave.

Because of their service at Vlotho, Mallory and Michael offered themselves as volunteers in Rupert's Lifeguard. Samuel Denby, unable to resist the call, rode with them, leaving Venetia to support her stepmother, Catherine. His first wife had died in childbirth, and he had married again, this delicate, pretty woman, not a great deal older than Venetia. A new family of brothers and sisters had arrived with depressing regularity, rendering her even more helpless. Venetia found that with her father absent, the steward, bailiff and tenant farmers were turning to herself for guidance.

It was hard to have to sit, listening to complaints, trying to balance accounts, while the weeks slipped by and her head was reeling with stirring tales sent home in letters by Michael or the brothers. Venetia was able to glut herself on news of the Prince, no man in England was given more flamboyant publicity by both sides. The King favoured him above all his advisers, granting him his own command, General of the Horse, with special permission to take orders from no one except His Majesty. His shock tactics of the headlong cavalry charge rocked the Roundheads. His daring excursions behind the enemy lines in a variety of disguises, his dramatic appearances when least expected, his phenomenal luck in coming out of the most desperate scraps unscathed, all added to the legend. The Roundheads began to look on him with superstitious dread, circulating stories of brutality and devilish practices.

At first, the Royalists had been confident of an early victory, for their army consisted, in the main, of aristocrats, officered by gentry whose education had involved swordsmanship. They had fully expected to put in their places the tapesters and tradesmen who were generally thought to fill the ranks of the enemy.

Lately, however, Venetia had been aware of a change in attitude; it was not going to be so simple.

A shaft of bright sunlight cut into Venetia's eyes, rousing her. Birds were whistling cheerily in the trees level with her window, and Oxford was beginning to stir into life.

She launched herself across the room, jumping on the bed, pummelling her sister. 'Ella! Wake up! Lord, what a sluggard you are!'

Ella grumbled crossly, tucking down under the quilt. 'Go away!' And it was not until Venetia shouted that there were half a dozen young officers clamouring outside the bedroom door, that her china-blue eyes snapped open.

While she dressed, Venetia reflected that no doubt the lie would be truth soon enough for Ella, just fifteen, was man-mad, and there had been a distinct shortage in their village of late. Meg, her maid, rustled about, unpacking bags, shaking the creases from hastily folded gowns and getting them on to hangers in the cupboards. She chattered breezily, hoping to convince the young ladies, and herself, that everything was normal and that they had not just been uprooted and flung upon the mercies of a strange town!

There was a hesitant tap, and the door opened wide enough to admit Aunt Hortense, all whispering black taffeta and clicking strings of pearls. She reminded Venetia of an agitated bat.

'My dears,' she smiled and bobbed, wisps of hair escaping from under her lace cap. 'Poor little lambs! I trust you managed to sleep. And your sweet stepmother, so near her time—and your father already departed to rejoin his regiment, such a conscientious spirit!'

Venetia thought it more likely that he had had enough of squalling brats and hysterical women.

'Oh, this war—this terrible war!' Hortense fluttered to the window. 'Oxford was once so peaceful, and now 'tis full of soldiers. You've no idea how disorderly they are! The tales I could tell you, were it not for the tenderness of your years! Why, not long ago, the Prince himself separated two quarrelling drunken troopers with a pole-axe!'

Venetia, washing at the pewter basin which stood on the flat top of the carved oak chest, managed to ask casually 'Prince Rupert? Have you seen him, Aunt?'

'I have caught a glimpse, once or twice, when he clattered by on that great black horse of his. A most restless person, I understand, always off on some skirmish with his troopers, spends little time at Court and practically none with the society of the town!'

'He's a soldier, aunt, and there *is* a war on.' Venetia stood still while Meg fastened the strings of the finely-pleated damask skirt which had gone on after the linen shift and a couple of petticoats.

'I know, dear, but he is also Royal, and people expect decorous behaviour from someone so eminent.' There was no doubt that Hortense was enjoying the war, it gave her endless topics for gossip. 'He has made himself mighty unpopular with the Courtiers. I hear that he is so proud and domineering, so hot-tempered and rude at the Council-table.'

Venetia eased her arms into the full sleeves of her bodice, turning to the mirror on the dressing-table to fasten the front. 'That is not what Mallory says.'

'Oh, Mallory!' Her aunt threw up her hands and eyes in mock despair. 'He will not hear a word against his chief. He is typical of the wild young men who positively idolize Prince Rupert.'

A commotion below in the courtyard announced the arrival of the Denby brothers and Michael, come to greet the newcomers. Excitement dried Venetia's mouth; though she romanticized about the Prince, it was Michael who had awakened her senses, rousing her body to passion. A desperate urgency thrust aside convention on their rare meetings; he had stopped treating her as if she were some untouchable holy relic, and they were both fully aware of his continual danger.

She quickly put the finishing touches to her toilet, and within minutes the room was filled with loud male voices, the glint of steel, flashy clothing and big boots. She was swept into Michael's arms, breathing in the sharp smell of outdoors while his mouth closed on hers, stabbing her with an instant reminder of stolen hours of love.

He released her and held her away, at arms' length, grinning with delight;

'Sweetheart! Here, let me look at you. Jesus! You grow more fair every time I see you.'

Sometimes his adoration worried her; she knew that she could not return it. They had been betrothed when she was still in her cradle, and the marriage had been arranged, as was customary, with lands, property and religion of prime consideration. They had played together as children, and he was always rather patronizing, provoking her into attempting to equal him in acts of daring; climbing a higher tree, swimming a more turbulent stretch of river, enjoying hearing the fear in his voice as her horse gathered his limbs for that spring over a more formidable obstacle than Michael thought it prudent to tackle. 'Don't, Venetia! You will get hurt!'

When he had come back from Vlotho, a toughened suntanned soldier, he had seemed even more superior, but had been packed off to London and the study of Law. He kicked his heels at the Inns of Court, chewed his pen, plagued his tutors and racketed around with the other students, glad when finally the call to arms released him. He came to say goodbye to Venetia before leaving for Nottingham and found that she had developed from a scrawny tomboy into a very beautiful woman. He had fallen in love completely and for ever.

She knew that she was very lucky for he was a pleasant person to be with; handsome, slightly built but sinewy, surprisingly strong, with a thin, sensitive face, shy hazel eyes under thick brown lashes, and quizzical brows over which fell untidy strands of pale hair. There was something endearingly vague and rumpled about his whole appearance, and he had a hesitant way of glancing across, as if for approval of what he said, and of laughing in mock dismay when anybody outwitted him.

Aunt Hortense was flustered by this sudden influx of hearty warriors, rattling their swords and scuffing her rugs. 'La, I don't know what things are coming to these days. Really, sirs, this is a young girl's bedchamber! Not one of your parade grounds or rude soldiers' quarters!'

'Nor the tents of the camp-followers, eh?' Mallory put in gleefully.

'Hush, sir!' she chided, mouth turned down reprovingly. 'Don't mention such loose wantons before gentlewomen! And surely Jonathan is too young even to know of their presence.'

Mallory threw back his tawny mane of hair and yelped with laughter. 'God dammit, he's seventeen! He's not confined himself to purely military activities, I can assure you!'

Michael's arm was around Venetia's waist again, pressing her to him while the Denby's engaged their aunt in conversation, their broad shoulders between her and the lovers.

'God, I must see you alone,' Michael whispered into the curls on her temple. 'It has been so long—'

Three months since she had lain in his arms, deep in the night when the whole household was asleep, on his last, snatched leave. Those thrilling, tormenting, unsatisfying embraces, marred because he was so afraid of making her pregnant; kind and thoughtful of him, of course, but she longed to be swept away by an impetuous passion which tossed caution to the wind. She was tempted to urge for permission to marry quickly, but there was a strange reluctance within her.

'I don't see how we can arrange it, with Aunt Hortense so watchful over my

24

morals,' she teased him, twining her fingers in his hair.

'The evenings are balmy in the fields by the river. Come there tonight with me,' he urged.

She prevaricated, while her mouth smiled and her mind boiled with the thought uppermost in it. 'You must first of all take me to see your Prince. This 'Rupert' that you praise to the skies.'

Because she felt guilty, she twisted away from him with a provocative rustle of skirts, leaning forward at the looking-glass to adjust the fine linen collar with its trim of point-lace, which draped the low neckline of her tight, high-waisted bodice. Sometimes she marvelled at her ability to be so two-faced, wishing Michael were not so easily duped, telling herself, crossly, that it was all partly his fault; he was forever talking about Rupert, whom he admired so much.

He frowned, his prime objective to make love to her as soon as possible. 'I'll see what can be arranged.'

'That is of no use!' Caution fled, and her voice betrayed her before she controlled herself, adding, more reasonably; 'I would like to see him today.' She gave a little laugh, slipping her arm through his. 'Really Michael, you have stirred up an almighty curiosity in me to set eyes on this paragon.'

TWO

Oxford had welcomed the King when he moved in to make it his headquarters in the winter of 1642. Undergraduates gladly forsook their books to join with the townsfolk in throwing up earthworks and digging trenches to strengthen the fortifications.

The more sober members of the community might deplore the fact that the University languished with so many scholars abandoning their studies, and complain about the drunkenness and brawling, but the tradesmen rubbed their hands in delight. Never had they been able to charge such high prices for food, drink and beds.

Now, in the place of gownsmen, it was a more common sight to see a gang of high-spirited horsemen, covered in dust, swirling their drover's whips and herding plundered cattle through the streets to the quadrangles where they were slaughtered to supplement army rations. Recruits were drilled in every available square, troopers and Courtiers billeted in spare rooms, and the whole exciting, colourful disruption worked its magic on the female population as it always will, when a sleepy city suddenly erupts into a garrison town.

The sight of so many virile males far from home, loved ones and restraining influences, expending their splendid energy on marching, training and learning how to kill, drove them mad. It was an irresistible challenge and the most demure damsel acted the harlot, while mature matrons behaved as if this was their last chance of youth, before old age set in!

Venetia needed no second bidding to snatch up a shawl and ride out with Michael through the wide, busy streets, in the direction of the meadows by the river where recruits were mustering for the Prince's inspection. Halfway there, they were met by two riders who hailed her brothers noisily and with much doffing of plumed hats and bowing when Venetia was introduced. They were as gaily dressed as for a party, one in green silk with gold swagging, the other in rose velvet, and they wafted a gust of musky perfume.

The green-clad beau was French with an impressive title which Venetia did not quite catch, but the others called him "Etienne". His slim companion, Adrian Carey, was given to graceful gestures and posturing, when he was not engaged in watching Etienne with shining eyes. He reminded Venetia of a rather pretty girl. He lost no time in acquainting her with the fact that he was an actor, which surprised her for she had not imagined that there would be players among the King's troopers.

'My dear, why not?' he said, toying with his red-brown ringlets. 'I don't say that I actually take sword and engage the enemy, but there are other ways in which one can assist. I was on the London stage, but since those confounded Roundheads closed the theatres, I have been on the road, following our armies, giving them entertainment.'

'Where is Madame d'Auvergne this morning?' Mallory asked the Frenchman, who heaved his elegant shoulders in a shrug.

'*Mon Dieu!* I defy anyone to get my wife out of bed at an early hour,' and he gave

Mallory an odd smile as he added: 'You should know that, Monsieur.'

They were blocking the road, starting an argument with a carter who wanted to get past. After a brief exchange of insults they moved on, still laughing, while Etienne waved and kissed his fingers to women who had come to the upper windows attracted by the noise. Venetia felt unreasonably irritated at the way in which Ella was goggling at him in open-mouthed admiration. She did not want to be bothered with her; as it was, her ears were still ringing with Aunt Hortense's reluctant goodbyes, after warning her for the twentieth time to be cautious, to be vigilant and to be sure to be home before dark!

The certainty that the outing was about to be blighted was increased by the sound of hooves behind her. It was the youngest member of Denby's first family, Timothy. He was spurring his fat pony after them, hair tousled, clothes flung on anyhow. Normally, Venetia felt very protective towards this boy at whose birth their mother had lost her life.

'Hey, wait for me!' He was shouting, making shopkeepers look round as they took down their shutters.

Ella tossed her head and scowled. 'Who wants a baby like you with them?'

'Baby yourself!' retorted Timothy hotly, his chin setting in that obstinate way which meant trouble.

'You cried because you had to leave your rabbits behind.' Ella delivered this home-thrust unmercifully, and Venetia's palm itched to slap her, well aware that Etienne and his friend were looking back with amused grins, while Mallory's expression grew dark. If they did not behave, he would wheel round and escort them home and her morning would be ruined.

Timothy had deliberately ridden his mount too close to his sister so that her beast swerved. 'You are just a great ugly girl. I'm going to ask the Prince if I can join his Lifeguard!'

It was still cool in the meadow, purple clover and blaze of yellow buttercups starring the lush green, a few tenuous strands of mist clinging near the water, and there was that clarity over all which promised a hot day. The recruits were beginning to straggle in, a motley assortment, armed with a miscellany of pikes, rusty swords and unwieldy ancient muskets. Their reasons for enlisting were as varied as their weapons, mostly in the expectation of action, looting and pay.

'Although there will be little likelihood of money,' remarked Mallory, casting an eye over them. 'I haven't had much since I joined. We mostly supply our own needs. The army is hopelessly in arrears and they'll have to 'live on the country' like the rest of us.'

'Plundering, d'you mean?' Venetia glanced at him, shocked.

Etienne was watching her in pleased contemplation as a man might look at a work of art, smoothing his thin line of dark moustache thoughtfully. 'Madame, if the Cavaliers take what they consider to be the spoils of war, remember that they are branded as Delinquents by Parliament and their own estates delivered up to swell the exchequer of the enemy. I am paying for the troop I brought over from France myself, and many are doing the same, providing equipment and meeting the running costs.'

'Of course, His Highness is used to this kind of thing,' Adrian's tone had the edge of malice. 'This is the way they do it in Germany. He will not think twice

31

about leaving plundered country behind him, saying that it is the need of war.'

Unhappily, they dwelt for a moment on every grizzly tale they had ever heard about the armies which ravaged Europe, while the sun shone from a cloudless sky on this typically English scene, where the windmills turned lazily on the horizon, and across the far side of the silver bank of the Cherwell, milkmaids approached the patient cows, armed with yoke and pail.

Beneath a clump of elm trees on the opposite end of the field stood a group of men, their horses cropping the grass in the shade. Their clothing and demeanour, the sound of their voices, cultured and confident, denoted that they were officers.

Venetia dismounted and, with her hand resting lightly on Michael's arm, walked over the sward. As they drew closer, one of those well-bred voices was drawling, 'Such wonderful news, Your Highness, that of Prince Maurice so soundly beating Sir William Waller at Roundaway Down.'

She did not need to ask which of the men was Prince Rupert; as soon as she saw him she knew how it would be. The flood of intuition and excitement stopped her voice for a second, then the words to

32

Michael flowed on, glad of something to say, so that she need not just stand struck dumb by the impact of the wonderful and incredible fact that he existed. He was only a few feet away from her, deep in conversation with his adjutants, different somehow from anything she had expected, her dream-picture instantly forgotten by the overpowering reality.

She had not realized his immense height. Mallory was six foot one, but Rupert topped him by at least four inches. He was lean and lithe, moving with an unselfconscious grace, and Venetia could not drag her gaze from his strikingly handsome face; that olive skin, those dark flashing eyes, the high cheek-bones and aquiline nose which gave him a hawk-like appearance. His mouth was beautiful; the upper lip finely cut with a curl which hinted at contempt for incompetence, while the lower was full and firm adding to the strength of his jaw with the slight cleft in the chin.

His hair was dark brown with highlights of rich chestnut where the sun played over his head and it fell from a centre parting, curling across his shoulders and chest. His manner was reserved, austere even, and yet, beneath this apparent control, lay a thinly concealed temper relentless and fierce. Venetia wanted to break through that veneer, to be caught up in the fury, the power, which lay just under the surface, not dormant but held in check.

He was dressed simply, in a well-worn leather doublet thonged down the front, a lace-edged kerchief knotted round his neck, plain burgundy velvet breeches, and boots pulled high up his legs, not rolled over into bucket-tops as were those of some of the other officers. A red silk sash spanned his narrow waist, and a serviceable baldrick carried the swept-hilt rapier which hung at his left hip. A page hovered nearby, holding his feather-loaded hat, his scarlet cloak, and a brace of pistols. At his feet lay a white dog of an unusual breed, shaggy and large, head resting on its paws while it panted in the heat, its black beady eyes fixed on its master through a thick mane of fur.

Mallory presented the members of his family, and he hissed in the ear of the stunned Venetia; 'Curtsey, you fool! He is of the Blood Royal!'

There was no need to remind her; every inch of him shouted the fact aloud. She obeyed her brother, dipping down, skirts spread gracefully then she rose, daring to look up into his face as if he were a god to be worshipped. This was the instant truth of the situation but she did not want it to be known to him; not yet. A brief smile lifted his haughty mouth, the sombre gaze met hers for a second, and when he spoke it was with an accent just strong enough to render the deep cadences of his voice even more fascinating. Its timbre scraped down her spine into her belly and she suddenly needed to sit.

Normally she was noted for witty remarks, well able to give a pert answer to any man. Now, infuriatingly, when she most wanted to make an impression, her mind went blank.

Timothy pushed rudely in front of her, gazing up at his idol. 'Sir, Your Highness...,' he blurted, red to the ears, aware of Ella behind him, arming herself with taunts to goad him later. 'Will you take me into your horse?'

The men laughed but Rupert looked at him seriously. 'A very young recruit, eh? How old are you?'

Timothy drew himself up proudly. 'Eleven, sir.'

35

'So...when I was your age, I wanted to be a trooper too, but they would not let me. You will have to wait, I fear. But you can study war, just as I did. There are many books which will make you a better soldier when the time comes.' He rested a hand on the shoulder of the crestfallen child. 'And what would your sister say if I took you from her? I already have two of her brothers.'

Venetia felt the meadow and everyone there melt away as he looked at her in that way he had, when he really concentrated, as if she was the only person of importance in the world. She was seized by a driving physical longing which astonished her by its force; she had never felt this desperate hunger for Michael, deprived, angry and jealous when the Prince turned away.

A groom was holding the fine stallion, ready for him, ebony coat glistening, leather trappings polished and immaculate. He put his foot in the stirrup and swung up easily, still talking to Timothy.

'I'm sorry to disappoint you, but get on your pony and come with me to review these new men. Then you can at least say that you have ridden with Rupert.'

'By God, he has a very high opinion of

himself!' thought Venetia, furious because he had not spoken to her like that. He wheeled his horse, turning on a couple of subalterns, all love-locks, laces, braid and flash, lounging against a tree-trunk, chattering to an entranced Ella.

'You there!' His stentorian voice brought them to attention. 'Enough of the fallals! We've work to do. To horse, Lieutenant!'

Venetia shivered at the sight of the black scowl on his stern young face. 'He is insufferably conceited!' she remarked to Etienne who was at her elbow, missing nothing of her reactions, raising his peaked, satyr brows quizzically. Everything seemed to amuse him and he laughed aloud when she added, 'I would hate to anger him!'

Rupert rode out into the brilliant sunshine, his eyes raking over the raw material before him and, more than anything on earth, Venetia yearned to be the horse between his velvet-covered thighs, or the reins under his sunburned hand.

' 'Sdeath! He's in the devil of a mood this morning.' Mallory shaded his eyes against the glare. 'Those poor bastards are in for a rough time!'

'Perhaps the Duchess of Richmond said "no" last night.' Adrian had disposed his shapely limbs in the grassy shade and was engaged in nothing more taxing than stringing together a daisy-chain.

Michael was spreading out his cloak for Venetia to sit on and frowned disapprovingly at him. 'He probably did not even ask her. Don't forget, she is the wife of his best friend, and Rupert is the soul of honour!'

He refused to elaborate on this tantalizing bit of information, sitting beside Venetia, elbows on his knees, watching the officers trying to make headway with the clumsy, inept levies. His face darkened as Etienne showed no such compunction, leaning on one elbow, looking up into her face, grinning puckishly, and gossiping.

'A mighty fine woman, Mary Lennox, Richmond's wife. They call her "Butterfly" and this sums her up.'

Mallory had gone to help the Prince. They were riding slowly down the lines, studying the shuffling men who fidgeted nervously under Rupert's eagle eye and Etienne told her some of the problems connected with turning them into competent fighters. The majority had never even heard the ordinary words of command, and were quite without any sense of military discipline. If they were needed urgently for an engagement, the most that the officers could teach would be the basic rules of taking their place in the line of battle, keeping their horses straight in the ranks and advancing to the charge without losing their order. Fortunately, most of the yeomen were used to riding as a matter of course, picking up sword-play as they went along. The foot were a more difficult problem, and the sergeants were sweating it out under the hot sun, struggling to pound a modicum of drill instruction into these confused amateurs.

Etienne watched Venetia watching the unusual beauty and regal bearing of the General of Horse, and murmured, close to her ear, '*Chérie*, your heart is in your eyes! Be more careful, lest Michael note it too.'

There was something about the Chevalier which encouraged confidences, it was almost as if he had been a close friend of long standing and she did not bother to disguise the savage note in her voice, speaking low, 'I want him!'

Etienne chuckled. 'So do many women, but they find him maddeningly elusive. He is dedicated to winning the war and thinks of little else. For one thing, he hasn't the time, and is forever in the saddle, so short on rest that bed, for him, means sleep. You must meet my wife, Damaris. If anyone can help you she will. Your brother Mallory, is very fond of her, by the by. Hasn't he told you?'

Venetia was nonplussed. 'Don't you mind?'

Adrian was on his knees arranging the completed flower wreath on her hair, head to one side, studying the effect. 'Mind?' he butted in. 'Why should Etienne mind? He has me.'

Etienne had been followed at a discreet distance, by two smartly-liveried servants who now brought over a picnic hamper, spreading refreshments on a damask cloth. Venetia was still digesting Adrian's remark and its implications when Rupert cantered up, waving aside the wineglass which the Chevalier proffered and taking a swig from a battered canteen handed by his page. He mopped the sweat on his face with this sleeve, speaking a few words to his dog who leaped high, trying to reach him. Venetia wanted to attract his attention, but she might not have existed as far as he was concerned and this nettled her; she liked to exist, most emphatically, and for men to recognize that she did.

The Chevalier had known Rupert since boyhood days at the Hague. Venetia could hardly have met anyone more informed and the morning slid away while she completely forgot Michael sitting beside her, growing ever more silent as her eager questions tumbled out and she drank in the replies.

Etienne soon had her laughing at his wicked impersonations of the commanders who had been offended by Rupert's position of seniority, calling him "The German", and hinting darkly, that if he took London he would send it up in flames.

'Ah, the quarrels and intrigues within our own ranks,' Etienne was finishing a dish of raspberries as a desert to hard-boiled eggs. 'Sometimes, I think that the settlement of their personal disputes is of more importance to many of them than beating the Roundheads! Not to the *Pfalzgraf*, of course, he merely wants to get on with his job, but he is hamstrung by the Courtiers.'

It was noon; the sun, a white-hot disc, glared against the azure expanse. A halt was called, and the men relaxed, glad to leave the ranks, knotting into little grumbling groups, seeking shade and rest. Venetia was making automatic responses to everyone in her circle, while her whole attention was focused on the Prince.

He turned his horse over to the groom, then got rid of his sash, stripping off his buff coat, jerking his cravat loose, opening the front of his shirt down to the ribbon-looped fastenings of his breeches. Sweat made great dark arcs on the fine linen under the armpits, across the back and up from the waist. His hair was plastered to his forehead, and he rubbed over his face and neck with a towel before stretching his arms, giving a wide-mouthed yawn and flinging himself down full length at the base of a tree.

The servants brought food which he shared with several troopers who had been given permission to sit with him. These tough, experienced veterans, their skin tanned by exposure to the elements, eyes crinkled at the corners with continually peering into the distance in search of an enemy, treated their chief with an enviable familiarity tempered with admiration and respect. He seemed to be at ease with

42

them, and while not talking a lot himself, he occasionally made some remark which evoked a burst of laughter. At one point, through the hum of conversation which dipped and soared, Venetia could hear him, using some strange-sounding tongue, guttural and harsh, when he spoke to a blond, bearded, leather-clad man who was spreading out charts for him to study.

The wine was strong and it made Venetia drowsy, fogging all thought but the one growing desire to lie at Rupert's side as his dog did; that fortunate animal who had the Prince's fingers fondling his ears and stroking over his fur. Etienne had told her that it had been given to Rupert to alleviate the boredom in prison and had been his constant companion ever since. It was called Boye.

The meadow had become very quiet, only the clink of harness broke across the subdued murmur of voices. Bees droned, filling the fragrant stillness with their soothing sound, and some instinct made Venetia raise her lids to find Rupert staring at her, his eyes slightly narrowed. Her face flamed. Though she knew that this was a God-sent opportunity which any sensible woman would use to give him a returning glance of bold invitation, she could do nothing but hope that he might recognize the adoration in her eyes, before she was forced to look down, nervously folding the pleats of her skirt one over the other, in an agony of longing, fear and embarrassment.

Etienne made Michael promise to bring Venetia to a supper-party which his wife was giving that evening. Venetia wanted to ask if Rupert would be there, but a warning spark in Michael's eyes silenced her. The Chevalier insisted on sending one of his own coaches to fetch her and she spent a couple of frustrated hours trying to decide which gown to wear.

The Frenchman had rented a handsome, red-brick house set in spacious gardens, with outbuildings at the back for the complicated work of his servants. Inside, it was given to solid comfort rather than fashionable furnishings, with big chimney-pieces, ribbed plaster ceilings, heavily-carved staircase and polished floors.

The drawing-room was already crowded when Venetia entered on Michael's arm, feeling her inexperience keenly. Mallory snatched a couple of goblets from a loaded tray carried by a passing servant, and Michael introduced her to some of his friends, young scions of good families, accompanied by girl-friends from every station. Venetia began to relax as she realized that she was being accepted, initially for the sakes of Mallory and Michael, and then very much on her own behalf as the gentlemen bowed over her hand.

A new world was unfolding before her, wholly different from anything she had encountered in the country, and she guessed that Mallory would not have brought her along had it not been that Michael had her in his care. It took a while to adjust to the uninhibited tenor of the talk which flowed around her, and the oaths which appeared to be high fashion. The accepted views of morality were changing fast, replaced by an indifference, cynicism and selfishness, which was worrying the older generation who blamed the war for it.

In the adjoining *salon* musicians had arrived, and couples wandered off to listen, applaud and commence dancing. Mallory's party weaved their way through the throng to where glass doors led out onto a terrace and the evening breeze fanned away the smell of stale perfume, tobacco and sweat. Etienne was lounging with his elbows on the stone balustrade by the side of a splendidly-built woman, who disengaged herself from him to reach up and kiss Mallory in an open, proprietorial manner.

'Mallory, my darling. So you are back in Oxford at last. I've missed you.'

He was grinning down at her. 'You are a very charming liar, Damaris. Come and meet my sister, and do not corrupt her.'

This worldly, laughing woman, stunningly beautiful with that unusual combination of raven hair and violet eyes, could have been intimidating, for she exuded all the confidence which Venetia was painfully conscious of lacking. But this certainty, this security in her own identity, made Damaris an extremely kind person so that she adroitly ignored Venetia's shyness. She was a talkative, outgoing, inquisitive creature, who was soon in possession of the relevant facts of her life and history, putting her at ease.

Damaris had been educated on the Continent and married to the Chevalier at fourteen, the alliance arranged by their respective families.

'And I think I was very fortunate.' She patted her husband's cheek affectionately. 'We get on mighty well. When he told me that he was volunteering to serve King Charles, I insisted on coming too. I've left the babies with my mother-in-law who has borne them off to her *château* in the heart of rural France.'

'How many children have you?' Venetia could never imagine Catherine abandoning her brood in such a light-hearted manner.

'Three—two girls came first, and I could see myself going on trying every year until we produced an heir, but, fortunately the next was a boy.'

'Thank God!' interjected Etienne, who was listening to her with an indulgent smile.

'Oh, come, Etienne, you are so ungallant!' She tapped him lightly with her closed fan. 'You know that you don't really mind if we bed together every so often to make a baby and keep your parents happy.'

There were strange undertones in their relationship. It was not until later, when the men had wandered over to the tables where ivory game chips and playing-cards were strewn, that Venetia began to comprehend the life-style of the Chevalier and his Lady.

Damaris was sipping the wine in her goblet, regarding her over the rim. 'Mallory tells me you are but lately come to Oxford from the country. No doubt you wonder if your brother is my lover, eh? Don't blush, child—of course the thought has occurred to you. Yes, he is, and you need lose no sleep on Etienne's account. I have my friends and he has his, an excellent arrangement and I am very fond of him. The only point at which there is any disagreement between us is our rivalry over the junior officers. But even then, we usually compromise and share them, each of us, in our individual way, giving them a new experience.'

Several times during the evening, Venetia had heard Prince Rupert mentioned as the men discussed his latest successes and the women sighed over his good looks and his inaccessibility. At last, she found courage to broach the subject to Damaris.

'Ah, I wondered when you were going to speak of him.' Her hostess had taken her to the buffet table, keeping up a light flow of banter with her other guests as

48

she passed among them. 'Etienne tells me that you have fallen madly in love with him, and who could blame you? But an amour will not be easy to arrange; he spends his time with his mercenaries, and has few close friends, perhaps only Will Legge and the Duke of Richmond. He is not easy to know, very aloof. If it were Maurice, now, that would be different. I'm sure he'd be only too happy to oblige you, but Rupert—he is certainly no squire of dames.'

The room was swaying for Damaris had been keeping Venetia's glass brimming, and she was glad to sink into a deep chair, filled with soft cushions covered in blushing velvet. She muttered something about Richmond's wife.

Mallory had left the gaming-table and now he and Damaris were eating from the same plate, and she licked her fingers clean from the grease of a chicken-bone before replying. 'Well, yes, there is talk. Mary is one of the Queen's ladies. The Prince seems to be somewhat smitten since he first met her a few days ago. I doubt that it will come to anything. He will value Richmond's friendship far beyond the enjoyment of any woman. He won't

49

betray him, so don't worry your head about that.'

Useless advice, when he was still as far above Venetia as the moon and stars, and his name was being shouted across the room, for the company had reached the stage of pledging everyone; the King, the Queen and each member of the Royal family. It was expected that gentlemen should honour every toast to the full; not a mere sip, but with glass or tankard drained to the bottom in one draught. Several weaklings had already succumbed and lay prone in corners whence they had been dragged by considerate comrades, so that people would not keep tripping over them.

A bustle in the hallway heralded the approach of Damaris, leading forward a new arrival, their progress halted until he could disengage himself from a group of girls in billowing satin dresses who descended on him with little welcoming shrieks and kisses, while fellow-soldiers gathered to pound him on the back in vigorous congratulation.

'Come, Harry,' Damaris was saying. 'Here is someone I want you to meet.' Her firm fingers were on Venetia's arm as she introduced him. 'General Harry Wilmot, fresh from triumphs over the rebels in Wiltshire.'

Wilmot's reputation had reached Venetia. Gay, witty dissolute, one of the King's top commanders, he fought boldly and well, when he was in the mood. He was about thirty, handsome enough in a raffish way, wearing all the exaggerated points of fashion so detested by the Puritans, his blue velvet sleeves slashed with white satin and frothing with lace, a great plumed hat cocked at an angle on his flowing brown hair, his moustache twirled up in a mocking flourish.

'This is Venetia,' Damaris was beaming. 'Isn't she lovely, Harry?'

'Charming, quite charming.' The sly, teasing eyes were going over her with relish, and he managed to imprison her hand in his free one; the other was clamped round the handle of a pewter tankard. 'Fit solace indeed for the weary warrior home from the toils of battle.'

With the practised skill of the experienced seducer, he soon had her penned in a corner. Venetia tried nervously to edge round him, sorry to give this cool reception to such a noted General. Wilmot did not budge an inch, taking a deep swallow before putting his drink down. He wiped his full lips on the back of his hand.

'Well, now, moon-flower of my middle years, I assume that you will want the conventional chatter to start with, though I can think of one or two things I'd rather we did. What shall we talk about?'

'Prince Rupert,' she said instantly.

Wilmot looked pained at this turn of events. 'The Prince? I' faith, why is it that every pretty wench I have a mind to lie with wants to discuss him?'

'You know him?' Venetia could not keep the eagerness from her voice.

'I have that doubtful privilege.' Wilmot pulled a face.

'You don't like him?' Her tone was accusing.

His eyebrows shot up. 'Tis nearer the truth to say that he does not like me!'

There seemed to be so many people with whom Rupert had quarrelled. 'Is he indeed such a very difficult person to get on with?'

'Difficult! He's deuced impossible!' Wilmot answered emphatically. 'I fought beside him in the Dutch Army, back in '35, and even then he looked down that long nose of his at George Goring and myself. Didn't approve of our drinking habits, and haughtily declined all invitations to join us! Dammit, he still does! He's not altered much, though I would say that his Austrian imprisonment did naught but aggravate his already hasty temper. Did you know that his nickname, home at the Hague, was Rupert the Devil?'

Two bumpers of wine later they were ensconced on a settee, half concealed in an alcove. A foolish move, Venetia knew, with this dangerous individual, but caution had fled before her obsession with Rupert. Here was a man who had spent many hours in his company, had been his comrade-at-arms, faced death with him, dared to argue, shot at, and oppose that passionate, determined will.

Laughing and exchanging bawdy jests and advice with his friends who had discovered their nook, Wilmot was well pleased with the situation, thinking that he was about to add Venetia's name to his list of easy conquests. He was prepared to indulge her a little longer by discussing his enemy.

'He demands his way on every issue,' he continued, settling back comfortably, amusing himself by trying to inveigle a hand into her bodice. Venetia wriggled away, not as tipsy as he was hoping she would be. 'My Lord Digby gave him the name of, "His High Illustrious Arrogancy", and the title has stuck! Very apt indeed!'

He was getting difficult to control and Venetia was thankful when Michael appeared, curtly informing him that she was his betrothed. The General eyed him up and down contemptuously.

'Don't ruffle your feathers at me, my game-cock! 'Tis not I who will endanger her virtue. You ride in Rupert's Lifeguard, do you not? My advice to you is to be negligent in your duty. Allow some Roundhead dragoon to shoot him in the back, if you want to keep her!'

At Michael's outraged expression, he suddenly roared with laughter, bawling to Damaris who had drifted across to see what all the noise was about. 'The lads don't know how to take their liquor, Damaris, my sprite! Bring me another bottle, and get rid of that young buck whom you intend to swive before the night is out! Come upstairs with me first, and I'll show you what a real man can do!'

One of Damaris' cardinal principles was

never to interfere in other people's lives, and she was liberal with her home, throwing it open to her friends. Later, Venetia stood at a window in one of the bedchambers, very much as she had done that morning, but now the steeples, the wide plazas, the quods, timbered houses and shops were shrouded in mystery under the wash of the sickle moon. Somewhere, beneath those dreaming spires, he lived and breathed. Did he too gaze out at the night from a casement beneath the eaves? Or was he lying with his friend's wife clasped in his arms?

Michael was a tender presence in the darkness, undressing her as carefully as if she were a precious piece of china, knowing the intricacies of hooks and laces almost as well as her maid. In the spinning blackness of the canopied bed, Venetia very nearly convinced herself that it was Rupert's large, aristocratic hands which caressed her. With her face buried in Michael's hair, she pictured those saturnine, proud features, and at the end, roused to a peak of passion, it was all that she could do so not to cry his name aloud.

Michael knew, with that sixth sense developed by those deeply in love, that there was something wrong. 'What is the matter, darling? Did I not please you?'

She was instantly contrite; he was so good to her. 'Of course you did, Michael. I think that I have drunk too much wine. It makes me melancholy.'

The nimble lies which sprang to her tongue surprised even herself. He said no more and she listened to his breathing, feeling the weight of his head on her breast. Silent tears spilled over, running back across her temples. Rupert's bravery, his Royal birth, his romantic history and personal beauty were deadly auxiliaries against any future peace of mind. And it was all so futile, she decided, with that desperate, small-hours finality; he could never love her.

THREE

Sunday turned Oxford into a city of bells. All day they had pealed, the noise vibrating in Venetia's aching head. In the evening, Damaris called for her and they rolled through the streets in her coach to join the crowds eager to catch a glimpse of the reunited Royal couple, as they took a stroll in the garden of Merton College after church.

Damaris had the effect of making every woman in her vicinity feel more feminine, her finger on the pulse of fashion. The Queen too was famous for her poise and faultless chic. Venetia was anxious to give a good account of herself, and dressed with care.

It had not been hard to keep abreast with the current vogues even in the Cotswolds. Pedlars called regularly, bringing a breath of the outside world, packs bulging with samples of material, ribbons, furs and laces. On market-days there were stalls where a woman might browse happily for hours, bemused by the antics of the wily hucksters who cried their wares, temptingly holding up a dazzling array of shawls, cuffs and collars of Flemish lace, fans, muffs, coloured hose, garters with sparkling paste buckles, and embroidered high-heeled slippers.

The country-bred girl learned the art of improvisation; Venetia had become an accomplished needlewoman, and had found a local seamstress almost as skilled in producing clothes economically, using materials to hand, or ordering them to be delivered with the next train of pack-horses. Damaris had been astonished to learn that the dress Venetia had worn the night before and now this outfit, had both been made at home. She commented approvingly on the way the green silk skirt was hooked up at one side for walking, displaying the contrasting tobacco-brown petticoat, admiring the cut of the bodice, with its basque and stomacher edged in the same shade of velvet braid, cunningly boned to fit Venetia's slender waist.

She had taught Meg how to help her copy the latest hair-style; her thick locks, the colour of sun-ripened cornsheaves, had been coiled into a bun, pinned high on her crown, while the side pieces were rolled into long, fat ringlets, the forehead line softened by a curling fringe.

'Faith, my dear, you show the same restrained elegance as His Highness,' Damaris exclaimed, the bunch of purple feathers in her wide-brimmed hat nodding in agreement as the coach jolted over the cobbles. 'He is most sparkish in his dress, and has a natural flare for rich dark colours set off against a sombre background. And he is so maddeningly casual about it all—it happens without any apparent effort on his part. All the young bloods strive earnestly to imitate his style, which does nothing to endear him to Lord Percy and Wilmot, who rather fancy themselves as leaders of fashion.'

A footman ran around to open the door, lower the step, and hand the ladies out. Within minutes, as they made towards the spectators lining the gravel pits, Damaris had formed her own retinue of gallants, each vying for her favours. The shoulders of their escorts cleaved a way for them towards the neat avenue between the boxwood hedges.

'There they are,' Damaris said on a sharp intake of breath, and all along the line men's hats were sweeping off, and women dropping into curtsies, like flowers bending before the wind. Erect and dignified, King Charles moved slowly past.

With almost superstitious awe, Venetia watched him; this was their King, the man they were fighting for, and there was a great regality about him, in spite of his lack of inches. His brown hair, beginning to streak with silver, brushed the shoulders of a beige satin doublet. His face was shaded by the brim of a black hat, and there were tight lines about his mouth which betrayed the nervous tension under which he now lived.

Henrietta Maria was a disappointment, thin and sallow, until one saw the vivacity of her black eyes, which changed constantly from sparkling merriment, flashes of anger and indignation, back to fun again. Today she was in a fine mood of triumph and optimism, as light-footed and dancing as the tiny spaniels bounding before her. She was exquisitely gowned, a flashing creature who reduced even the beautiful women who formed her train of ladies-in-waiting into cloddish lumps.

'That's Lord Jermyn, just behind the Queen,' Damaris was saying. 'He is her secretary, and some say her lover. She likes to think herself a fascinating spitfire.' Venetia wished that Damaris had kept that piece of information to herself.

She wanted to retain her illusions about the Royal pair, to think of them as a fairy tale King and Queen, presiding over a chaste, decorous Court. But the comments continued, for in common with Etienne, Damaris seemed to know all things, and

60

most people, nobles, Generals and ladies, a mine of gossip and information.

'Oh, look!' She gave Venetia a sharp poke with her elbow. 'There's my Lord George Digby, Bristol's son. Mark him well, for he is no friend to your Prince.'

He was a dandy, graceful of mien and gesture, his fair skin emphasized by black velvet, his expression that of a depraved choir boy. An exceedingly beautiful person indeed, slender and well-proportioned, with guileless blue eyes shadowed by feathery lashes, his oval face framed in golden curls, artlessly tumbling over his lace collar, adding to the cherubic appearance. His head was bent earnestly, reverently, toward the King, and his hands, smooth and dimpled, were in constant play as he talked.

Damaris was chattering about other notables, but Venetia was blind to everyone for she had caught sight of Rupert.

He was some way behind, slowing his impatient long-legged pace to match that of the woman walking with him. No one needed to tell her that it was Mary Lennox, the Duchess of Richmond. Venetia's eyes bored into her, trying to fault her beauty, miserably accepting that this was impossible.

Etienne was lolling on the day-bed when Damaris and Venetia returned, listening to Adrian who had abandoned his guitar for the spinet. The thin, plucked notes hung, clear-cut, on the evening air, the melancholy of the pavanne striking an echo in Venetia's soul.

Damaris shot her husband an annoyed glare. 'Etienne, I do wish that you would not wear your spurs indoors!'

He raised his head an inch from the pillow, squinting down the length of his legs which were draped across the couch with such a fine show of careless ease, arching an ankle to survey one of the offending articles attached to his fawn doeskin boots.

'*Chérie*, you know perfectly well that this season it is almost *de rigueur* for any man of fashion to retain his spurs on almost every occasion! Would you have me appear an uncultivated boor?'

'Thank God that these cushions are but rented and not our property,' she retorted briskly. 'And I hope for Adrian's sake, that you leave them on the bedside table at night, or he'll have the marks of rowels on that tender peaches-and-cream skin of his!'

'My dear, what a fascinating thought!' squeaked Adrian roguishly.

Etienne moved over, patting the place beside him when Damaris told him to be kind to Venetia because she was so unhappy about Mary Lennox.

'Oh, that bitch!' he remarked, filling her glass with splashing generosity. 'She'll lead a fellow on, but she's so damned faithful to her sobersided spouse that no one else could get even a blade of grass between those buttocks.'

Damaris kept a day by day journal of events and explained to Venetia, 'When the King is back on his throne, and myself once more incarcerated in the country, I shall write a book—my "Memoirs of the Great Rebellion!"'

'Not all of them, surely? It would never get an imprimatur!' Etienne gave a yawn, already acutely bored at the prospect of having to listen to her reading aloud extracts from her masterpiece. 'Moreover, women don't write books!'

'Then it is high time they started!' Damaris was one of those advanced thinkers who considered the female every bit as capable as the male, questioning their lordly assumption of superiority. With her eye for detail, good memory and flair for expressing herself, she was busy amassing material; every tract which came out of London, each public declaration by some important personage, now found its way into her collection.

Rupert was the principal target of the gutter press. To the impressionable Puritans, the alarming vision of this unusually tall, dark foreign Prince, wrapped in a cloak of hellish scarlet, accompanied always by a weird dog, seemed the very personification of evil. They were convinced that Boye was his familiar, able to make himself invisible and spy on godly troops, taking intelligence of their movements back to his Prince of Darkness. They almost ran out of epithets for him, the most polite of which were "Prince Robber", "The Diabolical Cavalier", "Plunder-Master-General", and "Ravenous Vulture!" He was cast in the role of the villain, a slavering ogre whose fiery breath stank of butchery, blood and Continental warfare.

'Is he really the "loose and wild gentleman" that they describe?' Venetia asked after reading an account of his hanging Roundheads at their own front doors and plundering wholesale. 'They say that he has shown no mercy to any that oppose him than to a dog.'

Etienne shook his head impatiently, filled with indignation at the lies spread about the King's finest General. 'The London newsmongers hate him because he is a hard-headed soldier and could see, after Edgehill, that the best way to finish the war quickly was to strike direct at the City. This stirred the merchants into a ferment, they feared for their property, so they put pressure on Parliament. A charge of High Treason has been drawn up against him and Prince Maurice, by the Commons.'

'He doesn't look like a brute.' Venetia visualized that sensitive face. 'I've never seen a more handsome man.'

Adrian was getting piqued by all this talk of Rupert, no one had even bothered to enquire about his latest performance.

'His nose is too big.' He posed against the spinet, so that his delicate profile was shown to full advantage.

'Oh, I don't know about that.' Etienne snatched at the small round handglass which dangled from a ribbon attached to Venetia's waist, gazing at his own rather pronounced features. 'I think that it lends a charming touch of dignity and strength.'

An attendant had come in with a lighted taper and was going round the room holding it to every candle. Damaris began to gather up her souvenirs to free the table for the supper dishes. As she swept towards the bureau, her arms full of papers, something floated to the floor and Etienne picked it up.

It was a letter, addressed to "His Highness, Prince Rupert", and someone had been scribbling sketches over the back of it, as if to pass the time in an idle moment. There were heads and human figures; a man with a pike borne on one shoulder, a girl's face, a boy with curling hair and a detailed row of buttons running down his doublet.

'I begged them from the Prince for Damaris' scrap-book,' the Chevalier informed Venetia. 'Did you not know that he is a most considerable artist.'

A letter had come from the bailiff whom Denby had left in charge of his house. Shortly after they had left, it had been occupied by a Roundhead company.

Venetia found it strange to imagine intruders moving through the pleasant

66

rooms, handling those personal belongings, rifling drawers, cupboards and chests. A crop-haired rebel Captain would now sit in her father's carver at the head of the table; some unknown person sleeps in the bed where she had dreamed her girlish fancies and, later, lain in Michael's arms. Another would occupy the chamber where all the Denby children had been born.

Venetia had little time to brood for Michael came next day, to tell her that the Prince was moving out of Oxford to attack the second most important city of England—Bristol.

Her reaction flattered him; he believed her distress to be on his account. 'Don't worry, love. To know that you will be here, waiting for me, will give me a magic immunity from harm. We march at dawn tomorrow.' He kissed her briefly and clattered away to his duties.

Venetia knew of one person only who could help her, and she found Damaris in the courtyard of her house, supervising the packing of her largest coach. It was a bright splash of sapphire, with gilt varnish and green leather trappings, and so heavy that six sturdy horses were required to pull it; especially with the added supplies of clothes, blankets, hatboxes, medicine chests, brandy-flasks, and cases of sack, which Damaris refused to trust to the covered carts. Two of these were coping with the overspill of luggage which a lackey was stowing inside with remarkable compactness to leave room for the personal servants.

'Are you going with him?' Venetia watched her helplessly; somehow she had not expected this.

Damaris was handing up a squat black liqueur bottle to her maid, Nancy, who tucked it away in a neat compartment under the seat. 'But of course, dear. I travel everywhere with my Etienne. How else should I know if he is having the right food? He has a delicate stomach, you know. I'm a very experienced camp-follower—in every way.'

'And this is permitted?' Venetia thought of the female riff-raff who trailed behind the armies as a collection of common harlots, she had not realized that married women were included.

'It is encouraged.' They sat on the coach step in the shade and let the lackeys finish loading. 'The Generals say that the men are better fed and looked after if their

68

wives go along. And we help with the wounded.'

The yard was full of activity with ostlers, footmen and pert maids scurrying to do madam's bidding. Her spaniel yelped as someone gave it a sly kick, and the kitchen cat did not blink a golden eye, his paws folded neatly under him, indulging his love of sun-warmed stone, too indolent to take up the challenge thrown out by a row of saucy sparrows perched on the guttering. But already Venetia could feel that chill lonely stillness which would descend upon her when Rupert had gone. If she did not act now, the chance would be lost, never to come again, she could not afford to hesitate. Damaris had said that no rumour had reached her of the Prince either sending for one of the camp whores, or having affairs with the Court ladies, yet he was only human. There must come a time when his high standards relaxed and, when this happened, Venetia was determined to be available.

'You'll take me with you?' It was more of a demand than a request.

'My dear child, it is no picnic, I assure you.' Damaris looked doubtful. 'And His Highness will be far too busy to notice you, were you to run around his tent stark naked! De Gomme and La Roche, his engineers, will be his constant companions, they'll be poring over plans together, you'll see.'

When she saw Venetia's desperation, and realized that if she did not aid her, she was likely to do something foolish, she relented. 'I don't know how we are to achieve your aim. Mallory and Michael will never countenance your joining the leaguer. You know how ridiculously touchy men are about the honour of their sisters or the women they intend to marry, no matter how much whoring they do themselves. You can ride with me, once we have put a good distance between ourselves and Oxford, but till then I think we had better hide you with the players. Adrian will help, he loves intrigue, and Jonathan is friendly with one of the girls.'

Early next morning she stole out to the stable calling softly to her horse, Orion, and he answered, whinnying gently while she patted his neck and harnessed him. Jonathan was waiting for her, and they rode to the fields beyond the town where a camp had been formed.

Jonathan gave the password to the pickets

and they trotted within the circle of carts, towards one at the rear. At Jonathan's voice, a girl's tousled head came out between the flaps at the rear, and the flickering light of the flares played on a pale face and slim, fragile hands which gleamed against the dark woollen shawl flung over her shoulders.

The two women eyed one another suspiciously for a moment, the sister and the mistress, then they smiled simultaneously and Jonathan sighed with relief; they were going to be friends. Now he could leave them with a contented mind, slipping back to rejoin his troop before it was discovered that he was missing.

The players had two wagons, and the largest was occupied by Meriel and her father, the actor who ran the show, Thomas Carter. It was not the time for introductions, for he and most of the other members were trying to snatch a little sleep. Meriel and Venetia conversed in whispers, peeping out at the smouldering fires, too excited to settle down.

As the sky lightened, a breath like a sigh stirred the waiting crowd as, sweet and high and far away, sounded the note of a trumpet, answered by another. From the West Port of the town came the noise of hooves and marching feet, and the rumble of heavy vehicles. This galvanized the leaguer into action; horses were backed between shafts, men cursing, blear-eyed, fumbling with awkward strappings, while fires were stamped out, children rounded up, dogs whistled to heel, and a rough column formed under the direction of the wagon-masters.

Louder and nearer jogged the cavalry, and, beyond a curve in the hedge, the banner of the Palatine came into sight, in the lead was Rupert himself, magnificent on his powerful destrier, the first sun-rays glinting on his steel corselet while the wind tossed the crimson feathers in his black beaver. His Lifeguard kept close beside him, followed by the troopers, a brave army of plumes, swirling cloaks, lace collars and gilt-chastened swordhilts.

The dragoons and infantry, musketeers and pikemen formed clumps of colour, the individual standard of each troop borne proudly, essential as a marker of headquarters when in billets, and as a rallying point in action. By the law of arms a company that lost its flag was barred from having another until they had redeemed their tarnished reputation by taking an enemy one.

After the soldiers came the Prince's sumpter-wagons and those of the principal officers, followed by lumbering vehicles carrying ironshot, match, barrels of gun powder, smiths' materials, the engineers' equipment, and the tents.

Behind the military jolted the coaches carrying either the wives of the senior officers, or bejewelled and feathered ladies who could make no such legal claim. A group of women riding side-saddle, cloaked and sensibly booted and attired for hard weather, were married to those of lesser rank, and the motley collection among whom Venetia was numbered, fell in at the rear.

For time immemorial a wandering army attracted a conglomeration of hangers-on. There were victuallers, tinkers, hawkers and sharp-dealers, musicians and play-actors. All were out to make a quick penny, including whores less fortunate than those borne in their splendid conveyances, brash, strident-tongued slatterns who obliged the soldiery for a modest fee.

The *cortège* moved off along the dewy, shadowed hillside, and Venetia, perched up in the player's cart, could feel nothing but happiness because she was a part of it; even the simple natural phenomenon of dawn was a miracle because the Prince was there.

At noon a halt was called, horses were fed and watered, weary troops chewed on bread, cheese, cold pies, slabs of beef, washed down with ale or cider. Venetia had brought food with her, packed in her valise along with a few simple necessities, and she shared what she had with the players. They were a convivial group, a dozen in all, living in the carts along with their costumes and properties, musical instruments, mummers masks, and thick bundles of scripts. Meriel was the only female, although several scruffy drabs hung around, attracted by the eloquent voices, the lordly airs affected by the actors. They were never short of stage-struck volunteers for crowd scenes. But all the roles, including those of women, were given to the men, although Thomas Carter, who had acted abroad, assured Venetia that this would not always be so.

At night the travel-stained caravan toiled upwards towards a village. The Prince and his staff commandeered the largest house, the officers took over the inn and, in the fields, the leaguer settled in for the night. The carts were drawn into a protective ring, lads were sent to search for firewood, and soon fragrant smoke circled lazily heavenwards. The seasoned campaigners slung iron pots on tripods over the flames, and in no time little family groups were squatting round the fires having their supper.

Meriel took Venetia through the camp where people greeted them with easy friendliness, and it became very clear that the rank and file adored their Prince, no matter how much he might annoy the nobles.

'Reckless young devil he is,' one grizzled battle-scarred warrior assured her, offering a slug of brandy from a blackjack. 'A grand fighter! Shot-free, so they say! D'you know he's never been wounded? He's ever foremost in the charge in the most exposed position that spur can drive to, chief object of the enemy's hatred, and yet he rides unharmed!'

'Not like Prince Maurice.' A younger, broken-nosed rascal was rubbing his chin through the stubble, eyeing Venetia with unconcealed interest. 'He gets hurt in almost every fight. Who are you with, sweetheart?'

Venetia ignored him, listening to the other man as he continued:

'Oh, yes, he knows what a soldier needs, by Christ! Worked his way up through the ranks himself, he did, in the German armies. He sees that we have food in our bellies, and something between us and the cold ground at night. Many's the time he's slept out in the open, along with us, and I've seen him, shirt stripped off, waist deep in mud, working in the trenches, digging under city walls to lay explosives. I was at Litchfield when he set off the first mine that had ever been used in England.'

He gave a rumbling laugh, taking a pull at the bottle, then going on: 'You should hear the lads yell when we storm through a city; "Damn us! The town is Prince Rupert's!"'

Wrapped in her cloak, gazing out at the stars through the half open flap of the wagon, Venetia hugged these words to her, and marvelled at the odd statement made so positively by Meriel. Everyone else had told her that she was mad to love him, that nothing could possibly come of it. Meriel

76

had merely said, with a strange, fey look in her eyes:

'You'll succeed, my dear. But I will not promise you happiness.'

FOUR

It took five days for the straggling procession to wend its way through the countryside to Chipping Sodbury, where the Prince rendezvoused with his brother who was serving with the Western Army under Lord Hertford.

On the second day, Venetia rode up nearer to the van and joined Damaris. Then she had better quarters, for the Chevalier was usually able to procure a room for his wife and Venetia shared with her. Mallory was furious at the deception played on him, but Michael, after the first shock, expressed nothing but happiness at having Venetia near.

She found no opportunity to meet the Prince; as Damaris had warned he was a very busy person, and extremely uncommunicative, apart from his chosen intimates among the professional soldiers. One night, when they had been forced to bivouac in the open, she saw him seated at a trestle drawn close to the tent entrance to catch the fading light, deep in consultation with the Captain of his guards, Sir Richard Crane. His hair fell forward across his face as he bent over papers strewn about the table. Boye was at his knee, tail thumping the grass, and Rupert absently fondled the dog's silky ears.

He glanced up as Venetia passed through his field of vision, and his eyes were as she had seen them when he was angry with his lazy Lieutenants, with something alight, like a flame, in their black depths. It was a look which sucked out all her strength. She was so disturbed, so racked with longing to kiss his perfectly moulded mouth, that she could not pretend to respond to Michael when later he pushed her back on the earth in the shadow of the wagon, twisting away, picking a quarrel with him to avoid contact.

The nights were short; His Highness's trumpeters had them up at three in the morning. Yawning, grumbling, shivering in the ground mists, they could do no more than snatch a hasty bite, bundle up their belongings, and be off as the first birds heralded the dawn.

Venetia was lucky to be with Damaris who was able to treat the march as an adventure, enjoying to the full the fun of living alfresco, while her servants performed the more unpleasant chores. It was impossible not to draw comparisons with the hardships that Meriel endured, forced to gather kindling, fetch water from the streams, and keep the cooking-pot well stocked. The actors had added poaching to their list of accomplishments, and there was usually a rabbit to be gutted, or a hen which had strayed from its own backyard.

It was Sunday, and the sound of church bells, ringing out from Bristol, was borne on the breeze to reach the Cavaliers as they entered a hamlet on the north side of the city. Their arrival caused the usual pandemonium, with the cavalry pounding in first, then the infantry swinging down the single street where the locals gathered to gape, bare foot urchins falling into step beside the column, and the village sluts well to the fore, shouting.

'I'll 'ave that little 'un, at the back!'

'Ho there, General! Mind you don't wear 'em out, with all that marching.'

'Uds Lud! Look at 'im! Cor, 'ee can come and quarter 'isself on me, any time 'ee likes!'

Prince Rupert requisitioned Westbury College, fanning all things into flame by the speed of his coming. Venetia found Meriel, on her knees by the brook, pounding linen on the broad, flat stones, her cheeks pink with the effort. Some of the other women had already finished, smocks and petticoats, shirts and drawers, baby clothes and diapers spread out on the bushes, bleaching under the blaze of midsummer.

'Damned war!' Meriel gave an extra hard slap with her father's hose against a slippery boulder. 'I shall be glad when 'tis over. Just imagine laying abed late, and then rising to find this done.' Meriel often spoke longingly of the kind of life that she had never known. She had been on the road since she was born, brought up by her actor-manager-adventurer father. Her mother had died young and from her, Meriel had inherited her appealing delicate appearance, and her psychic ability. Because she was not allowed to speak lines, though this was her ambition, she contributed to the show by telling fortunes;

but they were cautious, choosing customers with care, for she had no desire to be accused of witchcraft.

'I cannot predict for myself,' she told Venetia. 'But one thing I do know; I must love your brother Jonathan with every fibre of my being, while I am able.'

They were completely absorbed in one another, oblivious to mockery, wandering hand in hand, gazing into each other's eyes, whispering imbecilities. Venetia wondered how the family would react if he suddenly appeared with her as his wife.

For all her fine-boned slender build, Venetia had a strong constitution, an ability to adapt speedily to situations, and an iron will which enabled her to complete any project on which she had set her heart. Brought up among boys, she had learned early to out-hunt and frequently outride them; with screams and tantrums, or, if these failed, storms of tears, she insisted on being allowed to join in when they had their fencing lessons. She had been the despair of her nurse, who deplored such hoydenish behaviour, and strove to school her young charge to be ladylike. Later she had conformed, but now her old rebellion surged up. Resentfully, she watched the Prince gallop across Durdham Down towards the tower of Clifton Church spiking on a leafy rise.

The chaplains conducted a service in the open for the leaguer which was interrupted by the boom of cannon-fire blasting from the direction taken by the reconnaissance party. Venetia's heart plummeted, her thoughts fleeing into that wilderness of horror where she saw Rupert maimed or killed a hundred times over.

They clopped back unharmed, leaning against the cantles of their saddles, relaxed and laughing; Venetia could hear the Prince whistling to his dog; he sounded in high good humour. Michael said that while they were standing in the churchyard on the crest, the Roundhead gunners manning Brandon Hill Fort opposite, suddenly woke up to their presence. Two or three cannon-balls were sent crashing over, but no one was hurt and Rupert coolly continued to survey the city spread out in the hollow below. In answer to that challenging fire, he had put a battery there, leaving Colonel Washington in charge with his dragoons.

On Monday, the army deployed in full battaglia on the edge of Durdham Down. Maurice had gone back over the Avon to draw up the Western force in a similar manner on the south side. The sun sparked off breastplates and helms, the forest of pikes, sixteen feet high, and the wicked gleam of musket-barrels. The Royalist army marched wide, looking larger than it really was, all the panoply of death flaunting its gayest colours, and the great standard of Prince Rupert rippling out against the smarting blue of the sky.

It was a formidable spectacle, calculated to shatter the nerve of the defenders; and the Prince paraded them there long enough for the full impact to be driven home. Then he sent in a trumpeter with a formal summons to the Governor, Colonel Nathaniel Fiennes, to surrender the town. This was refused, as was expected, and the skirmishing began in earnest.

The defences of Bristol were strong and well planned; a wall and ditch protected it and there were four forts on the Downs side, with the River Avon making an awkward obstacle on the other. Royalist spies, busy within, sent cheering reports to Rupert. Optimism ran high among the besiegers, for Nat Fiennes was not the most valiant of men, and although Bristol was reputedly

Puritan, many leading citizens were for the King.

Rupert moved his headquarters further into the suburbs; the surgeons and their assistants turned a large farm-building into a hospital and, in the nearby fields of Redland, the women camped, waiting events.

Mining and sapping were out of the question on this stony ground, so every vantage point was seized, and the hedge-rows lined with musketeers. The gunners sweated to get the artillery into position, and soon this deeper roar thundered across the sporadic rattle of small-arms, a vigorous duel which lasted into the dawn. Leaving his men to continue the bombardment, the Prince crossed the river for a Council of War with the Western Army at Knowle.

And with all this excitement seething around her, Venetia could do nothing but wander after Damaris in an agony of concern for Rupert, who, with his usual indifference to danger, hourly took the most appalling risks.

Damaris became really cross with her, 'Oh, do stop fretting your bowels to fiddle-strings about him! Don't you know that the bullet isn't fashioned in hell yet, that can kill the Wizard Prince? What about your brothers and Michael, to say nothing of my own Etienne? Can you not spare a prayer for them?' She marched her to the surgeon's quarters. 'Do something useful. Occupy yourself in tearing linen into bandages.'

The Chevalier clanked into the big, stone-flagged kitchen, where several straw pallets were already occupied by groaning men. The scrubbed wooden table had been cleared for the use of the doctors, and on the hearth the fire roared beneath cauldrons of water.

Etienne wore his soldier's gear with considerable panache, although regretting that is was impracticable to don the full armour of a cuirassier for any other occasion than sitting for his portrait. Like most officers, he had compromised and settled for the more comfortable, if less safe, thick leather jacket which reached almost to his knee. While this would turn sword blows, it could not check bullets, so his gilded Milanese back- and breastplate were buckled on top. He made a splendid—almost heroic figure, and knew it.

Damaris beamed her approval, very

practical of a sudden, with her curls tied back, sleeves rolled up and a plain twill apron fastened over the front of her gown.

'Dearest, you look just as if you've stepped down from some tapestry depicting the ancient days of Chivalry.'

' 'Tis deuced hot!' Her husband eased his crested helmet from his sweat-drenched hair. 'Rupert has returned, and a full-scale assault is planned for early tomorrow morning. The password is to be "Oxford", and we've to wear green tokens and no collars, so that we may recognize one another and not shoot our own fellows by mistake.'

'He had no mind to sit it out and starve them into surrender?' Damaris drew off a mugful of ale from a barrel set on a bench in an airy corner, and passed it to him.

He gulped it back, perched on the edge of the table. 'That is what Maurice and Hertford wanted to do. But you know the *Pfalzgraf*, he has not the temperament for a drawn-out siege, and seems certain that the breastwork, on this side, is so badly manned that it will be easily carried by storm.'

Though worn out by bedtime, sleep did

not come easily and Damaris got up at last, going over to join Venetia at the window where the military masquerades made a fine firework display against the purple darkness.

'Just listen to that racket!' she complained, as the crash of ordnance tortured the air of the summer night which should have been soft and mysterious, full of stars and love, the sound of owls, nightingales, and the rustle of tiny furry creatures.

They went back to bed, and Venetia lay taut, worrying about her family, wondering what they had made of her hastily scribbled note, and if Catherine had started labour yet. Timothy's freckled face and babyish mouth, rose behind her closed eyelids. She hoped that he would not follow her example and run away to join up, and Ella—how long would it be before some irresponsible member of the Oxford garrison got that flighty little minx into trouble?

The firing had died and the silence was eerie, stretching endlessly so that sleep began to wash over Venetia, one face only filling her dreams—Rupert's, with its proud eagle lines and the dark fire of his glance.

Suddenly the staccato rattle of musketry, cries and cheering from the south, sent the Oxford commanders rushing from their billets, bawling orders as they ran. Drums were rolling, trumpets blaring out for "Boot and Saddle", and the Prince was shouting for the signal to be fired for the massed attack, before vaulting onto his horse and hurling like a thunderbolt towards the line between Brandon Hill and Windmill Fort.

Damaris fumbled for the flint and tinder to light the candle, consulting the enamelled face of her watch. 'It lacks two hours to the appointed time! I'll wager 'tis those fiery Cornish in Hertford's brigades wanting to snatch the glory of the first breach from Rupert's lads!'

Garbled reports of the battle came back to the leaguer with the injured. Venetia became numbed, unable to register shock, horror or pity, obeying the instructions of the surgeons, doing what was required of her. Now the hospital was very crowded, and the wives worked alongside the whores, enmities temporarily forgotten.

Jonathan limped in, his arm slung around the shoulders of a burly pikeman and his eyes were feverish with exaltation, his excitement so acute that he hardly felt the pain as the ugly gash in his thigh was sutured.

'We've broken in! And I was with them—Washington's men and Wentworth's almost quarrelling for the honour!' He held Venetia's hand in a vice-like grip. 'It was at the spur-work, just below Windmill Fort, where His Highness had said there was a weak point. He is always right! You should have seen Washington, driving us through that gap, yelling like a madman, "Away, away with them!" as if he was out hunting!'

'What of the Prince?' Venetia gave Jonathan a shake.

Aglow with hero-worship, he described how Rupert had flown up and down the line. He seemed to be everywhere at once, instinctively knowing where his presence was most needed; directing, encouraging, rallying and rebuking, his voice as keen as a trumpet. He stopped a retreat at one point where a sally had been repulsed, leading the waverers back. They attacked again and won, inspired by this creature of fierce and desperate purpose.

'And his horse was shot under him. A musketeer got it right in the eye, but he strolled off on foot, as cool as you please, till another was brought for him!'

Then Venetia looked at Meriel who had read her mind, and laid the exhausted boy back on the straw. He was trembling violently, his teeth chattering, and she tucked a blanket round him, bending to kiss his forehead, before following his sister. Only Meriel, who knew Venetia's inevitable destiny, helped her without comment as they went to the players' carts and found men's clothing in the property-boxes; and it was Meriel who laced her into the buff jacket, gave her a hat, discovered boots to fit, and fixed her up with a sword, remembering to pin on a green favour, and to rip the white collar from her shirt.

They saddled Orion, and Venetia found it strange to be riding astride, which she had not done in years. She bent towards Meriel, who kissed her solemnly, as if she were bestowing a benediction.

'The strength of your love will protect you—and him,' she said.

Orion was eager to gallop, and Venetia kept him at full speed, rejoicing to feel the lift of his withers, the strong thighs which bunched up under him as he leaped the wall. She leaned over and patted the proud curve of his neck where the mane blew about, and his ears pricked at the sound of her voice. But he checked, scenting the carnage with flared nostrils, needing firm urging as they came closer to where the throbbing force of battle shook the earth.

Venetia rode over the broken track, coming out into the open, facing a hill, thick with brambles and furze, crested by a great fort which crouched sullenly, belching out flames and smoke. To her left loomed another, rising high over the meadow which dipped between, where a large body of troops and horsemen gathered. The roundshot from the enemy batteries passed clean over them, while their own artillery, more cunningly positioned, gave back destructive answer.

She paused for an instant, but she had already seen him despite the distance. The scarlet cloak which he wore in sheer defiance billowed out behind him as he flashed across the grass with controlled speed, straight as the bolt from a crossbow, up to the break in the defences, where the activity was thickset. Nothing mattered but her compulsion to be with him. She ground her spurs against Orion's flanks, shooting him forward so that his charge almost shocked up against Rupert's stallion.

This was too much for Orion. He snorted, plunged and kicked, hurling Venetia straight beneath the trampling hooves. The Prince reined in smartly; his big beast reared upright, missing her by inches. Orion's legs coiled like springs, ready to launch him into flight, but Rupert's gauntleted hand grabbed the trailing bridle, pulling him up short with a jerk.

Venetia staggered to her feet and met the full blast of the Prince's rage, the dark brows curving beneath the peak of his helmet. Her hat had gone bouncing down the slope, and her hair glittered like bronze in the brilliant sunshine.

'God's wounds, a wench!' It was Sir Richard Crane, closing up beside his General, a wolfish grin on his craggily-handsome features.

Rupert did not find it amusing. 'Denby's sister!' He snarled. 'What the devil do you here?'

The moment had come but it was like a nightmare. She could not muster her thoughts, her head hurt, and her mouth tasted of blood where she had bitten her tongue at the impact.

'I seek to serve you,' she blurted.

'More like, she lusts to serve *under* you, sir.' Crane's smile widened. 'Why, she had already fallen at Your Highness's feet!'

More members of the Lifeguard had moved in round the Palsgrave. They sat their mounts and laughed, looking her over with the casual arrogance of experts; Rupert's select gentlemen volunteers who accompanied him everywhere. His angry, warning stare wiped the grins away.

'Get into the shelter of the wall and stay there!' The curt command scorched her ears. 'Don't try to ride that beast! You'll break your neck!'

He was an awe-inspiring sight in black armour, looming over her on his destrier, the white plume of his headpiece adding to his size—almost superhuman.

His mouth was set in a stern line, the sweat trickling down his smoke-grimed face, and he wore that wild battle-air, which men, used to fighting with him, easily recognized. Venetia cowered back, dragging Orion with her. One does not bandy words with an avenging archangel.

He had already forgotten her as he swung round to his staff. 'A messenger to go to Prince Maurice.' Hardly had he

93

voiced the request, before a dozen men leaped forward. He selected one whose horse was fresh. 'Tell him to come to me at once with a thousand of his Cornishmen!'

A galloper dashed up at full tilt with the news that a tertia had forced itself so near the quay that the shipping could be set alight. The town endangered by a blaze sweeping through its wooden structures would be easily subjugated.

'Sacrément! No!' The Prince thundered. 'I have sworn that the King shall have Bristol, not a useless heap of ashes! If the town is fired, tell them that they shall have Rupert to reckon with! Ride man, ride!'

He turned and was gone himself with such speed that sparks flew up from the stones beneath the hoofs of his charger.

Maurice could not spare that number of men, but he came in person with five hundred, and the Royalists surged through, past the inner defences, towards College Green and the Cathedral. The crooked alleys screwed down towards the sluggish River Frome and, in the din and reek, the sky rained shot from the tall grey gables which gave cover to the defenders. The afternoon heat grilled the tangle of men, locked in vicious combat on the blood-slippery steps.

At Frome Gate, they found themselves facing an army of two hundred screaming harpies, egged on by a forbidding Puritan lady, who had imbued them with her own fanatical determination that Bristol should not be crushed beneath the heel of the debauched Papist Cavaliers and their Devil Prince! They had blocked the gate with woolsacks and earth, putting up a hot fight against the swearing attackers who were half proud, half furious, at the vigour of these stubborn English wenches who put heart into their failing menfolk, yelling at them to go tell the Governor that they would stand firm and face the besiegers with their babies in their arms to keep off shot, if he was afraid!

With the clash of the striving city rising to join the defiant volley from the forts, Venetia crouched beside Orion. She gentled him as he shied and fretted every time a shot burst on the escarpment, and laid her face against his white forelock, wishing that a stray bullet would put an end to her misery.

There was a lull, and the commanders measured the work still to do, detailed their men and posted detachments to hold the outworks already gained. The mortars fell silent, and the forts waited in a stillness not at first apparent to those stunned by the bombardment. Rupert and his guard came sweeping back through the breach. He took up a position close by, where he could best receive intelligence and send directions, giving his adjutants orders to prepare to attack Brandon Fort. The fighting had dwindled; a drum sounded in the distance, and excited voices were shouting:

'A parley! They seek a parley!'

Rupert's trumpets brayed and the town was suspended in a weird hush as two Cavalier officers went in towards the castle to talk terms with Nat Fiennes.

Michael fetched Venetia, saying coldly that the Prince had sent him, and his silence, as they rode, hurt her more than the sternest rebuke. In the camp, women were weeping and preparing to bury their dead.

As the sun set, tired, hungry men returned to the camp, each with an exploit to recount. Venetia listened, and yet did not hear the talk which encompassed her, so absorbed in her own unhappiness that the tales of feats of arms, miraculous rescues and heart-rending agonies were like the outer ripples of a dream.

Damaris was folding gowns neatly, passing them to Nancy who packed them into a valise; they would be moving to Bristol in the morning. Like a mother whose first reaction to her child's narrow escape from danger is a burst of anger, so she lectured Venetia.

'What madness possessed you? You could have been killed!'

'I wish that I had!' Venetia answered between hiccuping sobs. 'He will despise me for ever. And Michael and Mallory are so cross.'

'Of course they are, and rightly so.' Damaris could be hard at times. 'You have exposed them to mockery. Their comrades lose no opportunity to exercise their wit at someone else's expense.'

The victorious troops were already celebrating, and filling their pockets with loot as soon as an officer's back was turned. Singing and hallooing, arm in arm with the recruits who had deserted over to their side, they barged into the houses of noted Roundhead supporters, pointed out by their new companions eager to

97

please. A mob swept on to Bristol Bridge where the shopkeepers were notoriously Parliamentarian in sympathies.

Mallory had been among those striving to keep order, knocking sense into the thick heads of some of the ringleaders. Rupert had told his Lifeguard that he hoped the soldiers would take the city without pillaging it, and they knew that it was not so much a point of honour as a religion to him, to make good his word.

Mallory trudged into Damaris' apartment weary enough to drop. He was not overjoyed to see the object of his angry concern sitting there. His mistress, glancing at his glum face, sent her servants scurrying for refreshment, and opened one of her bottles of sack. Mallory unfastened his sword-belt, letting it jangle to the floor, while Damaris fussed with the buckles of his corselet, getting him out of it.

The food revived him, but the wine made him argumentative and he quarrelled with Venetia, who hotly resented his overbearing attitude. As Damaris had surmised, the Lifeguard had lost no time in chaffing him.

'Leaving aside the raillery which I have suffered, you have succeeded in making

Michael a laughing-stock! Why, only just now, I had to rebuke a couple of subalterns whom I overheard saying that Prince Rupert will put a pair of horns on Captain Haywood as high as a stag's antlers!'

Venetia was seething with rage. 'You talk as if we are already wed!'

He jerked back his chair and stood up to cheat her of the satisfaction of being able to look down at him. 'Dammit, you are as good as married. D'you think I don't know that he lies with you? Forget the Prince! He is not for you!'

FIVE

"Bristol taken, Exeter shaking, Gloucester quaking", crowed the Royalist newspaper *Mercurius Aulicus,* showing Rupert with fulsome praises, and enlarging upon the difficulties which now beset gloomy London.

Fiennes was severely censured and very nearly court-martialled. The morale of the Parliamentarians was low and the leaders were quarrelling. Robert Devereux, third

Earl of Essex was their Captain-General, a sober God-fearing nobleman. But he was lethargic and over-cautious, a very strange heir for the dashing, turbulent Earl, whom the elderly Queen Elizabeth had loved, yet sent to the scaffold forty years before. The Cavaliers amused themselves with his foibles. They made up ribald songs about his wife who had left him for another man, calling him "The Great Cuckold!"

Sir Thomas Fairfax and his father in the North, and Oliver Cromwell in the East, were more stirring names. Sir William Waller was a favourite of the eager partisans who fretted at the dullness of Essex. But even he had gone back to the Capital under a cloud and was not on speaking terms with Lord Essex.

Bristol had been a tremendous fillip to the Royalist party, and all agreed that it could not have been stormed by anyone except the King's nephew. Meanwhile, the object of this acclaim was very busy squeezing contributions from the tight-fisted burghers, who found him unnervingly canny at driving a hard bargain, drilling the recruits which flocked in, strengthening the fortifications, and falling out with Lord Hertford.

'He and Maurice are a tactless pair!' Damaris was sitting with Venetia in a room at the *Bear and Staff* tavern, watching the actors rehearse. 'They were so pleased to be fighting together again, that they practically ran the siege between them, just as if Hertford were not there at all! I hear that the King is coming to settle their differences.'

'Rupert will get his way, no doubt,' drawled Etienne lazily, his voice coming from beneath the brim of his hat which was tipped forward over his face. He was slouched low in his chair, legs propped up on another.

'Oh, these soldiers!' Damaris, while acknowledging the Prince's capabilities, was fully aware of how his authoritative actions often exacerbated a situation. 'Rupert, so quick to criticize others, is only too compliant in his dealings with Maurice.'

'Ah, well,' put in the Chevalier, pushing back his hat and regarding them with a smile. 'Maurice is his brother, and not to be called to order!'

'My dear, we all know that he can do no wrong in Rupert's eyes.' Damaris would most probably have said just the same had the Prince been present. 'Was it not ever thus even when you were at Leyden University? He is really very naughty, and makes no attempt to get on well with the Council of War, dismissing with a "Pish!" anything with which he does not agree. It is not the spirit calculated to endear him to the nobles who consider themselves every bit as good as the son of a dethroned King.'

'That is half the trouble.' Etienne sat up, reaching for the brandy bottle and applying himself to it with extreme diligence. 'It is their poverty which makes the Princes so cursed touchy. Royal they may be, but they are also exiles, and penniless, dependent on their swords and the generosity of their relatives.'

'Could you please stop talking, over there?' It was Thomas Carter, in a ferment because the rehearsal was not going too well. 'We shall never be ready. Adrian—do concentrate, there's a dear! Stop looking at the Chevalier! Come, let us try that passage again.'

The landlord of *The Bear* cared little who was victorious, providing the conquering heroes were hard drinkers, and he welcomed Etienne's recommendation that the players would provide an added attraction. The inn was the finest in town, Etienne would never settle for less than the best, if it were humanly possible. An archway led into the courtyard where the building enclosed it on either side, and galleries ran all the way round each storey with flights of steps leading to them. It was very old with steep gables under a covering of age-sooted slates, its wooden struts elaborate with heraldic devices and grotesques.

Venetia shared with Damaris, a parlour panelled in oak, very dark, shiny and rich, with a massive chimney-piece heavily carved with biblical figures. Her bedroom was dominated by an enormous four-poster with faded brocade curtains, and there were cupboards, velvet-cushioned chairs, a mirror and dressing-table, and a closed stool with padded seat and chamber-pot; a civilized touch, so much more pleasant than having to use the communal privy in the yard.

The actors had been given much less grand lodgings at the back of the stables, but this suited them well; there was room to rehearse, and it was convenient for reaching the temporary stage which they had erected at one side of the courtyard. There was no scenery so, as was customary, they incorporated the gallery which became the upper windows of a house, the battlements of a castle, or a balcony for lovers, as the action of their play dictated.

Meriel, with Venetia's interests well to the fore, had suggested to Carter that they present a performance of "The Tempest", hinting that it might encourage some of the more wealthy citizens and officers to attend, if he could secure the patronage of the Palatine Princes.

'Excellent, my daughter! What a good idea! It will be a compliment to their Highnesses, for Will Shakespeare was dragged out of retirement to produce it as part of the wedding celebrations of their mother.'

The day had arrived at last. 'D'you think he will come?' Venetia asked Damaris for the hundredth time. She kept running to the windows which faced out onto the yard, but there was no sign of him.

'Maurice has promised to do what he can.' Damaris was fixing a star-shaped black patch in a provocative position near the corner of her mouth, while Nancy brushed and coiled, pinned and ornamented her thick hair, little threads of steam wisping up from the curling tongs.

Since the day of Bristol's capitulation, Venetia had glimpsed the Prince only from a distance. Her body still carried the bruises of her undignified tossing, but this was nothing to her mental hurt. Helplessness washed over her. It now lay in the power of those stars which Meriel said controlled their destinies to make him yield to the persuasion of Maurice, and his own curiosity to witness the play written for his mother.

With an unreal sense of ritual Venetia began to dress, her mind drugged with portents. Her gown was of soft, rustling shot-silk which shimmered with rose and green. Damaris advised her not to overdo the demure effect.

'Try a little of my paint,' she suggested, beckoning her to the mirror. 'Pull your collar lower, and don't forget to lean over when he speaks to you, so that he can look down into your bodice. It never fails! You do not want to give him the impression you are untouchable. I have already hinted to Maurice of your feelings; no doubt he will have related them to his brother. And yet, my dear, you do not want to appear a wanton. There are quite enough of those as it is, only too eager to warm his bed.'

Venetia nodded and listened to her friend whose advice was so sound; telling her that the Prince was a man, not a saint, and to treat him as such.

Nancy worked with the skill of an artist, enhancing Venetia's features with the subtle application of cosmetics. At home she had used some beauty aids, skin lotions brewed in their own still-rooms, creams for keeping the hands white, perfume distilled from rose-leaves, but never paints. Nancy emphasized her good points, brushing her cheeks with a hare's foot dipped in rouge-powder, reddening her lips with carmine, pressing a touch of blue shadow on her eyelids and blackening the tips of her lashes.

Etienne whistled wordlessly when he came in, turning her round slowly so that he could view her from all angles. *'Mon Dieu!* If this doesn't move him, then the *Pfalzgraf* must be gelt!'

Playbills had been pasted all over town in prominent places and had attracted a large crowd. The landlord kept his staff on the trot, bearing trays of foaming tankards, hot meat-pasties, crusty bread and fresh cheese to serve the customers crowding the

106

benches in front of the stage. Bristol had been starved of entertainment during the dismal Roundhead occupation. Now trade was booming again. The Royalist soldiery spent their money freely; shopkeepers, warehouses and taverns benefited hugely, even if it was at the expense of those citizens who complained that they had been pillaged.

Carter was wearing the grey beard and flowing robes of "Prospero", and leaned out of the window of the dressing-room, raising an anxious eye heavenwards; 'Pray God that it keeps fine!'

The courtyard was open, and a sudden deluge, making patrons dash for shelter before the hat had been passed round, could be disastrous to their erratic fortunes.

Meriel, hooking the back of Adrian's gown, answered him cheerily. 'There's not a cloud in the sky, Father. We shall do well today.'

The actors were suffering from their usual jitters before the show, but Venetia felt that no one could be as nervous as she, sure that she would never survive if he did not put in an appearance. Even the fact that she caused a minor sensation when Michael took her across to their seats, was of very little consequence compared with this huge emotion which was shaking her to pieces. Afterwards, she never knew how she kept up that inane chatter, talking about nothing of any importance, while within her resounded one prayer, 'Oh God! Let him come!'

She had never felt herself to be on particularly close terms with the Almighty, but it seemed that He heard, for there was a sudden commotion at the archway leading into the street, and Rupert strode abruptly out into the sunlight, his head rising high above his gentlemen; only Maurice was nearly tall enough to look directly into his eyes as they talked.

A spontaneous cheer rose from the crowd of troops and tradesmen, apprentices, and citizens on a spree. Hats came off, the men bowed while the women curtsied, peeking up to catch a glimpse of him. He uncovered and acknowledged the homage with a solemn returning bow, and the throng parted to let him through.

The Royal brothers took their seats on the other side of Mallory who occupied the place next to Venetia. Rupert's eyes were on her, his lips curving faintly in greeting. She could hear his voice with that foreign intonation, and Maurice's halting English, and she wanted to leap to her feet, thrust Mallory out of her way, hang on to Rupert's sleeve and tell him that she adored him.

Damaris, leaning across Etienne, was making some remark to Maurice, tapping him on the arm with intimate fingers. Behind them sat Rupert's friends, Richard Crane, Major Will Legge and Charles Gerard, in that privileged position of knowing him well enough to bend across his shoulder and address him. There were a bunch of his mercenaries near at hand, lean and war-worn, throwing their weight around, with bearded jaws, manes of unruly hair, and flashy weapons, laughing and joking and ogling the women.

Michael had grown very quiet, his fingers still laced with hers.

'He knows,' she thought sadly. And how could anyone not be aware of the current pulsing through her, directed towards the Prince?

The noise died down as the play began. The actors were good, and held the interest of the audience. Venetia had seen them rehearse so often that she knew precisely where each well timed piece of business

109

was worked into the plot. She was glad that everyone's attention was on them and ventured a glance sideways to Rupert's profile.

It was perfectly true that, as Adrian had remarked, his nose was large, curved like one of his falcons, but this fierce aspect was softened by the sweep of black lashes. Although they sat on the shady side, there were beads of sweat on his upper lip which was already darkening; because he was so swarthy, his beard showed quickly, giving him the predatory look of a brigand.

He sat with elbows resting on the arms of the landlord's best chair which had been dusted and put in the place of honour, and he was bareheaded, his hair rolling into thick rings past his shoulder-blades. He was wearing burgundy-coloured plush, and his jacket was richly laced, with the top buttons fastened and the rest left undone in that casual, careless way so fashionable at the moment, displaying an amount of puffy lawn shirt. The sleeves were slashed to the shoulders with more shirt bulging through, ending at the wrists in wide, tight cuffs. His breeches were straight and decorated with tiny velvet buttons running down the outer seams from the thigh, meeting his supple leather boots which had the tops flopping over below his knees.

He was listening attentively to the play, smiling occasionally, making comments to Maurice and, without taking his eyes from the stage, reaching down a hand to silence Boye who was getting fidgety. Between scenes, he accepted a glass of sack, unfolded seemingly endless legs and stood up. And, with every heart-beat, Venetia was becoming more spellbound, the whole sequence of events taking on the ramifications of a dream.

The shadows were lengthening when, amidst wild bursts of applause, the actors took their bows. They were presented to the Prince who discussed the performance with Carter. Maurice was grinning at Damaris in a way which made Mallory bridle. She was playing them off against one another, languid and cynical, regarding all men with a kind of amused contempt. She was fond of Mallory, but the ease with which he usually cleared the field of rivals, piqued and provoked her; she fancied the younger Prince.

Michael wanted Venetia to go with him;

he had booked a private room in another tavern, but she impatiently tugged him across to join the Chevalier and his wife, determined to be introduced to Maurice, and through him, to contact Rupert.

It was a daunting experience to be stared down on by the two hawk-faced Princes, so alike, and yet so different in personality. Maurice had the same type of over-pronounced good looks, but Rupert had a double share of strength and beauty. Maurice was a year younger than he, and in him that inner fire was damped down; Rupert, when annoyed, smouldered, whereas Maurice only succeeded in looking sullen. It was significant that one of his nicknames was "Twin", and that he was known as Rupert's faithful "Shadow". His men had affectionately dubbed him "the good come-off", because of his adroit management of retreats.

Damaris had told Venetia that Maurice was very popular with his troops, easy-going, not a particularly brilliant com-mander, but having a staunch reliability and the will to fight very stoutly when the occasion arose. Some people found him rather a boor and a little uncouth because he was not familiar with English manners and customs. But he had many attractive qualities, not the least of which was his gallantry in action, and his unquestioning devotion to his brother.

His warm brown eyes followed Damaris, bedazzled, like a rabbit before a stoat, and he alternated between speechless shyness and coltish confidence, stumbling over difficult English words.

The Chevalier, that wonderful friend to all lovers, prevailed upon Rupert to be his guest at supper. At first he had wanted to return to headquarters but, seeing Maurice's regretful face, he shrugged and relented.

Damaris organized the seating arrangements to suit her own plans. Rupert stood back so that Venetia might pass through the narrow space between the tables and himself to take her place further along the settle. As her hips brushed his thighs, she felt his sudden startled flinch, followed immediately by an involuntary returning pressure. Trembling, she was glad to sit down. The possessive Michael put an arm around her and she wished him miles away.

She toyed with her food, appetite gone, trying to catch what Rupert was saying to Maurice, but they spoke in French; a curious French, interpolated with Dutch and German phrases, and this gave them ample opportunity for sharing private remarks and jokes which made them laugh, shutting everyone else out. This was a rude habit, which even Venetia had to admit was irritating, well understanding how it must madden the Courtiers if they did it at the Council-table.

At Etienne's end of the board, the subject had come round to General George Goring, who had been captured by the Roundheads at Wakefield. It was natural that such a convivial atmosphere, coupled with flowing ale and the company of pretty women, should bring him to mind.

'No one enjoys parties more than Roaring George,' said Damaris, adding with a sigh, 'Such a shame that he cannot be here.'

'Will you be able to exchange him for a Roundhead prisoner, sir?' Richard Crane enquired of Rupert. ' 'Tis a pity to have him cooped up in captivity when we could use his services.'

A frown darkened the Prince's brow, he remembered him from pre-war days, though he had not yet met him in this conflict. 'I shall see what can be done when we get some equally important officer to barter. He is a good soldier, when he's not as drunk as a fiddler's bitch!'

With a quirk of his humorous eyebrows, Crane tried to draw Venetia into conversation, winking at her when Michael was not looking. Damaris was flirting outrageously with Charles Gerard, whom Venetia had not met before, though Damaris assured her that he was one of Rupert's favourites and a valiant fighter.

Cards appeared as soon as the supper dishes had been removed. Goblets were kept replenished, and clay pipes sent up fragrant smoke to coil around the low, crooked beams. Some of the Cavaliers still wore their soldiers' garb, smirched by rough usuage, others had changed into a blaze of velvets and damasks. Their cloaks, slung over the back of chairs, sent out flashes of gold and silver lace as the tapesters brought in candles. In the background, Adrian was playing his guitar, and they started roaring out the chorus of "The Whore of Babylon", beating time with tankards and sword-hilts.

Taking advantage of Mallory's interest in the gaming, Damaris slipped out and, as if drawn by invisible threads, Maurice rose and followed her. They were not gone for long and when they returned, she seated herself demurely by her husband. Mallory glared at her, and she smiled sweetly back at him. Presently she came across and whispered to Venetia:

'He desires you. I've been talking to Maurice. Why else do you suppose we went up to my room?' Her violet eyes slanted with laugher; a delicious wanton, opulent and gamey, completely incorrigible. She assured Venetia that Rupert was definitely attracted, and a woman like Damaris was not apt to misread a man's signals.

Venetia could not imagine how the objective was to be reached; Michael was glued to her side like a limpet, while the Prince ignored her, talking to Boye who had jumped up onto a chair beside him and was being fed with the tastiest morsels. But, in his misery, Michael had been gloomily drinking a large quantity of ale and was forced at last to seek the privy. Maurice stood up, with the faintest flick of a wink at his brother. Crane and Gerald, grinning, scraped back their stools and accompanied him on his mission to make sure that Michael was detained. And

Will Legge, that solid, dependable friend to all, puffed at his pipe and watched these elaborate courtship dances with mature tolerance from behind a screen of smoke.

Then Rupert turned to Venetia; their elbows touched, eyes met and conversation began. It was so easy that she could hardly believe it. His shoulders obliterated the rest of the company and her heart was thudding so hard that she was sure it might leap into her throat and choke her.

'How does the little she-soldier find herself?' he enquired seriously. 'I hope that your fall did you no harm.'

Venetia was thankful that someone, probably Damaris, had kept topping up her glass. She was full of alcoholic *savoir faire*. 'A few bruises, nothing more, Your Highness.'

She sat at his side and shook at the thought of her own boldness. Something in common; bricks on which to build an affinity; a lifeline. She asked him if he had enjoyed the play.

He shrugged. ' 'Twas pleasing enough, though I have seen my sisters act as cleverly.'

Her ears pricked. Sisters? She wished that he would talk about his family, but

117

he had fallen silent, looking at her in a most disconcerting way. She stabbed about for something stunningly deep and clever to say, knowing full well that when it was too late, she would be brimming with wise and witty remarks. Nothing came.

Boye pushed a damp nose into her hand, his bright watchful eyes going from the Prince's face to her own. The dog and Lintz. Her words rushed out and she was asking him about his imprisonment. He expressed surprise that she knew of it, and told her what it had been like to be shut up for three years.

'Boye was a present from Lord Arundel, the English Ambassador in Vienna. A small, woolly puppy, weren't you, old fellow?' He ruffled his pet's fur and was licked by a pink tongue. 'Someone else gave me a wild hare, and I trained them to live together in harmony. But I let it go, it found captivity as irksome as I. God, it was so boring! They let me have books, and I studied the technical side of warfare. I drew a lot, played tennis, walked about the castle grounds, dined with Graf Kuffstein, who was the Governor and my gaoler. My confinement was close. I think they feared rescue bids. Kuffstein had been

118

instructed to try and convert me to the Catholic Faith.'

His brown fingers played with the stem of his goblet, watching the swirling golden liquid as he brooded on the frustrations of Lintz.

'I suppose it was good for the character. It taught me how to endure celibacy when necessary.' His eyes were on her face and there were tiny sparks, jets of amber, in his blackly-dilated pupils.

With admirable aplomb, Venetia managed to say, 'Were there no women in the castle?'

A faint smile tugged at the corners of his mouth. 'There was a girl—you remind me of her—she too was fair, and had the same colour eyes. Her name was Suzanne and she was Kuffstein's daughter.'

'Did you make love to her?' The impertinent question burst out, and Venetia was too drunk to care.

His smile was mocking. 'How eager women are to know that! When I finally went home, it was one of the first things my sisters asked. "We've heard about you and Suzanne Kuffstein! Did you make love to her?" My mother was more concerned as to whether she had managed to convert me to Catholicism. To both queries I could answer, quite truthfully, no!'

It was foolish to feel this uprush of relief. Why should it matter to her that he may have loved some girl out of boredom and despair.

'In any case,' he added, 'her father had been kind to me. It would have been ill repayment, on my part, to have seduced his daughter.'

Venetia did not want to think about Suzanne any more, so she asked him if the Elector Palatine had been captured also.

Rupert gave a sharp bark of sardonic laughter. 'Charles Louis? Not he! He always manages to save his own skin. He escaped, fleeing from the battle, and fell into the river Weser on the way. Yet even so, our mother made it known that she was much relieved that "he whom she loved best" was safe. She has always preferred him—he is a true Courtier. Now he spends his time flitting between the Hague and Essex House, currying favour with Parliament, apologizing to them because his wild brothers are traversing the country like freebooters!'

He was so furious that Venetia sobered, afraid that she had gone too far and that it would cross his mind that it was time this forward hussy took herself off and left him to his comrades.

'He is not for the Roundheads, surely?' she ventured.

'Charles Louis is for no one but himself!' He bit off the words with a savage snap. 'He lingers about his friends in Westminster, begging that they will not stop his pension because of me! I hope he dies of ennui, listening to the long-winded Puritan sermons! I'll wager that mother still dotes on him, although he is betraying the King. I was never a *beau garcon,* as he is, to make her easy with me—she was forever telling me this. No doubt she corresponds regularly with him, and she hasn't written me a single letter since I came over!'

He spoke so passionately, mouth so sulky, eyes so reproachful, that Venetia suddenly realized that this untamable creature could be very capable of jealousy over precedence, position and power, childishly furious because his mother dared to prefer the suave, unprincipled Charles Louis, to himself. Elizabeth of Bohemia must be a remarkable woman indeed, to rouse such resentment in her stubborn, wilful son. Etienne had hinted of trouble between them; the Queen had borne thirteen children, nine of whom still lived, and Rupert was the one with whom she quarrelled most frequently. They were too much alike, so the Chevalier insisted.

Venetia attempted to put this into words, and Rupert glowered, muttering something irritably surly in one or two languages. She was afraid that he was going to retreat into himself.

But he spoke again, giving a low laugh with an edge of bitterness. 'She cared little for any of us when we were children. As soon as we were old enough to travel we were packed off to Leyden, some three days journey from her house at the Hague. She much preferred the company of her monkeys and dogs, and those friends who adored her so faithfully, squandering their fortunes to keep us all. Sometimes she would send for us and parade us before some notable person, like a herd of stud horses! Best of all, she loves to hunt. I have yet to meet the woman who can ride like my mother!'

The roisterers were bawling toasts, and some of the young bucks, with bared blades held aloft, had their feet on the table, sending the goblets crashing. The Prince swung round.

One dapper gallant, with a blue ribbon in the lovelock which swung over his left shoulder, pledged him, and added:

'We'll drink to His Highness's dog too! Glasses raised, gentlemen—to Sergeant-Major-General Boye! Who puts the fear of God, or the Devil, into those canting, snivelling rebels!'

The cheering made Boye leap against Rupert, barking indignantly. He patted him reassuringly, eyeing his men, none too pleased. 'Hush, my Boye. 'Tis only your comrades, few of whom will be fit for duty in the morning.'

Venetia laid a hand on his arm, emboldened by wine and the fear that he would leave. 'Don't you ever forget the army?'

He was instantly guarded, experienced enough to recognize the worship in her eyes which he had become accustomed to seeing so often since the war began.

'I have no time.' The well-worn excuse sprang to his lips.

'You had time enough to dally with Mary Lennox!' She was angry and desperate. Very well. Let it hurt his damnable pride to know that he and Richmond's wife were gossiped about! She would sting him to rage, if nothing else.

A dark flush spread up under his bronzed cheeks, astounding her by the sudden revelation that beneath his apparent confidence he was uneasy with women.

Rupert shot her a wrathful glare. ' 'Sblood! What time did I spend in dalliance at Oxford? Three days, that's all! Much good did it do me!'

Elation surged through her. Mary had roused but not satisfied him. She began to feel her own power; the Prince and she were both becoming equals in this struggle to hide feelings and put up a sensible front. His face had set into moody lines with pouting mouth and heavy eyelids. Venetia wanted to run her fingers through his hair and kiss away the look of baffled anger.

He was talking again and she had not the faintest idea what it was about. She reached out and covered his hand with hers. In the candle-lit dimness, she could not tell his reaction, but he did not withdraw from her touch, and his eyes slid from her face, past the line of her throat to her high rounded breasts, and they narrowed, in a way which she recognized, hard and wary.

He drank down the last of his ale. She could smell the faint odour of it as he breathed, combined with the heavy masculine sweat on his clothes, the scent of leather and horses.

Rupert stretched and lounged to his feet. 'It is very hot in here. Nightingale Valley would be refreshingly cool. Shall we go for a ride?'

Cool would hardly describe her feelings when in some secluded leafy glade with him, but the hope in his words dizzied Venetia beyond speech. Walking on soft billowy clouds of intoxication, she was carried safely past the eyes which marked their progress to the door, amused, mocking or envious; and there was Mallory, dice-box in mid-shake, registering shocked alarm.

In the stable, Rupert's page appeared, catching the hat which he tossed over and receiving his order:

'Take Boye back to headquarters, Holmes: I shan't need you any more tonight.'

In a swift movement, the Prince put his hands round Venetia's waist and lifted her up onto Orion's back. It was the first time that he had touched her and she was sure that the air about them crackled. He said nothing, but mounted his own horse and together they rode out under the archway.

SIX

When they reached Durdham Down, the Prince spurred to a gallop, his hair streaming in the wind. Venetia suspected that he was doing it out of devilry, and also to test her ability against some yardstick of his own, most probably that Diana of the chase, his mother.

She flicked Orion with her whip, giving him the rein, determined to prove that she was no novice. His winged speed, the rush and whistle of the air, cleared the wine fumes from her brain. But the stocky pony was no match for the stride of Rupert's big animal, and he reached the rim of trees first, checking the courser, drawing him into a walk.

The view was wild, forest and cliffs intersected by the winding River Avon which had carved a deep gorge. Out towards the estuary, a ship, with sails spread before the breeze, was carried on the night-tide. It was a still evening. Faint and far away, the bell-ringers were practising for Sunday.

Rupert helped Venetia dismount, standing for a moment with his hands at her elbows.

'You ride well,' he said. Praise indeed from the finest horseman in Europe.

They led their mounts along a narrow path where the soil of the dusky forest floor was dotted with flowers which, when crushed by the hooves, sent up a sharp odour of wood-vetch and leek. As they passed through open spaces in the woods, they came across several late picnic parties, people resting, reading, playing with their children, and, in the seclusion of the undergrowth, couples were making love.

Curious stares followed the aristocratic young man and his beautiful companion. They were a striking couple, more richly dressed than most people who frequented Nightingale Valley, and their beasts were well fed and glossy. It could have been dangerous to come there alone, for there were footpads, working in gangs, ever on the look-out for victims, but the sword swinging at Rupert's hip, and the pistols in holsters each side of his saddle, would prove protection enough. It was not a healthy place to be in after dark, and some of the holidaymakers began to stir and gather up their belongings, casting speculative glances at the sky. Sunset-edged evening was throwing mysterious shadows, filling the gully with blackness.

The Prince tethered the horses in a glade, and they pushed on further among the trees, where he had to hold back brambles which threatened to tangle her hair. He hardly spoke and she found herself gushing information, about her home-life, her family, the people she had met in Oxford, and she listened to the words falling over themselves and thought, 'Who is this fool?'

The branches arching sombrely over his head reminded her of the fan vaulting of a great cathedral—the correct magnificent setting for the pomp which would attend the nuptial of such a renowned Palsgrave, and there would later be a great State marriage-bed, with a fortunate Princess waiting for him among satin pillows. Venetia felt cheated because she could never be that bride: but even so, she would not have him take her casually like any back-street trollop. She needed time to develop the relationship so that friendship overlapped passion, affection blended with lust. Their first mating must not be done in stealth with the constant threat of interrogation; a hurried groping, quickly over for him and as soon forgotten, and completely unsatisfying for her. If she did not please him, he would not bother with her again.

All the time, she was seeing the light dappling over Rupert's face, running into his eyes, slanting across them, spilling out again down to his mouth, and she gave up the struggle, unable to stop staring at his lips, so finely chiselled, cruel yet sensitive, rarely smiling. He took her hand to help her down a difficult bit and they both stopped. He smelled of heat, and of the spicy perfume which he used on his cheeks after shaving. The combined effect was so overwhelming that she put her hands behind her, seeking the rock-steadiness of a tree-trunk and leaning against it for support.

The Prince rested an arm on either side of her, so that she was enclosed, and bent his head to kiss her. His mouth was unexpectedly gentle, almost hesitant, as if he were not too sure of her acceptance. This moved her deeply; she yearned for, and sorrowed over him. He should not feel uncertain ever, not Prince Rupert, and she slid her arms about him, her lips parting, tongue seeking his in welcome and celebration.

Venetia could feel herself dissolving, wanting only to be devoured; she rejoiced that she was no inexperienced virgin. Michael had schooled her well. Rupert pressed her back against the tree, his body hard and demanding, his kisses hot on her face, neck and shoulders where he had pushed her bodice aside. He was fully roused, desperate for relief, as if he had not had a woman for a long time. This was what she had wanted since the first moment that she had seen him, towering and godlike, in the meadow; his wildness, his roughness, and his need, were so exciting that she was sliding rapidly towards surrender and had no inclination to stop. But it must not happen there.

She heard herself saying "No!" several times. He ignored it and she broke away

130

to stand, panting, on the other side of the path.

He looked down at her with the blackest scowl that she had ever seen on a man's face. 'What's the matter? D'you expect me to woo you with soft words? Find a silken Court fop, if that's what you need. Don't play games with me!' His hands shot out like talons, ready to rend and tear at this woman who was frustrating him, fingers biting into her shoulders as he shook her. 'Answer me! Do you want it or don't you?'

He was hurting her, forgetting his own strength, but she stood her ground. 'My God, if only you knew! I've never wanted anything else! But I'll not let you swive me in the bracken, like a peasant!'

Rupert released her, so abruptly that she almost collapsed. He turned and went crashing through the scrub, nearly tripping over a pair of lovers lying in the grass. Venetia, catching up with him, met his gaze as if to say, 'D'you see what I mean?'

She had no idea of his intention, miserably certain that he was going to escort her back to the inn. Silently, he helped her into the saddle and she could not bear it, wanting to fling her arms round his neck and beg him to take her, then and there, on the ground, like an animal, any way he wanted, but not to leave her. Who was she to dare dictate terms to him—of all people?

The road was unfamiliar and he drew rein at last at an imposing gatehouse, set in a high wall. In the courtyard beyond, Venetia looked up at the colours of the Palatine, flying high above the chimneys, silhouetted against the dark perimeter of the sky.

The back of the house was deserted, although cheerful sounds came from the direction of the kitchen, a clash of pans, and the smell of suppers being cooked.

'Get down, and wait for me there,' Rupert said curtly, pointing to an open doorway, before riding across to the stables, leading Orion.

She shrank back into the gloom, obeying his order, nettled because he did not want her to be seen, trying to convince herself that he was considering her honour, while the new cynicism, which she was rapidly developing, insisted that it was more likely his desire to retain that reputation for stern self-sufficiency which was part of his

132

mystique. He was respected as an austere, abstemious man. *Il etait toujours soldat!* as one of his acquaintances described him.

Then he was at her side, sweeping her up a twisting stairway to his bedchamber, flooded with the scarlet of a dying sun. Only his valet, De Faust, occupied the bare, functional quarter, and, after one startled glance at the Palsgrave's face, he could not get out quickly enough. Venetia was trembling and unable to control her breathing, wanting Rupert so badly that she did not know how to cope with the reality of having him.

His arms encircled her waist, dragging her hard against him.

'I am afraid,' she said.

'Why?' He was muzzling her ear, the rasping of his jaw sending shocks down her spine.

'Because I love you so much and you are going to hurt me.' The last of her pitiful defences was being stormed; now he could destroy her with mockery or contempt. If only he would say that he returned her love, even if it was untrue. But he did not; Rupert never lied. Instead, his hand came up to stroke over her hair, and he was gentle, so strangely gentle, that she

133

was lost; condemned to belong to him for the rest of eternity.

He lifted her against his chest, running his tongue over her tears, then locking his mouth on hers with a hunger which emptied her of all thought. He pulled her down into the canopied bed, caressing her inexpertly, with the eagerness of a young man who has been used to the offices of harlots. Venetia envied the leaguer drab of some foreign army who had initiated him, early in his teens.

His possession of her was quick, as impetuous as one of his famous cavalry charges, and she wanted it that way. At the moment when cautious Michael carefully withdrew, Rupert was beyond control. Venetia did not care; it would be no disgrace to have His Highness's bastard.

He lay quietly, his mouth on her breast, and she smiled into the dusk, aware that there were hours ahead till dawn, plenty of time to show him just how clever she was at loving; she would give him slow, lingering delight. She had experimented with Michael, developing an unerring knack for finding out and exploiting male sensuality. Rupert should benefit from this.

Let him rest awhile, and then she would use her skill to rouse him to an ecstasy which he would never have experienced with his whores. She would be imaginative and tender, because she worshipped him. He was her soul, a part of herself.

Damaris had been right; the Prince was an instinctive rather than an expert lover, and it was easy to believe that he was more at home with his gunners and his horsemen than with women, snubbed by his mother who had so often told him, when he was a shy, awkward boy, that he was too rough to please ladies. He shied away from emotional involvement, afraid to put his masculinity to the test, feeling that it would diminish if he could not win and keep the devotion of a desirable woman.

The accolades heaped on him early in his career had given him an exaggerated sense of his own importance. He had been thoroughly spoilt by the indulgent Prince of Orange in whose army he had first served. The admiration he had won, during his captivity, added to his self-esteem. Conscious of his own abilities and claims to distinction, he adopted that arrogant manner which gave such offence

135

to Courtiers and Councillors. Yet Venetia recognized that beneath this apparent conceit, there was still the child, one among so many clever siblings, scrambling for a crumb of attention from that careless Queen who seemed blind to the thwarted love of her hero son.

'You have made me so happy,' she whispered.

He stirred and touched her cheek. *'Liebling,* don't cry. *Ach Gott,* can it be that you really do care for me?'

He would need to be told repeatedly and then still doubt it. Her fingers were tracing across his body in the dimness. 'You are all I have ever wanted in a man. I've longed for you for years. Ever since I was a child I have been in love with you, though you were just a name.'

'All moonshine, surely?' He sounded pleased, though still deprecating. 'Girls are always dreaming, my sisters do it all the time.'

'Time will show if I speak the truth, Highness.' Even at the closest point of contract, she had not dared to use his name, and he had not suggested it. Now she added: 'Can I stay with you tonight?'

She felt his wariness; although they were

still clasped close it yawned like a chasm between them. Venetia took no notice, continuing to caress him as if it were already agreed that she should remain. She was beginning to know Rupert; he would have perished by protracted torture rather than admit he needed her.

'It will be the talk of the taverns tomorrow,' he warned.

'I'll wager 'tis already, they all saw me leave with you.' Her new confidence was amazing.

'What of your betrothed? I don't want him to hate me,' his voice trailed into silence as she wriggled against him, warm and voluptuous.

'You did not speak of that a little while ago,' she reminded gently. 'Did you expect to hand me back to him when you had finished? Don't worry, I will manage Michael.'

He no longer mattered; nothing was of any consequence beside her consuming passion. Oh, Rupert would be very difficult. There would be no placid areas of tranquillity as there had been with Michael; it would be like living on the rim of a volcano. Three-quarters of his mind would be shuttered against her and with this she would have to be content, checking her feminine desire to probe and peel away layers. She would have to be patient, subjugate her own personality to his, gladly paying the price for this enviable position where so many women wanted to be—in Prince Rupert's bed.

Sometime during the night, the poodle whimpered and scratched persistently at the door and Rupert got up to let him in, making him lie at the foot of the bed, instead of in his usual place, on his master's chest. Annoyed by this banishment, Boye retired resentfully to a chair where the Prince's cloak lay. He bounded onto it, turning round several times to get comfortable, and tried to settle down. His ears twitched, thoroughly disturbed by the vibrations in the atmosphere, eddies of powerful emotions which made him uneasy. His Prince's voice was different, low, vibrant, caressing, and there were the alien noises of the woman, her soft laugh, and gasps of pleasure.

When the sounds stopped, Boye came across, whining, to lick Rupert's hand questioningly. He rested his front paws on the quilt, unhappy to see the woman with her face buried against the moist hollow of Rupert's shoulder, her hair splayed out, mingling with his dark, tangled locks. Boye gave a sharp bark of protest, but though the Prince's hand half raised to quieten him, it dropped back and they were both deeply asleep.

Very early, Rupert woke Venetia and, reluctantly, she dressed and followed him out. Boye was before them, scrabbling down the stairs while Rupert hushed him with forcible Low Country oaths. The yard was grey-washed with dawn; they paused in the doorway and Venetia clung to him.

'Ich liebe dich, Ruprecht,' she whispered, trying out the phrase he had taught her during the night. He was still so beautiful to her, though he was dishevelled and in a desperate need of a shave, clad in hastily donned shirt, breeches and boots.

His even white teeth gleamed in a grin. 'Good. Your pronunciation is perfect. Tonight, you shall learn to say it in Spanish.'

She knew that he spoke six languages fluently; the prospect was delightful, but the chill finger of doubt touched her, 'You won't forget?'

'Sweetheart, how could I forget such a night?' He was laughing and relaxed. 'If we dwell on it more, I shall be forced to take you upstairs again, and I have work to do. Holmes will bring you to me this evening.'

He saddled the horses himself, there were no grooms about yet, and she helped him in the hay-sweet stable. This simple humdrum action and the way in which the animals responded to his sure touch and the sound of his voice, threw them into a rapport deeper than they had known in sexual congress. The world was so still; it was as if they were the only people living.

At the gate, Rupert became a General again, giving a sharp reproof to the sentinel nodding over his musket. They jogged between hedges still wet with dew. When they reached the turning which led to the inn, somewhere among the hawthorns, a blackbird began to sing.

As they parted, he leaned across to kiss her cheek with a look which was like fire and wine to her. Then he wheeled, and dug in his spurs, yelling over his shoulder to Boye, who careered after him, barking joyously as they raced for the Downs.

Venetia started up the gallery steps,

wanting to reach her room and think about the past hours, reliving every moment. She was nearly at the door, when it was flung open, and Michael loomed over her.

'Where the devil have you been?' he demanded, grabbing her wrist and snatching her up close to him. His eyes were bloodshot, his face haggard and his clothing rumpled. He had been waiting all night, drinking heavily.

Before she could answer, he jerked her inside and slammed the door. The noise woke Mallory, who, keeping watch with Michael, had fallen asleep in the bed. He raised himself on one elbow, scowling across at her.

The sight of him made her furious, she could feel pity for Michael in his jealous misery, but resented Mallory's interference. She twisted free from Michael's grasp, rubbing her chaffed wrist. 'I went for a ride with His Highness,' she answered sullenly.

Michael's eyebrows shot up and he regarded her intently. 'You must have covered a good many miles!'

Venetia could not decide whether it was sarcasm in his tone, unable to believe if he guessed where she had been—that he would be so controlled.

'We lost count of the time.' As she gave this lame excuse, she knew that it no longer mattered what they believed. From now on she would live under Rupert's aegis, and her eyes went over them scornfully, there was nothing they could do about it.

'Don't bother to lie to me. I know where you have been and what you have been doing.' Although his voice did not rise, he was murderously angry. 'What kind of a fool d'you take me for? Don't you think that I've seen the way you look at him, with drooling admiration?'

'If you know about it, why ask me?' she said tartly.

His face twisted with rage; this was a man she had never known existed beneath the quiet, gentle Michael whom she had taken so casually for granted. For one terrified instant she thought that he was going to strike her.

Mallory intervened, though wanting to thrash her himself, no man must lay a hand on his sister. 'Give her a chance! You have said often enough that Rupert is no lecher!'

But Michael was beyond reason, ex-hausted by jealousy and sleeplessness, his

142

eyes boring into Venetia as if he would unravel all her secrets.

'The Prince is human, and you are desirable.' He spoke between clenched teeth. 'It is useless to deny it. I know by your face that you have been lying with him. 'Tis true, isn't it?'

He ended on an imploring note, begging her to release him from his torture, willing to accept a lie, if it would blanket his mind from the obscene images which had filled it through those hellish hours.

Venetia stood fronting them with lifted head and steady gaze. It was as if some of Rupert's courage had poured into her along with his passion.

'Of course I bedded with him!' There was a ring of triumph in her voice. 'And I shall do it again!'

Michael's face was suddenly grey and old; his fists clenched till the knuckles showed white. 'I'll kill him,' he ground out. 'Mallory, will you act as my second?'

'Don't be a damned fool! You know he's an expert swordsman and a crack shot!' Mallory treated Venetia to a raging glare. 'You slut! See what you have done! He was one of Rupert's most devoted officers!'

'Still the war, and the prospering of the

war!' Venetia thought savagely. 'They are as bad as the Prince! A pox confound all men!'

'You should never have come with us!' Mallory continued to nag. 'The leaguer is no place for you.'

She rounded on him, blazing. 'Oh, no! Not good enough for Mallory Denby's sister, but what about your whores? You are mighty prudish over my morals, but never slow to take your own pleasures where you will!'

'That is different,' Mallory stated emphatically, but he frowned in perplexity.

She was repeating views being voiced loudly by many of the younger women now. If they were to be forced to endure the miseries and heart-break of a war which was not of their seeking, then they too wanted a share in the freedom. Mallory's mouth tightened; letters from Oxford had not been reassuring. Catherine wrote that they were having trouble with Ella, their house swarming with junior officers and students. Sisters were the very devil!

Anger, affection and shame warred in him. 'God, Venetia, be sensible! D'you really believe that you mean anything to him? He is forever on the move. Women come and go—many offer themselves. Sometimes he takes them—more often he turns them over to Maurice. He probably won't even remember your name.'

'That's a damnable lie!' He was putting into words her own sickening doubts. 'I am to go to him again tonight.'

Michael groaned, burying his face in his hands. 'I swore to serve him to the death. There is no man on earth I love so well. In truth, could never bring myself to harm him, but do I have to sit back while he rides you like a rutting stallion?'

Silence stretched across the room. Outside, the inn was waking. In the yard, someone was applying energy to the pump handle which wheezed in protest, buckets bumping beneath it while servants chattered, maids whisked into bedchambers with pitchers of water, or trays of newly-baked bread and sizzling bacon.

The confident tones of Damaris rang along the gallery, and a tall form passed the window to go clumping down the stairs. Mallory drilled Prince Maurice's uncaring back with wrathful eyes. He had problems of his own.

'Those damned Palatines!' And he was gone in the direction of Damaris' room,

145

where the sounds of a quarrel immediately ensued, with the clang of pewter as she hurled the breakfast dishes at him.

Michael did not stay, recalling his duty; his sense of honour compelling him to endure the agony of close daily contact with his rival—and chief.

As the door closed behind him, Venetia swirled round and ran to the mirror. Surely a woman who had been loved by Rupert must look different from common mortals? She almost expected to see a luminous aura, and was disappointed that her appearance was not changed, except that her hair was snarled and there were faint blue smudges beneath her eyes.

In a churning state of nerves Venetia could hardly believe it when Robert Holmes was announced early in the evening. She had been ready for hours, but now she had Damaris and Nancy searching frantically for last minute essentials, her scent-bottle, a fan, a clean kerchief. Then she swept out in a froth of petticoats, her velvet hooded cloak flowing behind her, while young Holmes smiled and held the door wide.

Rupert was worried. While they supped, she listened to his grievances. The crux of the matter this time appeared to be over

146

the Governorship of Bristol.

' 'Sblood, that they dare to question my right to be Governor!' the Prince exploded imperiously. 'I *took* the bitch of a city!'

Venetia, watching him cracking a nut-shell in the palm of one hand as if he wished it were Lord Hertford's head, had to admit that she had never seen such self-will and arrogance stamped across one face before. 'Someone should have whacked your backside early in life, Rupert le Diable!' she thought.

Maurice's inferior position under the Marquis had rankled the prickly German brothers for some time. His appointment as Lieutenant-General to Hertford had brought no satisfaction to either.

'He fancies himself slighted because I didn't go into a lengthy consultation with him over the surrender terms.' Rupert was in a very irritable mood. 'I wanted to get the matter settled quickly without giving Fiennes the opportunity to hum and haw. Hertford would have wasted time thumbing through half a dozen text books on correct procedure. Now he's damned well gone behind my back and given Sir Ralph Hopton the post, without a word to me about it! He knows that I will not set up another officer against Hopton. I esteem him highly, he's a gallant soldier and one of my mother's best friends.'

'What will you do?' Venetia was refilling their wineglasses. The Prince had dismissed his staff, and they were supping alone at a table drawn up by the windows which faced out over the garden.

'Do?' Rupert gave a sudden, frank laugh. 'I forestalled Hertford days ago. When I first wrote to the King, telling him the good news of the city's fall, I requested to be made Governor and he readily assented. The trouble arises because Hertford has publicly declared Hopton's appointment.' His eyes glinted wickedly. 'There's one hell of a row going on in Oxford about it now!'

Naturally, there would be; once more Rupert was involved in trouble. Venetia felt sorry for King Charles, called upon to settle the disputes of his quarrelsome Generals, a kind of minor civil war in itself.

'He arrives tomorrow,' Rupert announced. 'And he'll do as I want. He always does when I am nigh. But when I am not with him, the others undermine my advice—the Courtiers, and Digby!'

He was lounging moodily in the large padded chair, one leg slung over the arm, and the other stretched out before him. He seemed so preoccupied that Venetia thought he had forgotten her, but he suddenly beckoned, and she went over, sinking to her knees beside him, her arms going about his waist, head pressed against his ribs, hearing the steady pounding of his heart, feeling the heat of his body, the firmness of his muscles beneath the thin linen shirt.

'You won't be able to stay all night,' he was saying, his fingers against her lips as she started to argue. 'I must be up betimes to greet His Majesty.'

De Faust woke her a little after midnight, and she sat up, dragging the sheet around her, catching sight of his dour Flemish features above the glow of the candle, registering disapproval at this relaxing of the Palsgrave's high-souled austerity.

'Holmes is waiting to take you home, madam,' he told her stiffly.

Venetia propped herself up on one arm, able to take her fill of looking at Rupert now that he was soundly asleep. In repose, his face was poignantly boyish, with the frowning lines smoothed away, the lips

149

pouting slightly, not compressed, and the eyelashes lying in dark semi-circles against his high cheek-bones. A haughty, lonely young patrician, who had taken so much responsibility onto his shoulders. Tenderly, she pulled the blankets up more closely across his chest, bending to press her lips against his damp forehead, brushing back a heavy lock of hair which straggled across it.

She gathered her scattered clothing, dressed and went out, closing the door softly behind her, anxious not to disturb him. She knew how hard he drove himself, often in the saddle for fourteen hours at a stretch, up before anyone else in the mornings, and last to bed.

In the antechamber, she found Major Will Legge chatting to Holmes. He was thickset, of medium height, with nothing particular to distinguish him, except a pair of kindly, observant eyes. Universally known as "Honest Will", he seemed to be able to get on with everyone, and had taken the Palatine Princes under his wing as soon as they set foot in England. He was especially devoted to Rupert, recognized in him a plain-spoken fighting man, like himself.

150

Venetia had the distinct feeling that his care for the Prince explained his presence there at that moment. Women were a hazard, they might be rebel spies, or even hired assassins. No doubt, he had taken the trouble to vet her background before encouraging her access to the Palsgrave.

'Well, my lass,' he said, heaving his heavy shoulders from the mantel where he had been leaning. 'I see by the stars in your eyes that you have been enjoying yourself in there.'

Will insisted on escorting her back to the tavern himself. In the stable yard the horses were waiting and, from Orion's back, she looked down into his face as he warned her, with rough compassion:

'It is not wise for a young lady like yourself to fall too deeply in love with His Highness. He is dedicated heart, soul and mind to the happy outcome of the war. He spares neither himself, nor those about him in this resolve.'

'I cannot help myself, Major Legge,' she replied simply.

Will shook his head, sorrowing for this lovely, spirited creature, so fit a mate for Rupert, but doomed to unhappiness if she tried to shackle him.

151

'I've been with him from the first—I know something of his devils and his deeds, so take my advice, girl, make no demands on him, he must be as free as air.'

He heaved himself onto his horse, giving it a prod with his heels. 'Come on there, you old dung-bag!' And, before they left the circle of light flung by the lanterns hanging from brackets, he turned to Venetia with a final word; 'I think you will be good for him...I've never met a youngster so full of tension...he needs to unwind. Stay with him, if you can, for he is a very great gentleman, but be prepared to bleed!'

She recalled those words many times during the following days. Useless to fume, weep, sit at the window waiting for Holmes, or De Faust or even Will, to come with a message. The Prince was busy.

King Charles detached Hertford from the West by the flattering request for his company at Oxford, then he made his nephew Governor of Bristol as he promised. Rupert, having got his own way, readily appointed the faithful Hopton as his deputy, intimating that this meant virtually the Governorship in practice as he would not be there much. Spirited arguments began as to the next move to block Essex and make a successful advance towards London.

Not even the bonfires and revelry with which Bristol welcomed the King could rouse Venetia from her despondency. She hardly showed any interest on hearing that he had taken up residence in the mansion of the Colston family in Small Street, and that the city fathers were finding entertaining the Court an expensive honour. They were already contributing to a gift of ten thousand pounds wrung out of them by Rupert as a testimony of the "love and affection" which the town felt for the Sovereign!

'He could have written to me,' Venetia lay on Damaris' bed in a welter of misery. At first, she had not wanted to wash, sure that as long as a trace of his sweat lingered on her skin, some magic would bind them together. But now even the visible tokens of passion, the purple bruises left by his love-bites, were beginning to fade.

'Did it really happen?' she burst out, thumping the pillow with her fists.

Damaris was sitting in the middle of the counterpane, occupied with an intricate bit of embroidery. In and out flashed her

153

needle, an exotic pineapple springing into being in a blaze of yellow silks. 'Yes, my dear, it happened right enough! And don't I know it, having to listen to you babbling on about it ever since. I vow and declare that I know exactly what he said at any point during the proceedings, also what he did, and how he did it, with as much clarity as if I'd lain with him myself.'

Seeing that tears were about to start afresh, she changed the subject. 'How is Michael?'

Venetia rolled over on her stomach, turning a woeful face to her. 'I haven't seen him or Mallory.'

'Your brother is not pleased with me.' Damaris bit the thread and selected another colour from her basket. 'He is being very miserly about Maurice. But that dear child moves out tomorrow, taking a train of artillery to besiege Dorchester. He is ridiculously pleased with himself, now that they have made him a General and given him command of the Western Army. Aren't men vain?'

At dusk, Venetia started up when she saw a shadow at the door, uncannily like the Prince, but her cry of delight was arrested on her lips when he entered. It was

Maurice, come to take farewell of Damaris. And Venetia could not corner him, as she wanted to do, and demand if his brother had spoken of her; her awareness of his rank made her shy. Damaris had no such inhibitions, pushing him into a chair, setting food and brandy on the table and perching herself on his knee while he tried to eat, then, catching the urgent appeal in Venetia's eyes, asking after Rupert.

'Ah, well...my brother is rather angry at present,' Maurice replied, munching cheese-cake and apple-pie, one arm around the distracting Damaris. 'Those fools around the King...there have been high words!'

Damaris sat bolt upright and raised her eyes to the ceiling. 'La! There always are! The trouble with him is...now listen to me, Maurice!... You always present cloth ears and a blank expression when anyone faults him! Even you, and this imbecile, besotted wench here, must admit that His High and Mightiness is not at his best in the Council-Chamber! He goes to every meeting as if it were a skirmish with the enemy, and well you know it!'

Before she carted Maurice off to the bedroom to bid him goodbye in earnest,

Damaris said to Venetia: 'Send Rupert a letter. Maurice will act as post-boy,' and she dropped the key of her writing-case into Venetia's lap.

Damaris was a great scribbler, and never travelled without materials. Venetia spread out a sheet of paper, dipped the quill into the ink-horn, hesitated for a moment, and then started to write:

'My beloved Prince,

Since your brother has graciously consented to bring this to your notice, I will tell you of my deep unhappiness when denied the joy of living in your presence. I could bestow one side of this paper in making love to you; and since I may with modesty express it, I will say that if it be love to think of you, sleeping and waking, to discourse of nothing with pleasure but what concerns you, to wish myself every hour with you, and to pray for you with as much devotion as for my own soul, then certainly it may be said I am in love. I implore Your Highness, that you will send me word that you have not forgotten me, for, if this were so, it would be the greatest kindness to draw your sword and deal a deathblow to, Sir,

Your Highness' most faithful, passionate and devoted servant,

Venetia Denby.

Bristol. August 3rd, 1643.

Tears fell across the paper, blotching it; Venetia left them, hoping to touch his heart. She had no seal, so secured the letter with a strand of amethyst silk, twined with tinsel threads, borrowed from Damaris' work-box.

Maurice stood, regarding her very solemnly, just before he left, and he gave his word he would place it, personally, in Rupert's hands.

No reply came from the Prince. In desperation Venetia took to hanging about on College Green which had been worn bare of grass as the tertias were drilled. Rupert was strenuously training the recruits with exemplary care, refusing to waste his time attending banquets given by aldermen who hoped to placate the King. Venetia watched him from a distance; he was completely absorbed in his work rarely losing patience, cheerful and encouraging. Once, he noticed her, his eyes sharpening in recognition, and he was about to come across, when an officer galloped up and engaged him in earnest conversation. He made a gesture of regret to her and rode in the opposite direction.

Rupert was so offended because his propositions for the new siege of Gloucester had been overridden that he refused the command; none the less, he was going to accompany the King. Damaris predicted that it would not be long before he turned up in Oxford.

Venetia agreed to travel back with her, immediately regretting her decision when she stood waving to the army as they marched out through Frome Gate, with the Prince and King Charles at their head, the whole town resounding to the tread of soldiers, the challenge and answer of trumpets, the rolling of drums. Too soon they were gone, leaving only the garrison behind, and an air of anticlimax, a hush, and a waiting.

Dragging unhappily back to the inn to commence packing, Venetia found a messenger there with a letter. It was sealed with an immense blob of blue wax, deeply imprinted with the Palatine arms. In a rush she tore at the seal and it was a second before the words took shape and meaning.

'My dear Venetia,

Certes, you have no reason to think that I have forgotten you. My time has been engaged with the levies who know so little of war that they are like to ask for "mercy", instead of "quarter", though now grown so big with pride at their attainments, that they will deem it a dishonour to request either. The King would not heed the soldier and the advice of Rupert to take Gloucester by storm, fearing to repeat our losses here, and deciding to sit down before it in a formal siege, which may be a protracted affair which I like not, for it will give my Lord Essex time to come to their aid. I desire that you repair to Oxford, and there remain under the charge of Madame d'Auvergne, where, as soon as this business be settled, you will assuredly be joined by your loving friend,

Rupert.

Bristol. August 8th, 1643.'

Hardly a romantic love-letter; the sort of communiqué which he could have penned to a member of his staff, but its military brevity was softened by a funny little sketch of Boye, prancing on his hindlegs. It was an instant reminder of their last evening together when the Prince had put him through his paces, showing the tricks which he had patiently taught his clever pet.

Venetia laughed and cried over it, running to flourish it under Damaris' nose, kissing his name repeatedly, as if it were a holy relic.

SEVEN

The coach lurched over the ruts in the dry road and Venetia, wedged in a corner beside Meriel, was having difficulty in keeping awake. They were on their way to Oxford, a small convoy consisting of the d'Auvergne vehicles and those of the players. They did not anticipate any encounters with the enemy in this vicinity but Damaris had, early on in the war, obtained a pass as a French citizen, permitting her to go quietly about the country, even to London, without hindrance, members of the Parliamentarian forces being commandered to treat her with civility if she happened to cross

160

their territory. As a Royalist adherent this amused her. She could not wait to seduce some repressed Roundhead officer, and then tell him afterwards that he had shared her body with the hated Prince Maurice, and that despised debauchee, General Wilmot, to name but two odious Malignants!

'What shall you do now?' Venetia asked Meriel.

'Pa will find a tavern where we can stay for the winter. The troops will want entertainment when they are in winter quarters. There is a lull in activities then, though the Prince, without doubt, will be leading raids into the neighbouring counties to keep all fed and paid.'

Venetia pressed her hand against her bodice where his letter lay, warmed by her naked flesh. 'There will be ample occasion to see him.'

'The Duchess of Richmond will be there also,' Damaris reminded.

Venetia could now almost pity Mary Lennox, very superior. She had known Rupert, and Mary had missed her chance! Damaris had it on the best authority (that of Maurice with whom Rupert had discussed the matter) that he had found the experience both shattering and astonishing! Adding that Venetia had all the tricks and abandon of a harlot, without the coarseness, and he was hot to repeat it.

Thinking of this, she sat and glowed. 'I no longer fear her. He is mine now, and what can she do anyway, she is married?'

'That never stopped a good woman!' Damaris replied firmly.

She had her feet braced against the opposite seat, and, as they bumped over a particularly deep rut she began to curse the state of the roads, and the inadequacy of the springing of this English coach. As if to add to her annoyance, the driver suddenly braked with a force which nearly hurled them to the floor. Damaris thrust aside the leather window-curtains, ready to give him the trouncing of his career. She found herself staring down the wrong end of a pistol-barrel.

'What the devil...?' she began, flabbergasted by the sight of the mounted man who had ordered the coach to stand. Two or three others, on foot, presented muskets at them from the hedge.

'Madam, a thousand apologies for our unceremonious behaviour.' Their assailant's voice was full of a lazy humour, and his eyes glittered through the slits in his black vizard. He bent almost to his saddle-bow in ironic courtesy. 'My friends and I are but poor fellows, torn from hearth and home by this plaguey war, striving to seek the wherewithal to keep body and soul together.'

'Why are you not with the army?' Damaris' eyes were running over him as if he were at stud, for he was showily dressed, his body broad-shouldered and powerful, and he sat his horse well.

'I'faith, we were, still my troop is but thin since Lansdown fight. What were left of them lost heart, and went home to look to the harvest. With humble duty I request a contribution, my lady, and be pleased to make haste about it. Your gold, your jewels, anything of value will suffice!' He cocked his pistol.

Damaris was intrigued, and in no mind to lose her possessions to this Reformado officer turned highwayman. 'How now, sir, would you rob honest supporters of King Charles? Go, seek a rich Parliament man!'

As she spoke, a couple of his henchmen eased forward and pushed their carbines into her coachman's back. He was shaking with fear, his face turned imploringly to his mistress.

'Hold!' Damaris shouted. 'God damn you, sir, d'you think yourself a gentleman? Call off your jackals. We are close friends of His Highness, Prince Rupert.'

The highwayman paused. 'The Prince Robber?' he said in a slow considering way, and then he laughed and reached up, and removed his mask. 'Well, in truth, wolves do not prey one on t'other. I have a fellow feeling for the Plunder-Master-General. His whores, if that be what you are, can go unmolested.'

He was laughing again...laughter seemed to be as natural to him as breathing—a handsome man with plenty of natural audacity, his thick curling yellow hair making his brown face seem darker. But his hellions did not think it amusing, starting to growl and complain, their small mutiny quickly silenced when he knocked up the pistol of one, and rapped another smartly over the head with the butt of his own weapon. Then, wheeling his bay, he ranged in beside the coach.

Damaris' lips were glistening with such invitation that Venetia guessed she would no longer be pining for either Mallory or Maurice. 'Get your disorderly soldiers together, Captain, and come to Oxford with me. You may join my husband's troop, when he returns from Gloucester. You'll be paid, never fear. We need men of experience.'

They clattered through the West Port and along High Street in style, with a fine escort, led by Captain Barney Gilbert, mounted on Damaris' spare horses, which she had loaned with the brisk warning that, should they be tempted to abscond, she would report them as deserters and see that they hanged at Carfax gibbet.

It had been arranged that Venetia would live with Damaris, but a visit to her aunt's house could not be avoided if only because she had money there, the remains of a small legacy left to her by a godmother. There was a painful scene with Aunt Hortense who did not mince words, a tearful scolding from Catherine, still weak from childbed fever, and a galling encounter with Ella, grown yet more precocious in the hectic atmosphere of wartime Oxford. Venetia left, vowing it would be a long time before she visited again.

She turned to the Chevalier's house very

depressed, sure that she had made herself an outcast, lost the man who really loved her, and for what? Two nights in the arms of a Prince who must look upon her only as some passing light-o'-love. Damaris was in the hall, on her way to a party, squired by Barney. He had slipped very easily into her life, this burly, boisterous blade, typical of the rapidly growing Cavalier legend; brave, devoted to the cause while it profited him, reckless and raffish. A member of the younger element who strove hard to be the complete antithesis of the Puritans, overdressing, drinking to excess, roaring about the countryside, wenching and leaving behind a trail of bastards, choosing to forget that no one led a more chaste life than the King who they supported so noisily. His estates, much as they were, had been sequestrated by the Parliamentarians. He had no alternative but to live by his wits.

He gave Venetia a lopsided grin and made a bow, sweeping off his beaver. Their companionship made her feel even more lonely; though Damaris was smiling at her.

'*Ma petite,* I'm so glad that you have come home early. You have a visitor. He is in the withdrawing-room.'

And she was gone, with a laugh, a wave, and a flick of purple silk, the door closing with a bang behind her and Barney, leaving a strong trail of perfume in their wake.

The black and white tiles of the hall shone like water. Beyond the high, narrow windows at the end, a great solemn sunset was tipping the spires with scarlet. Venetia hesitated at the drawing-room door, firmly quelling the wild hope which had flooded up at Damaris' words. Of course it would not be him! There was little chance of his appearing in Oxford yet. It could not even be Michael; he would be protecting him in the Lifeguard...

For a moment she was blinded by the evening rays pouring across the large, elegant room, then, stepping aside so that the damask drapes shielded her eyes, she saw someone leaning against the fireplace. It was Rupert.

Venetia stood perfectly still, one arm braced against the wall, then she was running across the room while he came half way to meet her, swinging her up in his arms with a great whoop of laughter at her surprise.

She managed to gasp out breathlessly:

'Highness, what are you doing here?'

His expression changed, his fierce eyes gazing down at her under their heavy lids. He gave an impatient snort. 'Forth is in charge. I'm not welcome at Gloucester. I'll be better occupied reorganizing and increasing my horse.'

He was dirty, his high boots caked with dried mud, and it was obvious that he had come directly to her after hacking back to headquarters. Still shaken and hardly daring to believe her good fortune, Venetia questioned him and, finding that he had not eaten for hours, she had a hand on the bell-rope for the servants.

'Have them bring a meal up to your bedchamber,' ordered the Prince.

Venetia hauled off Rupert's boots for him herself, without waiting for a manservant; he threw aside his sword, cloak and doublet, and the bed creaked as he flung himself across it with a deep sigh, stretching his great arms until it seemed that he would go through tester and panelling alike. They supped off salad and cold chicken from a tray placed between them on the quilt, washing it down with wine, and she produced a long-stemmed pipe and tobacco, getting a flame going with flint and steel while he puffed. He unwound and poured out the indignation of his soul into her eager ear, and although Venetia was impatient for him to make love to her, this rapport was so sweet that she kept asking him leading questions to prolong it.

'Holy God, if I could but have a free hand with the King,' he burst out. 'But there is always some Courtier or elderly commander who will oppose me. Forth is deaf, past his prime and too fond of the bottle, stepping into the place of Lord Lindsey with whom I fell foul at Edgehill. He swore that it would be the last time he'd go to war with boys! Prophetic words! It was there that he received his death-wound!' A grim smile played about his mouth.

It was getting dark and his pipe had gone out. He laid it aside, turning to take her in his arms, running a finger round the low-cut edge of her bodice.

'I like your dress,' he said in dusky undertones which made her want to tear it off. 'Let us make the most of tonight for I must be away again in the morning.'

Venetia was awake long after his breathing had become deep and steady, watching the patterns of moonlight shift across the shadowed room. This would be her life from now on; his sudden flying visits, a few snatched hours, then the waiting when he had galloped back to the knife-edge of danger. Every time he left, she would have to come to terms with the knowledge that she might never see him alive again.

The siege dragged on as Rupert had predicted. Sweaty messengers on foam-flecked horses thundered into Oxford with news, none of which meant much to Venetia except the horror of hearing that a grenade had been thrown into the Royalist trenches, missing the Prince by inches, while a few days later, his pot-helmet was knocked sideways by a stone hurled from the walls. She deplored his rash insistence of lingering about with the sappers, and spoke her mind on it when next she saw him, ten days later. But he only laughed and teased her and hauled her into bed without preamble, sparing her but an hour of his time.

Rupert was in an angry, sardonic mood; trouble was brewing between himself and Henrietta Maria. She was viciously jealous of the way in which Charles leaned on his nephew, blaming him for the move on

170

Gloucester when she had wanted an attack on London, managing to persuade herself and those closest to her that he had agreed on the siege, not from military motives, but from personal spite directed against herself. At this juncture, three Puritan peers had quitted Parliament, and sought to be reconciled with the King.

'The damned woman received them with contempt!' Rupert flung aside the bed-clothes and stood up. ' 'Sblood, couldn't she see that there was nothing to be lost, and, in probability, much to be gained by encouraging them? Now her silly action will discourage similar desertions which might be of service to us!'

Venetia listened to him raging as he dressed, moving about the room with restless, animal grace, muscles rippling beneath his smooth skin. How that proud little Frenchwoman must hate this dominating man who had exercised so much influence over her husband during the months that she had been abroad.

'They came wandering down to Gloucester and I took them to kiss the King's hand.' Rupert was frowning while he knotted his cravat. 'I gather the Queen is somewhat annoyed with me.'

171

The siege proved fruitless and the Royalists had to withdraw. Lord Essex, with a large army, speeding up his usual lingering pace, moved purposefully to relieve the city. Wilmot, with cavalry from Oxford, tried and failed to delay his advance. Finally, there was a battle at Newbury but the King's ammunition failed, and he retreated, leaving Essex with the way to London open, and the advantage to the rebels. What could be done to retrieve the Royalist fortunes the Prince did, but nothing could stop the sheer weight of numbers of the Parliamentarian side.

It was a dispirited General of Horse who came seeking his mistress when the army tramped wearily into Oxford. He told Venetia all about it, and she tried hard to understand the military jargon, and to say, "yes", or "no", or "did you" in the right places. One thing was very clear; he had played his part to the full, which was more than could be said for some. Facets of his uncle's character were becoming clear to the Prince; his stubbornness, and the way he vacillated between modes of action, too ready to reflect the opinions of the last councillor to advise him.

When he had talked himself to a standstill, Venetia was able to tell him that she was going to the supper-party which the Queen was giving to welcome them back. Rupert looked uncomfortable, though his hand still continued to pass over her hair, coiling the tawny locks round his fingers.

Stung by the thought that he was ashamed of her, she jerked away from the caressing hand under which she had been almost purring in sensuous enjoyment. She stared up into his strongly-cut intense features, filled with the urge to drag her nails down each side of his face, drawing blood and marring the perfection of his smooth cheeks.

' 'Tis because of her, isn't it? Mary Lennox!' she accused. 'You don't want her to know! So, tomorrow night, I must stand by while you ignore me. Oh no, we must not offend the pure Mary by letting her suspect that Prince Rupert sleeps with a leaguer-bitch who threw herself at him!'

'I am but trying to shield you.' There was a tightness about his mouth and warning sparks in his eyes. 'You have no notion of the cruelty of their tongues.

I would not have you hurt, so you had best obey me!'

He dragged her against him roughly, holding her by the hair, excited by the challenge of her anger. 'Come, kiss me, *liebling*. I did not come here to argue. God knows, I get enough of that elsewhere!'

Queen Henrietta Maria's drawing-room was packed with Courtiers. The ladies were resplendent in silks and taffetas of the pastel shades so popular that year, although black tended to predominate. An almost hysterical gaiety prevailed, a desperate determination to forget that Death waited for their men beyond these cloistered walls. It was the same spirit which had closed their eyes to reality before the war, when, beneath the hunting, the stately masques, the regal grandeur, the slowly seeping poison of rebellion had been spreading, soon to engulf the nation in a torrent of blood.

The room was hot; a thousand points of light from chandeliers sparkled on satins and jewels, sword-hilts and insignias. Their Majesties, seated on chairs upholstered in crimson velvet with their sons on either side, held out their hands to be

174

kissed. When everyone had been presented, formality was relaxed as the buffet supper was served and the musicians at the far end of the room struck up for dancing.

Henrietta Maria, so tiny and volatile, had a passion for company; wherever she happened to be, a miniature Court sprang up, where she surrounded herself with her sycophantic friends, her poets and artists. Every interest was concentrated there, each political or social intrigue gossiped about, places canvassed and schemed for; behind the suave masks and polite conversations, the gravest mischiefs were concocted. Her winning manner and brittle charm threw a fatal fascination over all who succumbed to it, none more so than King Charles who watched her constantly, like a man in a trance.

Venetia held her head high, but she was nervously aware of so many pairs of eyes coolly appraising, murmurs running round behind spread fans, with feminine giggles and low male chuckles. "How much did they know of her?" she wondered, panicking, or was this just their usual reaction to any new element which might threaten their tightly-knit cliques? Etienne was at her elbow, immensely kind, knowing just how to deal with malicious beau and spiteful lady alike.

Rupert arrived late, bursting in like a blast of fresh air through a hothouse, causing a stir, snapping them out of their lazy indifference into a kind of bored curiosity. Seeing him against the back-cloth of Courtly life, Venetia felt lost, cut off from him. It seemed quite incredible that only a few hours ago they had shared a cosy domesticity. Then, sunk deep in the feather mattress, tinglingly alive from his recent love-making, she had watched him as he stood, clad only in his linen drawers, grimacing in the mirror, scraping away at his beard with a cut-throat razor, cursing violently when he nicked his chin.

Now he looked so Royal, dressed in claret velvet and silver lace, wearing the wide blue ribbon of the Order of the Garter across his chest, with its flashing George. The gulf which stretched between them was emphasized when he leaned towards the Duchess of Richmond, who greeted him with the familiarity of an equal.

Venetia felt certain that being broken on the wheel could not have caused her more suffering than seeing Rupert lead the Duchess out in a coranto. For so large a man, he moved lightly, a natural dancer. It was a slow, stately measure, full of formal posturing, requiring skill, elegance and concentration and its very nature prevented any opportunity for flirtation or talk, which afforded Venetia a little comfort. Her face felt stiff with the effort of keeping that fixed smile; she was sure that in a moment it would crack across like porcelain. She wanted to turn tail and fly, but Etienne was holding her close against his side, understanding and wise:

'See, *chérie*, those are the members of the Council of War who vex your Prince.'

King Charles was conversing in his slow, hesitant way with Sir Edward Hyde, a bulky, rather pompous-looking individual who had studied law before devoting himself to the King's service. Etienne added that Sir Edward did not much care for the Palatine Princes.

'And those others are Jack Ashburnham and Harry Percy. They are both in Rupert's black books, being in charge of money and ammunition respectively. Powder, bullets, carts and horses provide endless sources of dissension.'

'My dear Chevalier, will you not present me to your charming companion?' There stood George Digby, a seraph in shining black satin, with white boots of the softest kid.

Introductions were made, with flourishes and curtsies and small-talk. Venetia noticed that Digby's mouth was not in harmony with the rest of his bland countenance. It quirked up at the corner in the smirk of a spoilt child who intends to do something naughty out of sheer obstinacy. No, on the whole, she did not much like the pretty Lord George Digby.

'I trust, sir, that you are quite recovered from your injuries?' Damaris was fluttering her eyelashes at him over the edge of her fan.

'Dear lady, 'twas but a slight hurt,' Digby drawled. 'During a brush with the enemy up on the Berkshire Downs, some poxy rebel discharged his carbine in my face. Thanks to my helmet, I was only stunned, a little scorched, and blinded by the powder.'

'I hear, my Lord, that you have His Highness, not your helm, to thank for your rescue.' The voice was familiar; Venetia glanced round and saw General Wilmot looking at her with his sensual smile.

Digby flicked an imaginary crumb from

his immaculate lace collar. 'I pray you, dear boy, do not bring the matter up should he join us, or we shall be launched into a tedious reconstruction of the whole campaign. So boring, and 'tis the only subject on which His Highness will discourse at any length.'

'At least Prince Maurice is not here to act as his echo, and remind him of fascinating details which he has omitted.'

'Thank God for small mercies!' Digby lifted hands and eyes to the painted ceiling, then they both indulged in wicked impersonations of the rather stiff Maurice with his thick German accent, and Rupert's curt speech and brisk soldierly movements.

Attracted by the laughter, Ashburnham and Percy came across to see what it was about, leaning on each other's shoulders, breathing brandy and smelling very high of orange-flower water. Digby loved an audience and responded with his cat-like grin and further pantomiming with his delicate hands, but his eyes kept sliding across to where Rupert was still dancing, adroitly changing the subject when the Prince took Mary back to her husband.

The Queen's shrill laugh and fluting treble swooped and soared above the hum of conversation, her bright eyes resting on her husband's face, and then going to Rupert, when they hardened. Her Courtiers were urging her to tell them again of her ride from Bridlington to York. She had enjoyed every moment of it, heading an army of two thousand Cavaliers, and needed no second bidding.

'I was their She-Majesty and General-issima! Their rallying cry was, "For God and Queen Mary!" Ah, such a valiant retinue of soldiers.' Her voice rose imperiously to include the young man who was persistently ignoring her. 'Rupert! Have I told you how it happened?'

The Prince gazed broodingly at her as he leaned back against the wall, his arms folded across his chest. 'You have, Madame, several times!'

The Queen smiled teasingly, but her tone was shrewish. 'You men try to convince us females of what a terrible time you go through! Why, it was just like a hunting party, but more exciting. Would I had donned the great helmet of my father, Henri de Navarre, and led my troops into battle against this pack of base-born rebels! I'd not be bringing them to kiss the hands of the Sovereign whom they have betrayed!'

Having loosed this shaft, she glared up at the exasperating individual who was no longer the gangling, attractive teenager whom she had petted in his first visit to England years ago, when Van Dyck had painted his portrait and Oxford bestowed upon him her first honorary degree of Master of Arts. He had been so appreciative, imbibing the states of his connoisseur uncle, developing his talent for drawing, and shyly adoring his aunt.

He was looking at her with a strange, aloof expression as if he could not for the life of him see why his uncle placed such great store by her. It was very offensive, and she whirled round irritably, catching sight of Boye making overtones to her lapdog.

'Rupert!' she shrieked in alarm. 'Get your great brute away from my spaniel! She's much too small for him. He'll give her huge, hideous puppies which will kill her!'

'A dog? So that is what it is. I thought it was a muff on legs!' remarked the Prince sourly as he prised free the unrepentant Boye, clouting him, and handing him over to Holmes.

'I am surprised that Madame's refined pet aroused him,' said Digby *sotto voce*, staring at Venetia in a way which made her want to toss her wine in his face. 'He is a foreign cur with a predilection for low company. No doubt, like his master, he would prefer to mount a mongrel bitch?'

Wilmot guffawed; even Ashburnham and Percy permitted themselves a snigger. But Digby's aside had not been quiet enough, and Rupert's hearing was keen.

'You spoke, my Lord?' His eyes flashed balefully as he rounded on him, hand flying to his sword-hilt.

'Your Highness?' Digby turned languidly, an eyebrow raised; all knew it was illegal to draw in the King's presence. 'I did but jest with my friend, General Wilmot.'

'If it be a good jest, all should share it!' Rupert said, on a note of snarling menace. He had not moved, but the air gathered tension about him, and people began to look around for he had not bothered to lower his voice.

'We English have a peculiar sense of humour, sir,' Digby dabbed at his lips with his lace kerchief. 'It is not readily understood by foreigners.'

182

Rupert's face was livid, a vein standing out on his forehead, but King Charles was glancing across at them in reproval—they must not brawl in the Queen's drawing-room.

'Your Highness, I was but congratulating Lord Digby on your remarkable rescue of him at Aldbourne Chase,' Wilmot breathed admiringly, the respect of his words belied by the impertinence in his eyes.

'I did not ask for your opinion, sir!' Anyone but Wilmot would have buckled under the lash of the Prince's scorn. 'Save your breath, and use it to give me a satisfactory explanation as to how you let Essex give you the slip and get through to Gloucester. Were you too busy "jesting" then, mayhap, to attend to your duties?'

That started a rip-roaring argument which rattled back and forth, impossible to carry out with any decorum for, when heated, Wilmot could shout almost as loudly as Rupert. Ashburnham and Percy joined in, trying to hush this unseemly commotion, but they succeeded only in bringing down the wrath of the Prince on themselves. He jabbed a finger at Percy.

'And what happened to my supplies for which we waited in vain?'

Percy bowed so low that his fair curls almost brushed the floor at the Palsgrave's feet, but though he grovelled, his voice had a sarcastic edge. 'Your Royal Highness, pray forgive my presumption, but may I remind you that you did not return the carts which had borne the previous load.'

'You should know by now, Percy, that His Highness has a weakness for taking wagons unto himself, particularly if they be heavy with plunder.' Digby was being deliberately provoking, goading Rupert into losing his temper, so that the scandal-mongers might tattle of this further display of ill-manners on the part of the Prince.

Venetia watched their faces, Digby's so round and feminine, and Rupert's as darkly handsome as the Devil, each determined to have his way. England was not big enough to hold them both.

Rupert swore between his teeth, 'My Lord, you lie like Satan, and do it as if you were quoting the Bible!'

Unruffled, Digby threw him a taunting smile. 'Your Highness is, perchance, more fortunate than I in knowing this, being on intimate terms with that personage.' Never before had he shown his dislike of the Prince so blatantly, but tonight there was an effervescence about him, an air of conspiratorial self-satisfaction, and he added: 'Possibly, such an ability may be of assistance in my new post.'

'And what, in God's name can that be?' enquired Rupert nastily. 'The Queen's lickspittle?'

Digby was buoyant, relishing every word as he answered: 'I have given my services readily on the field, suffering wounds, bleeding for my King, but now I am content to exchange my regiment of horses for the political scene.'

'Sweet Jesus, I cannot imagine how the army will survive such a blow!' sneered Rupert.

'Alas, such sacrifices have to be made for the good of the country,' Digby said piously. Before the Prince had time to give vent to his feelings, he continued: 'The tragic death of Lord Falkland at Newbury leaves the office of Secretary of State vacant, and His Majesty has graciously asked me to fill it.'

There was a long, tense, funereal silence; then a rush of effusive compliments from the Courtiers.

Rupert's voice slashed across the flowery speeches. 'Well, my Lord Digby, I fear that the Roundhead marksman who killed Falkland, dealt a more fatal blow to our cause than we have yet realized.'

Then he turned on his heel and swung out of the room. Digby stared after him with narrowed eyes before excusing himself and going to lean over the back of the Queen's chair, all flattering attentiveness, while she smiled up at him in welcome.

Venetia wandered down lengthy corridors lit by smoking torches and patrolled by uniformed men-at-arms. Pages and attendants played cards in ante-rooms, forever on call; lackeys skittered up from the depths of the building bearing salvers and decanters. She was searching for the closet. Though the apartments were so fine this office was, as usual, tucked away in a remote corner. The floor was wet, and she held her skirts high fastidiously, the latrines which Rupert insisted that his sappers dug whenever the army pitched came were far better.

On the way back, she paused in an alcove which gave onto a small balcony. She was looking out across the dark, tree-rustling garden when someone spoke behind her and arms went round her waist.

'Beautiful Savage, you starve me of hope, and for all others extinguish desire!'

It was Harry Wilmot, drunk and waxing lyrical. His hands were cupping her breasts and his moist mouth was kissing her neck and bare shoulders. Venetia struggled, but he found her lips, his breath retchy with wine and tobacco. She wrenched her face away, twisting in his arms, putting up her two hands and giving him a hard shove. He was unsteady on his feet and tottered back with a grunt of laughter.

'Why so reluctant? Damn and sink me to hell, 'tis common knowledge that you are Rupert's whore!'

Haltingly, she tried to tell him of her love for the Prince, not wishing to hurt his feelings by rejection, hoping that he would understand and leave her alone.

'Love? You love him?' Wilmot screwed up his eyes, trying hard to focus. 'Bah! There is no such thing between man and woman. One can love one's fellow-soldiers, one's King, one's country—even one's horse! But woman—never!' He made another grab at her. 'Come, confess that you are no better than the *hurweibles* who blooded us when we were boys in the good old Netherlands armies. The *Pfalzgraf* too!

Damme, his sword was not all that he fleshed in the campaign at Breda!'

'Wilmot, you drunken sot!' The gigantic shadow of the Prince blotted out the light as Venetia's tormentor was picked up bodily and hurled into the passage. He dragged slowly to his feet, all the breath knocked out of him, while Rupert roared as if he were dressing-down a corporal. 'When I have finished crushing this rebellion, I shall give myself the pleasure of killing you, after I have dealt with Digby! You may choose your own weapons—rapier, pistol or what you will!'

Venetia clung to that big, protective shape and his arm came about her. 'Get your wrap,' he commanded.

She hung back, although he had hold of her hand and had started off towards the door. 'I thought you did not want them to see us together?'

He paused and, sensitive to every nuance, she could tell that now he had erupted into violent action he was feeling better; he had been wanting to punch someone all evening. 'I have told you, I care naught for their good opinion of me. You have seen for yourself how they are. Overnight they can destroy a woman's reputation with their tongues but, if this does not trouble you, then we will stand together.'

'Are you quite sure?' Venetia was thinking of Mary Lennox, and how he had gazed into those laughing eyes.

'God damn them to hell!' said the Prince savagely.

EIGHT

When Rupert and Maurice had first entered Oxford in the autumn of the previous year, they had taken over the house of the Town Clerk as their headquarters. Now, it was once again the season of dead leaves drifting across the gardens and mellowed colleges, muffling the noise of wheels and horses' feet, while the smoke rose from bonfires, a sad nostalgic fragrance which touched Venetia's heart.

She could not understand this melancholy; she had everything she could possibly desire. Rupert had relented and allowed her to move in with him, with a smile, a shrug and a warning that it was on her own head. He had a large staff of loyal retainers, known as his "family", many of whom had been with him since early days in Bohemia. Venetia was sharply aware of their suspicion; his chaplains made no secret of their disapproval; De Faust was very starchy and correct, trying hard to ignore the feminine garments which now bestrewed the Palsgrave's bedchamber. Rupert advised her to give them time, which was all very well for him as he was away a good deal.

Meanwhile, she hobnobbed with young Holmes, and struck up a curious friendship with that despot of the kitchen, the master-cook, Pierre Belfort, whom she had met when meandering down into his domain to find a bone for Boye, or collect a tray of food for Rupert when he blew in unexpectedly at some ungodly hour when all the servants were in bed. Pierre never seemed to sleep, snatching catnaps, nodding in his chair in the chimney-corner, hands clasped over his prodigious stomach.

Another ally was a voluble, energetic Welshman, Arthur Trevor, the Prince's new Secretary.

'What happened to the old one?' Venetia wanted to know.

Rupert was leaning over the table, frowning down at a map which he was trying to study. 'Blake? Oh, I got rid of him after Edgehill. We took the enemies' wagons and among their correspondence, I found reports of my own proceedings, sent to Essex by Blake, and a letter from him demanding an increase in pay. He was already getting fifty pounds a week for selling information!' The parchment would not lie flat under his hands; with an oath, he struck his dagger in one end and unrolled it. 'He was brought to Oxford, tried, sentenced as a traitor, and hanged.'

Trevor and Venetia exchanged a glance; the post was certainly no sinecure. There had been no regular secretary since Blake, though Will Legge had helped when he could, and now Trevor faced the enormous task of answering the mountain of letters. Rupert suggested that Venetia might like to assist him, and, all afire with his trust in her, she set to work with zeal, and was often present at important meetings, learning quickly how many difficult issues surrounded each project, and how little ease and pleasure it was to be a King's General.

Rupert did what he could to maintain order, to answer the innumerable demands, sort out the confusion concerning the allotment of quarters between different regiments, the clashes over lodgings and forage which regularly occurred. Everyone lacked arms and ammunition, and their wants were poured out to the Prince, whose own supplies were wretchedly insufficient.

Trevor shook his head in despair, sheafing together a batch of replies which required Rupert's signature. 'Was there ever such a difficult army as this? Made up of gentlemen who, while scorning to take orders from one another, show themselves equally averse to obeying a foreign Prince, while displaying a remarkable willingness to do anything rather than that which they are required to do! It is far too small, undisciplined, continually on the verge of mutiny for want of pay, scant of all save bellies and grievances!'

Rupert was never idle; with his cavalry he harried the Roundhead garrisons and towns within easy striking distance, making a series of swoops around the countryside. This guerilla warfare suited his horsemen, providing adventures which gave lift to ordinary army routine.

'*Mon Dieu!* I thought we should be settling down here, warm and snug for the winter!' Etienne came stamping into his wife's parlour, slapping his arms against his sides to get the circulation back into his hands, wearing his high leather boots and long cavalry cloak, his brown hair wet and the feathers in his hat dripping with rain. 'But not he! The worse the weather, the more he seems determined that we shall be out in it!'

'Never mind, dearest heart,' Damaris wrapped a cloth round her hand and seized the handle of the posset-pot standing on a trivet over the ashes of the fire, pouring scalding ale onto the sugar and cinnamon in a tankard and passing it to him. 'I've nearly finished another set of hose for you.'

The house resounded to the click of needles these days; Damaris had all the female servants knitting woollen stockings. There was a pair ready to despatch to Maurice who had been ill with paratyphoid which was raging through the armies of both sides.

'Lord, I hope they are big enough,' she stretched them energetically. 'He has huge feet.'

The disappointing end to the victorious summer had brought a harvest of recriminations amongst the Cavaliers. Venetia watched the pressures from all sides taking their toll of his temper. He had been speaking the truth when he had told her, early on, that he had no time for love; sleep was at a premium, sex a luxury. A few hours leave were enough to put him in a towering rage. There were brief interludes in his exacting duties, giving him no opportunity to consolidate his position with the King.

'Why does Lord Digby hate Rupert so?' Venetia asked Etienne, as he thawed out by the fire.

'Trouble started as soon as they met. He had a high command in the army and the Prince was placed over him. Rupert understands war and he does not. His schemes are wild and fantastic, whereas Rupert's are practical and based on experience in the field.'

'His is an unquiet, mischief-making spirit,' Damaris added; 'He is very busy feeding the Queen's overactive imagination, and she needs but little encouragement.'

Venetia fretted when Rupert was away, wanting to ride with him, but he would not hear of it, saying, with maddening superiority, that she must stay at home and be about women's work; she could embroider a baldrick for him, if she liked, or knit him a crimson silk scarf to wear across his breastplate. She suspected that she was the victim of his dry humour for his tone was teasing and he knew only too well how such talk would provoke a high-spirited girl, having had experience with his wilful sisters.

Fuming, she made him his scarf, giving it to him for his twenty-fourth birthday on December 7th, and he went off on a foray flaunting it. Venetia, nose pressed to the window, watching him ride out of the yard with his Lifeguard through a light flurry of snow, prayed that it would never be used as a sling to help carry him, if he was wounded.

'Now stop moping. If you went with him it would add to his hazards,' Damaris said soothingly. 'You are lucky, he thinks a great deal of you.'

'Not enough to marry me.' Venetia was in a discontented mood, forgetting that, not long ago, she had sworn that just to breathe the same air as he, would have been sufficient. 'I haven't even his portrait to look at. I've begged him to have a miniature painted but he just snapped my head off and said that he hadn't the time to sit.'

'And you know that this is true.' Damaris strolled across to the fire, spreading her hands to the flames. She had a fur-lined cloak flung over her shoulders, for this winter it was so cold that it was necessary to wear one all the time indoors, not only when passing through the draughty passages. 'As for him marrying you—I thought you had accepted the fact that this is impossible. He could not, even if he wanted to. I don't think he will ever wed, sweetheart. I suppose you have heard that he finally refused that heiress who has waited so long?'

Venetia drew the curtain back into place with a sigh. Yes, he had told her, and she had been vastly relieved.

'Did you also know that King Charles, loath to let such a prize escape, wrote to Maurice offering her to him? Maurice showed me the letter. He suggested that Maurice should "take his brother handsomely off". Needless to say, he turned her down as well. Even eighty thousand pounds a year could not induce either of our Palatines to sacrifice their liberty!'

Oxford was preparing for Christmas, and gay—very determinedly so. There were balls, masques, parties and entertainments, with Thomas Carter's players in great demand. Young men galloped over the ice-hardened road on snatched leaves, citizens braved the frost to go to Christchurch and see the King and Queen dine in public, and, in spite of shortages and sickness, the old traditional merry-making was in full swing.

In the small hours of Christmas Eve, Rupert had come dropping into bed without bothering to take off his clothes, a habit of his which had started the rumour among the Roundheads that he had sworn a solemn vow not to undress until he had brought King Charles to Whitehall. Actually, it was a matter of expediency, but it did not make him the most fragrant of sleeping companions; it was rather like going to bed with a horse, as Venetia had complained to Damaris. Either that, or he would strip and, chilled to the marrow from the night ride, coil about her, rubbing icy feet down her legs, pushing her nightgown up round her shoulders, intent only on extracting every vestige of comfort from the warmth of her naked flesh, using her just like a fire-brick!

Venetia surfaced as it was getting light. Rupert was already wide awake, lying on his back with his hands clasped beneath his head. Outside their snug curtained cocoon, a servant was raking at the ashes, humping logs, busy with the tinder-box, so that when they decided to rise, the room would be warm. Venetia turned drowsily and snuggled against his side, feeling velvet under her cheek, reaching up to run a hand over his face, tracing the firm jawline, the high-bred Norman nose, the deep eye sockets.

'Damaris is giving a party tonight,' she reminded gently. 'You did say that we could go.'

He encircled her with one arm. 'Sorry, *liebchen*, I'm taking my brigade out to relieve Grafton House.'

'But it is Christmas Eve!'

'That won't stop the war!' he grunted. 'You know that the Puritans treat it as an ordinary day...that is how it must be for me also.'

All those festivities which she had been looking forward to sharing with him; now she would as soon spend the time shut up in their room, awaiting his return. 'When will you be back?'

She could feel him growing impatient, the way men do at things which worry women. 'How can I say? I hope that it won't be long.'

Sadly, she conjectured that this earnest hope was engendered not by a desire to speed to her side, but merely to press on to the next stage of operations. Why could he not catch some disease, like Maurice? Nothing serious, just bad enough to lay him up for a few weeks, so that she might have him all to herself. But he was so superbly healthy; one of those insufferable people who never ail and have little sympathy for those who do.

She sighed and delved under her pillow. 'I have a present for you.'

It was fashionable for the Cavaliers to wear bracelets plaited from strands of their mistress's hair, and she had ordered Nancy to take the scissors to her own locks. Now she fastened the result on Rupert's left wrist, unbuttoning his cuff, feeling the broad bones, the urgent pulse, under her fingers. She leaned over to kiss him.

'Wear it for me, my Prince, and God keep you safe.'

He pulled back one of the bed-curtains to examine her gift more closely, turning his wrist this way and that, the gold clasps glinting against the dark hair on his arm. He shook his head wonderingly, puzzled, strangely pleased, and his eyes, impenetrable in ordinary light, showed reddish depths, like a stag's, in the weak sunshine which slanted across the pillow.

'You loving little fool,' he said softly. 'Are you aware that your infatuation is the joke of the regiment?'

Venetia stiffened. Damn him! Why was it that he could never accept anything graciously? He still doubted her sincerity, even now. 'I am glad,' she tried to sound coolly sarcastic, 'to be able to provide amusement for your soldiers.'

Rupert roared with laughter, pulling her down on to him with both hands, tormenting and tickling and contrite, while she swore at him, vowed that she hated him, and beat at the muscles which scarcely felt her blows, then he was suddenly serious and passionate.

'Love me quickly,' he said harshly. 'The

trumpets will be blaring to horse at any moment.'

When he had gone, and the room had fallen back into that dead pool of silence and desolate emptiness, Venetia stood by the rumpled bed, stretching out her hand to smooth away the impression where his body had rested, so that no evil spirit should lie in it and gain ascendency over him. On her pillow lay a small red velvet box. She pressed the catch and inside, against a cushion of white satin, lay a locket, circled by seed pearls and rubies, with a slither of gold chain. Rupert's dark eyes gazed humorously up at her from the exquisitely painted miniature.

Lonely? Well, not exactly. How could she be lonely in that hive of activity, the quarters of His Highness, where there were always people coming and going. Hollow, was perhaps a more suitable description of how she felt—barren within and without, when Rupert was absent. Oh, she kept up a brave face, bright and cheerful, but down in the warm dark womb of the kitchen where she was wont to seek comfort, Pierre Belfort cast a wise eye at her and said:

'You've had no letter, madame?'

Venetia shrugged and shook her head, building castles on the table with his pots of spices; exotic odours excited the nostrils.

Pierre was stirring a sauce which he had invented to serve with pork for supper, adding sage, a stream of melted butter and verjuice, gravy and the brains of the deceased pig. He ruminated, as the big wooden spoon scraped against the sides of the skillet. 'The *Pfalzgraf* is an indifferent correspondent, madame. Queen Henrietta herself has chided him about this.'

Venetia shifted impatiently, reflecting Rupert's irritation with his aunt. 'I know, and she chose to do so at Bristol, of all places, right in the middle of the siege, adding a postscript to one of Percy's letters containing her hope that his success at arms would not make him forget his civility to ladies! Treating him like a naughty schoolboy!'

Pierre dived a hand into a wide-necked stone crock, coming up with a fistful of currants which he scattered into his sauce. 'He is unlike his mamma. She is a great one for dashing off letters to everyone all over Europe.'

'Except to Rupert,' Venetia could not

forgive the Winter Queen this omission.

'I think, madame, that the Roundheads may have intercepted the mail from her. She would have written—I am sure of it—although they had a furious quarrel just before he left for England.' Pierre lowered his bulk carefully on to a stool, ordering a minion to keep the sauce stirred and not to let it burn, on pain of being skewered on the jack and roasted over a slow fire! A bottle was produced from its hiding place, a rare old brandy which Pierre shared only with his favourites; two glasses were filled and one pushed across the table to her.

'You see, madame, she envies her swashbuckling warrior sons. A very marvellous lady, tall and robust—she would be riding at the head of the troops herself, all suntanned and rosy—inspiring them! This she would enjoy but, as she cannot do it, she is jealous of their freedom, finding fault, bringing out the worst in our Prince, turning him always into a defiant, bad-tempered young oaf! There is an eternal springtime gaiety about her—not that youth-seeking madness of Queen Henrietta—one forgets that she should be a staid matron of nearly fifty, and is only aware of her vitality.'

This dazzling mother of Prince Rupert, her radiance blinding her sons to the qualities of any ordinary woman, what an impossible rival she made!

Pierre had served the Palatines for years and Venetia spent hours in his company, listening to anecdotes of this remarkable family. There was the tale of Frederick Henry, who would have been the heir, but, victim of their attempts of economy, he had been drowned when an overcrowded boat on which he and his father were travelling collided with another in freezing fog.

'So sad, madame,' Pierre would say, with a deep sigh, 'only fifteen, the pride and joy of his father. They found his body next day, tangled in the floating wreckage, his cheek frozen to the mast. The Elector took it badly, dying himself not long after, still hearing his son calling to him over the black, icy waters, "Help! Father! Father!" '

Pierre could be very dramatic and this story never failed to raise the down all along Venetia's limbs. It was more comfortable to hear about Elizabeth, the studious eldest daughter, or the madcap Louise. 'So like our Prince in appearance and temperament, madame!'

And while Elizabeth and Louise, clever and witty, wrote pages to Rene Descartes, the French philosopher, and filled innumerable canvases under the able tuition of the resident family portrait painter, Gerard van Honthorst, the gentle Henrietta made sweets in the Royal kitchen.

Two sons were still at university, dark handsome Edward, and fair shy Philip, and the Queen had had her share of heartbreak; two babies had died in infancy, and her last-born, Gustavus, had not lived longer than nine years, silver-fair, angelic and fragile, he had been an epileptic.

'One of the sharpest members of the family is Sophia,' concluded Pierre, 'such a shrewd little lady, doesn't miss a trick!'

Oh, Rupert, Rupert, how many days must she endure before he came home? Venetia counted them in her head, and then again on her fingers to make doubly sure, and, to pass the time, went off to bath Boye, rendering that indignant animal into a soft white bundle of fleece, spending ages working at the tangles in his fur.

'We'll clip him again when the weather is warmer,' said Holmes, clearing away the mess.

'And don't you dare go out into the

205

stable yard and roll in the mud!' Venetia held Boye firmly by the ears, looking into his black eyes. He licked her nose.

At night they shared Rupert's bed, consoling one another. Boye pined as much as she did, when parted from his god, but it was not always possible to take him.

The excitements of Christmas being over, Oxford became more aware of its discomforts. There was an acute shortage of domestic staff, not enough laundresses, the influx of population had put a great strain on the scanty water supplies and sanitation, drains and conduits became choked and army fever flourished.

There was the usual crop of plots and counterplots boiling between different factors, culminating in a plan supposed to have been devised by the Peace Party in London. They had sent one Ogle to Digby with an understanding that the Roundhead Governor of Aylesbury had been bribed and was prepared to admit the Prince into the town.

He had been home for three whirlwind delirious days, and now prepared to depart again, striding round the bedchamber, gathering up essentials, huge and alien in a massive goatskin coat, embroidered with bizarre designs, lined with shaggy fur and smelling strongly.

'Given to him by one of his Transylvanian godfathers,' Pierre informed Venetia, adding, with a touch of pride, *Dieu*, he looks just like his ancestor, Attila the Hun!'

Rupert had a hat to complete this extraordinary outfit; a scarlet velvet montero, edged with sable, and with flaps, usually buttoned on the crown, which could be pulled down over the ears.

'Warm,' he grunted by way of explanation, tugging on his boots while she dithered, getting in his way. 'Very sensible headgear. Hats blow away in these gales, helmets are deuced uncomfortable.'

Holmes and Boye were allowed to go along, but not Venetia; no amount of pleading would alter Rupert's decision. Some hours after they had left for Thame on the first stage of the trip to Aylesbury, a galloper arrived with the news that it was a trap, and Essex was boasting that he would have Rupert, dead or alive.

Trevor sent for Barney and gave him his instructions, while Venetia fled upstairs and changed, catching him in the hall on his way out.

'I want to come!'

'Don't be silly, sweetheart,' Barney tried the fatherly approach, wrapping his cloak around him, ramming his hat down, knowing he was in for a cold, tough ride through the darkness to catch up with the Prince.

She gave him her most melting, madonna-like look which never failed to move every man—except Prince Rupert.

'Oh, very well, but you'll get me shot!' Barney capitulated with as much grace as he could muster.

In the stable a lantern glimmered, their own and the horses' breath hanging like fog on the cold air. Orion nuzzled against her gently, nosing in her pocket for an apple, then crunching noisily while she swung onto his back. Barney primed his pistols and produced a leathern bottle from his saddle-bag, taking a swig and passing it up to her. It burned her throat, and made her choke, but sent warmth tingling to the tips of her toes. She felt ready for anything.

The moon had come up, and the hoarfrost glistened. The hunting and hard riding of Venetia's childhood stood her in good stead. Barney was a rock, always optimistic, shouting encouragement, ready

208

with his flask, pleased and surprised at her determination to keep up with him. On and on, through the weird gloom of copses, between hedges, over wide moors where the wind sawed at the tortured lungs like knives, then, at last, a pale coppery sheen creeping across the east, and witch-fires and the pickets of Thame.

Rupert had already gone. They were told that he was halting at Lord Carnarvon's manor, planning to reach Aylesbury that night. No respite yet for cramped muscles and frozen extremities, and they clattered across the cobbles of Carnarvon's courtyard as the grey daylight grew stronger.

Barney went to find an officer and Venetia watched the scene from her saddle, the steaming horses, the activity of the soldiery taking on a dream quality. Even the cobwebs were spangled, rimmed with a million frozen droplets, the most commonplace objects transformed into crystal by the frosty touch of Faerie. Then Barney was at her stirrup, grinning waggishly, calling her "comrade", making the other men laugh. She slid awkwardly into his arms, he tucked a hand firmly under her elbow and guided her into the house.

The Prince was in bed but he shot up, instantly awake, while Boye's yelping protests changed to delight as he rushed across to leap at her, nearly knocking her over.

'Venetia! What in hell's name are you doing here?' Rupert roared, his black brows almost meeting in fury.

In jerking, disjointed words, she tried to tell him of the peril. Barney broke in, giving relevant details, and Rupert's expression was none too pleasant.

'That traitor Ogle! I knew that he was not to be trusted, but my Lord Digby was so confident. The fool! Ogle shall hang when we get back to Oxford. We'll continue to Aylesbury, and he'll march in the van to share whatever hot welcome they plan for us!'

Now he was safe, she could allow the backwash of terror to swamp her; for hours she had been dead to all save the horror of Lord Essex's net closing over her Prince. Life was coming back, agonizingly, into fingers and toes, so that she sobbed with pain. Holmes had appeared, astounded at the sight of her, kneeling to pull off her boots, then Rupert had her under the covers beside him, thrusting her numb hands beneath his doublet, warming them against his body. He asked Barney one or two more questions, commended him for his action, promised reward and dispatched him with an adjutant to find some breakfast.

He was angry and troubled because she had been exposed to risk, proud of her too, although she smarted under his tirade. She began to feel rather pleased with herself, now that it was all over.

Succulent chops were rushed up from the kitchen, clapped between two silver platters set over a chafing-dish to keep hot, and served with thickly buttered rye bread, and plenty of sack. Sitting up in bed, pillows stuffed at their backs, they ate, throwing titbits to Boye, and Venetia said:

'I'm never going to be separated from you again.'

'You might have been killed—supposing your horse had slipped on a patch of ice, or you'd run into a Roundhead ambush?' Because he was worried, he sounded cross, and Venetia rested her hand gently against the side of his face. He seized her wrist, turned his head slightly and kissed the palm, and she put her arms round him

211

and held on tightly, tipping up her face so that he could kiss her mouth instead.

'Can you understand now, how I feel every time you ride away?' she asked softly. 'I die a thousand deaths for you.'

Rupert was unfastening all the small buttons down the front of her jacket and the shirt underneath. 'You make a handsome lad. But do you not know that the army has issued a proclamation forbidding our soldiers to hide women in their quarters disguised in men's apparel?'

Venetia was luxuriating at his touch, her fingers in the dark curls which swung forward as he leaned over her. 'You are his General, surely you are a law unto yourself?'

His mock severity became serious. 'On the contrary, I should set a good example.'

There in the privacy of his hair, just below his ear, she breathed in the heart-breaking fragrance which was always Rupert to her; his unique skin, the outdoor freshness, with a hint of tobacco, wine and pomade.

'Rupert—' even now, the name seemed a shocking familiarity, 'they say dreadful things about you, that you drink the blood of innocent babies, and eat their flesh.'

'I know it,' he answered, and she could tell that the absurd, vicious attacks rankled. Then he laughed: 'Shall I devour you too?' His mouth came down to nibble across her throat. Later, he said: *'Sacrément!* I must get some rest if I'm to make any showing at Aylesbury tonight.'

Venetia woke up enough to demand: 'You'll let me come with you?'

'If I say "no", I suppose that you will only disobey me,' he was smiling, though his eyes were shut. 'Really, darling, you are the most mutinous of my soldiers. But, seriously, you must do as I say on the instant, if you ride with us.'

She promised and then surrendered to the urgency of slumber. Outside were the sounds of a military encampment, but in the room there was peace, broken only by the tick of the Prince's pocket-watch on the table, the crackle of logs, sending up an occasional shower of sparks, and the noises made by Boye, scratching on the rug.

As soon as it was dark, the Prince assembled his officers, giving instructions and ordering Ogle to be brought to him. The wretched turncoat stood, shuffling his feet, between grim-faced guards, while

213

Rupert, eyes hard as granite, loomed over him and told him exactly what he thought of him.

'I shall see that you accompany us to Aylesbury!' the Palsgrave's voice was as cold as the blizzard outside. 'You'll ride right at the head of the column—with me!'

They dressed Venetia in a breastplate and pot-helmet, and there was a new kind of admiration in the eyes of Rupert's Lifeguard, something other than the praise of virile men for a pretty woman.

A blinding snowstorm gave way to sleet as a thaw set in. Moving prudently, the army approached the silent town. Then a couple of videttes sought out Rupert, bringing with them a lone scout who carried the unconvincing message that they were to push on at once to Aylesbury as everything was ready for their reception.

'And we know, don't we, Ogle, just what sort of welcome that would be, made up of steel and shot!' Rupert said grimly.

The scout lost his nerve when confronted by the terrifying apparition of the Prince in his outlandish raiment, more than half sure that all the tales told him were true and that he was an emissary from the Devil.

'Tie him up!' thundered that awesome figure. 'Send me Colonel Gerard! We'll assault the opposite side of the town, where we are not expected!'

They rode as fast as darkness and treacherous ground would permit, through rain which had increased to a downpour. By the time they reached the far side of Aylesbury, the river was so swelled with melting snow, as to be impassable. Nothing remained but a speedy retreat.

Venetia decided that hell must be very cold and wet, not fiery, as she struggled through the lashing wind, blackness, rushing water and driving rain. Above the uncontrolled roar of the elements came the jingle of harness, the clank of arms, men cursing, and the Prince's voice cutting across the confusion, encouraging his troops, rounding them up, going back for stragglers, thudding up and down the ranks.

At daybreak they reached Thame, with Rupert in a black rage at the waste of time, waste of men, for some had drowned in the river. It was as well for Ogle that his life did not depend on the Prince's mercy that day.

NINE

The newly-created Earl of Holderness and
Duke of Cumberland (some punster had
already travestied it into "Plunderland")
was standing like a collossus at the head of
the staircase, bellowing for De Faust. King
Charles had made him a "free denizen"
and peer of the realm, in order that he
might sit in the Royalist Parliament, now
summoned to Oxford. He was late, and
could not find his insignia—a rich stream
of oaths rolled out, mostly concerning
his valet's parentage and the morals of
his mother in particular. It was the day
after the fiasco at Aylesbury, Rupert's
mood was still foul, and someone had
to bear the brunt. He had already reduced
Venetia to tears, upset Holmes, and ranted
into the kitchen, bawling at Pierre over
some imagined fault with his breakfast
which would have gone unnoticed at any
other time.

Pierre ducked, and kept his best crockery
out of reach, saying happily to Venetia:

216

'Just like when he was a little boy, red with rage and roaring, and his mamma, equally furious and determined to thwart him. You could almost see the sparks fly! He will enjoy an argument with my Lord Digby today.'

Much later, Venetia went to find him in the indoor court, working off his temper in a hard game of tennis with Prince Charles. The boy adored his cousin and, whenever he could, Rupert spent time with him, trying to mitigate the influence of his tutors, the domination of his mother, and the fussy, vague attentions of his father. Charles, just fourteen, was a tall, quick-witted lad, with glossy black curls and humorous dark eyes. His features were heavy, and his skin so swarthy that it bore evidence of the Moorish ancestry of his mother.

He thrived in Rupert's company, impressed by his talents, his ear for languages, his knowledge of books and art, science and mathematics. His audacious exploits were bound to endear him to a lively youngster, and, beneath that shell of haughtiness, Rupert was very understanding of the sensitivity of children.

'We'll make a player of you yet,' the

elder Prince mopped over his face with a cloth handed to him by Holmes.

Boye got up, his feathery tail waving, hoping that this might be the signal for a speedy departure out of doors, glad that his master had finished pursuing that silly little ball, one, moreover, which he had been sternly forbidden to chase.

Charles was buttoning his green satin doublet, his bold eyes going to Venetia. 'You may present the lady to me, cousin.'

With a lift of an eyebrow, and a perfectly serious face, Rupert made the introductions. She found it odd to be dropping a curtsey to this ugly-handsome boy who was looking her over with such precocity; hard to believe that he was the heir to the throne. Women would find him irresistible soon, and men fall under his spell, for he oozed that dazzling charm which the Stuarts possessed in an almost unfair measure.

'You are fortunate, Rupert, to have such a beautiful friend,' he remarked, his knowing glance assuring them he was perfectly aware of the nature of their relationship.

A chill, muttering wind swept past them as they left the tennis-court. Venetia had her arm through Rupert's, while Charles loped on her other side, giving her sidelong glances of admiration, and Boye rushed ahead, barking.

They took a short cut through the churchyard, with the poodle bounding in and out among the headstones, lifting an irreverent leg against the weathered inscriptions.

'Where will you be journeying now, cousin?' Charles wanted to know; then, without waiting for an answer, adding rebelliously: 'Why can't I ride with you? 'Tis wicked folly to be forced to work at one's books when there are father's enemies to beat!'

He was suddenly a child again, moodily scuffing the gravel of the path with his toe, hands thrust deep into his pockets.

Rupert smiled, sympathizing with the boy's indignant feelings. 'I am leaving soon to start recruiting in the Welsh Marches. My headquarters will be Shrewsbury.'

'Are you going with him, madame?' Charles was amused by the languishing look in her eyes whenever they rested on his cousin.

They had paused by a stile bridging the dry-stone wall; the fields beyond glittered frostily beneath the misted copper ball of the low sun. The bells of Oxford sounded thin and dismal, their peals muffled by the fog which was drifting over the flooded meadows. Rupert's hands were resting each side of Venetia's waist, ready to lift her, and he was looking down in that compelling way of his, straight and unblinking, which always made her breath shorten, and scattered her wits so that she forgot what she was about to say.

But this question had been hanging between them for days. Now she voiced it: 'Will you take me?'

Her worship in turn irked and flattered him; naturally he enjoyed it, but did not want the responsibility, really far too busy to stop and ponder where it was leading. She adored him, offering herself whole-heartedly and without reserve, a balm to his wounded self-esteem when there were so many people against him. Now he laughed and embraced her; there were compensations for the problems she brought, and he said:

'How could I endure the wilds of that barbaric country without you, *liebchen?*'

The horsemen breasted a rise. It was a

keen February afternoon and the northerly wind, blowing up the slope, set the feathers in their hats fluttering, and tossed the fringes on their sashes.

Below them lay a manor house, nestling in the valley, mellow stone walls, lichen-shaded slates melting into a background of soft greens. Rupert the artist saw it as an etching, while the General in him listed the dry moat, thick walls set with arrow-slits which could become musket-loops, and the easily-fortified gatehouse, now standing innocently open. He turned to his quartermaster.

'We'll stay here tonight.'

They moved down the gentle incline and Venetia was at Rupert's side. This never ceased to amaze her; every time Orion swung into an easy rhythm matching that of his own horse she could still not quite believe that it was true. They were on their way to Shrewsbury, and, when the scouts reported a clear road ahead, with no Roundhead pickets, he allowed her to jog up to the van.

In the paved courtyard, enclosed by the house on three sides and with the protective walk and battlements on the fourth, the owner waited apprehensively.

He had harboured the earnest hope that he might be able to keep out of the war in such a sheltered backwater, nonplussed at finding himself suddenly confronted by this stern, unusually tall young man with the foreign accent who introduced himself without dismounting.

'I am Rupert. No doubt, sir, you are loyal to the King. I seek quarters for the night, food for my men, and fodder for their horses.'

The Prince's tone indicated that he had not even considered the possibility of a refusal and his enforced host recalled every wild story which was told about him. His only aim was to get out of a tricky situation with the least damage to his property.

He pressed his lips to the back of the sinewy brown hand extended towards him. 'Your Royal Highness—such a great honour. We had heard that you were in the district—but never dreamed that we should have the pleasure—most unexpected. By all means, use our stables. You want to take over the meadow for your tents? Make it your own. There are officers needing rooms? My wife will be only too happy to air beds for them, won't you, my dear?'

In a nervous spate of words, he

introduced himself as Miles Farnaby. His wife, in a plain wool gown, a small cap covering her hair, seemed far less flustered than he. In fact, Venetia had the impression that she was rather enjoying this change from routine, it would give her something to talk about for months to come, and certainly Rupert was at his most courteous, bowing gravely over her hand, making his requests with a hint of regret at upsetting her household arrangements.

They dined by candlelight in the hall, where logs roared up the wide chimney, and Farnaby's hounds, stiff-legged, bristled at Boye who issued throaty challenge from between Rupert's feet, under the table. There was an awkward moment when Mistress Farnaby first realized that the leather-jacketed, booted and spurred stripling at the Prince's elbow was a woman, and, although playing her part as a good hostess, Venetia kept finding her looking across with scandalized eyes.

Farnaby began to feel easier with his alarming guest, even formulating, in his mind, the phrases in which he would describe to his neighbours how the most famous young Prince of the age had spent a night under his roof. His son, seventeen and impressionable, was listening, open-mouthed, to the soldiers' talk which rattled round the table. 'You'll be needing levies, Your Highness?' he burst out, interrupting his father who had embarked on a rambling account of the local hunting facilities.

Rupert saw the anxiety which sprang into Mistress Farnaby's eyes, and his mouth tightened. Fighting he could control and enjoy; military operations were a challenge, but dealing with personnel, their problems, their complaints and unhappiness, irritated him.

'Indeed, we need all the men we can get. Doubtless Major Legge will advise you.' Uneasy under the silent reproach of the mother, he turned to Farnaby, suddenly very correct and businesslike. Venetia knew this change of mood; here was a situation which troubled him, therefore he would concentrate on more straightforward matters. 'Sir, this is a fine house which could be useful to the enemy were they to capture it.'

Pride, puzzlement and apprehension chased across Farnaby's features in rapid succession. 'The Roundheads! Is it likely that we may expect a visit from them soon?'

'They will not bother you, 'til they know Rupert is well departed,' stated the Prince drily. 'In the circumstances I can offer you three alternatives—to man and defend your house yourself—to have it occupied by a garrison of my choosing—or to blow it up!'

Venetia's heart ached for these civilians dragged into a conflict which was none of their seeking. The Farnabys, in common with the majority of the people, wanted nothing but to continue their lives in peace. Now they faced disruption; their son would go to fight and perhaps to die, their house would resound with the tramp of booted feet, and they would be left the poorer. Rupert's vigorous decisions were often hard in individual cases. Love him to idolatry though she did, Venetia could not blind herself to this fact—he had war in his bones!

Her depression refused to be shaken off, hanging like a pall over her when she went to him that night, in Mistress Farnaby's best bedchamber. 'What will you do when the war is over?' she asked him.

He looked at her blankly for a moment, as if he never thought beyond the one objective of placing King Charles back in

225

his palace at Whitehall.

'Years ago my uncle wanted to make me Governor of Madagasca.' He was prone across the bed, fingers laced under his head. 'I planned to lead an English naval expedition to the Indian Ocean and conquer the island. We spent a deal of time studying ship-building—I was to have twelve warships—we even went into the details of arming and victualling them. My mother was furious when she heard, writing angry letters to poor old Sir Thomas Roe, who was doing his best to bearlead me. "No sons of hers," she wrote emphatically, "should go for knights-errant." '

'And that is exactly what has happened.' Venetia filled his brandy-glass, bringing it over to him.

'It seems like another life. I remember the wrench of leaving, when they recalled me. I think I was more upset than I had been at anything since my father died. On that last morning, we went hunting, and I told the King that I wished I might break my neck, so that I could leave my bones in England.'

As he was feeling reminiscent, she asked him if he remembered staring at her on that hot summer afternoon when they had

226

met. She half hoped that he might say that he had fallen in love with her at first sight, though she knew perfectly well that he never would.

'Of course I was looking at you,' he answered tersely. 'I was making a drawing of you, in my head, 'tis a habit of mine. The play of the light, the curve of your neck, made me want to sketch you;' he paused and grinned, '—in the nude.'

She should have known better than to angle for compliments, so set up the chessboard instead. He liked to win and usually succeeded. Now he was studying the pieces closely, scratching his head, tugging at his curls with his free hand. He cornered her queen and she spent some time deliberating her next move, but they had had a gruelling ride and her eyes were heavy. Bemused she stared at the tiny monarch, his pawns, his bishops, and his knights.

'Would you have liked to be ruler of that island, Highness?' she asked. What an Emperor he would make!

Rupert was asleep. Venetia had got used to his habit of suddenly dropping off, a trick he had learned in boyhood campaigns, snatching rest when he could.

His doublet was slung over the back of a chair and there was a rip in the sleeve where he had caught it and freed himself with an impatient tug. Venetia found needle and thread and sat closer to the candle to repair it. It was very shabby and when she had mentioned getting a new one, he had given his habitual reply—'No money.'

'What are we to do with him, Boye?' she sighed, and he looked up, head cocked at the sound of his name.

Miles Farnaby and his wife watched the brigade march out at dawn. Rupert, on his black steed, bowed from the waist in salute as he passed. Although he could ill-spare them, he had left muskets, powder and shot to supplement their meagre arsenal, and instructions on how to make further bullets, in an emergency, by melting down the lead guttering. Farnaby had elected to defend his home himself, promising to assemble a garrison from the village. His son rode confidently in the reserve, head high, clad in an antique cuirass and morion which had adorned the parlour wall for years. His mother's face was like a death-mask as she waved to him.

The Prince occupied the same house which he had used seventeen months before, when Shrewsbury had harboured the King and his forces for a while. It stood opposite the turnstile of St Mary's Church, large and comfortable and belonging to Mr Jones who moved in with relatives while Rupert was in residence.

The needs of the north were pressing, but there was much work to be done before Rupert could go to their aid; hostile interests to reconcile, powerful families to be placated, harbours fortified, contributions fairly assessed, commissions distributed, recruits made, trained, clothed, armed and, if possible paid.

He arranged his own commissariat, fought, by letter, with Lord Percy for every cannon-shot, and with Jack Ashburnham for each instalment doled out to his men, and argued with the whole country around him for every soldier's ration unwillingly bestowed.

Arthur Trevor had remained behind as Rupert's agent so now two of the chaplains struggled with the letters which arrived daily, all urgent, all demanding the Prince's personal attention. Venetia helped to sort through his correspondence. Any written on scented notepaper in a suspiciously feminine hand which proved to be yet another female offering her money, her estates and, mostly, her body to Rupert, she removed. The promises of cash were investigated, the others went on the fire and it gave her a primitive satisfaction to see those words of admiration, sent in by women who had fallen in love with his reputation, consumed in the blaze, leaving her sole possessor of the real man; in so far as anyone could be said to own that self-willed individual.

Rupert was in an exasperating mood, this kind of employment did not suit him, and he drove Trevor to despair by forgetting to answer letters, by signing bills of exchange without letting anyone know and by making wildly extravagant demands, on the principle that if he asked for more than he needed, to be delivered at once, an adequate supply might be expected to arrive somewhere near the actual time that it was really required.

They had been joined at Shrewsbury by a contingent of Irish soldiers, under their commanders Colonels Broughton and Tillier. Stout fighters, with experience behind them, Rupert much preferred them to the Welsh. They needed all the men they could get if the pressing demands for help from Newark, and Lord Derby's pleas that Rupert should go to the relief of his Countess besieged at Lathom House, were to be met.

Venetia saw even less of him than she had done in Oxford as he darted about the associated counties proving himself a most uncomfortable neighbour. Nowhere could the enemy feel free from the threat of his lightning raids. Amusing letters were captured, in which captains, holed-up in some remote fastness, sent frenzied appeals to their commanders for aid—; "I hear that Rupert is coming!" and then, in a terrified postscript—; "Rupert has *come!*"

And not only rebels were shaken by his unannounced appearance at any time of the day or night. He called on all the different detachments which were to accompany him on his march north, and little bands who had settled down comfortably, up to any number of profit-making wangles, were thrown into outraged consternation when he swooped upon them with his eagle scrutiny which missed nothing and would not countenance laxity. He was particularly dreaded by shifty aldermen, doing very well out of the shortages; their dreams of military neutrality were shattered when the Prince strode across the scene.

Damaris arrived from Oxford, causing a stir in the old market town, bowling through in her coach, finding her way to the house of Mr Jones. Venetia was overjoyed to see her, running out as she descended in a flurry of stiff silk skirts, her personality as glittering, as elemental, as barbaric as her beauty; sleepy Shrewsbury had never seen her like before.

'And where are the men?' Damaris was carefully working her fingers out of her fringed, perfumed gloves, evaluating the furnishings of the parlour where nothing was later than the reign of Elizabeth.

'They've gone chasing Roundheads at a place called Drayton. The scouts reported its being occupied by important enemy Generals whom they intend to capture or drive out.' Venetia ordered refreshments from Powell who had materialized even before she rang for him.

'Ah, a modest little exercise which, I doubt not, your beloved will complete before dinner.' Damaris could rarely mention Rupert without irony. 'And how is our magnificent *Pfalzgraf?*'

Venetia sighed deeply. 'Oh, he is always so busy and preoccupied. I sometimes feel that the only time I meet him is when we are abed.'

Damaris laughed, arching her slim throat. 'Dearest, don't tell me that this displeases you! 'Tis the one place where I can tolerate men! The vexing creatures! And I suppose Le Diable is being as difficult as ever, riding roughshod over everyone?'

'If he were less domineering, nothing would get done!' Venetia sprang to his defence, her eyes flashing. 'You have no idea how hard he works! Each time a Roundhead outpost is conquered an enlistment takes place, more or less freely.'

'They are all mad,' Damaris yawned, and removed her Cavalier hat, patting her ringlets into place. 'Particularly these Welsh, so I hear. Still, I suppose it is better to enlist than to hang!'

'He doesn't hang them!' Venetia's denial held a vehemence which made Damaris lift questioning eyebrows. It was true that, since knowing Rupert intimately, ripples of disquiet ruffled the serenity of her faith in his chivalrous nobility. Sometimes a chill ran down her spine when she looked into his face and read there his obsession with instilling into his soldiers the discipline of that strange, harsh communal life of the mercenary.

'Have you seen this?' Damaris was rummaging in her valise. 'Digby is losing no chance to flourish it while pretending to be wild with indignation at its imputations. Fortunately, King Charles has treated it with the contempt it merits.'

No, his latest insult to the Prince had not yet come with the post. Venetia read it through once quickly and then, as the full import hit her, sat down to study it more closely. It was titled, "A Looking Glass, wherein His Majesty may see His Nephew's Love, who secretly under pretence of Assisting Him to gain an absolute Prerogative or Arbitrary Power, will disthrone him to set up himself."

It was an unsavoury piece of poison pen literature, written by an anonymous "Wellwisher". Phrases stood out among the black lettering, as if written in blood—"Thus, Prince Rupert is so near the Crown, if law and Parliament be destroyed, he may bid for the Crown, having possessed himself of so much power already—"

'This is monstrous!' Venetia's hands were trembling.

Damaris retrieved the tract, eager to keep it for her collection, afraid that her friend might be tempted to cast it into the fire.

'A man such as he will inspire devotion in his troops, deepest loyalty in his friends, but he will also make enemies,' she said soberly. 'Rupert has offended a great many important people. It might be better if he had learned to be more suave and patient, like Digby, better attuned to the vagaries of the Courtiers.'

'Never!' Venetia was pacing up and down, her skirts rustling, driving her fist into the palm of her hand. 'He is too honest! Quite incapable of intrigue, deceit and wanton backbiting. Digby appears to be a master of it! I would like to see him face Rupert, sword in hand, then it would be a different story.'

Damaris was cautiously sampling the home-brewed metheglin which had been given by some of the Welsh gentry. It slid over the palate very deceptively smooth, taking several moments for the full devastating effect to be experienced.

'You've heard what Etienne has to say about Digby and Rupert, I suppose?' she asked. 'He believes that Digby may have rather fancied the Prince when they met. There are rumours of his Lordship's exotic inclinations; Etienne swears that his taste runs to boys, and he should know. Even if this is not strictly true, I expect he wanted to be the close companion of such a renowned Prince, and visualized them leading triumphal processions together. Digby must have been disappointed that his charms did not impress Rupert. I think he rather snubbed him, and, unwittingly, made a dangerous enemy instead of a doting friend.'

She stood up, and then sat down again abruptly; 'My God! What did you say this stuff is? Mead? Brewed from honey? What do they feed the bees on in these parts, for Heaven's sake!'

Venetia ignored her, head lifted. With that extra sense which she had developed, she felt, rather than heard, the pounding of hooves.

She turned to the door. 'He's here!'

'God has arrived!' announced Damaris.

The cavalry were blown but victorious,

and Rupert elated by the brisk fight and the hard ride home. The room seemed to explode as he came in. And there was Jonathan, waving aloft the captured colours of Sir Thomas Fairfax with its bold lettering, "For Reformation".

Everyone was talking at once, filling bumpers with mead, sending down to the cellar for more, and, between the disconnected sentences, the boasts, the forgivable exaggerations, it became clear that the Roundheads had fled, leaving the Cavaliers the richer for goods and prisoners; an important part of the booty, representing so much ransom-money in proportion to their rank.

Rupert's eyes were seeking Venetia, over the heads, through the confusion, and his lavish physical presence took her breath away. She waited her cue. Sometimes he took little notice of her in company; his Calvinistic upbringing, which demanded almost Puritanic standards, was constantly at war with his pride and his need for rich, varied experiences of the senses. Now she sat beside him, watching him raptly, with the afternoon faded into evening, the golden light deepening, making little pools of blood beneath their goblets.

His officers were full of drink and brag, and he smiled indulgently, pleased because they had taken Drayton without any loss of life on their part, clapping Richard Crane on the shoulder affectionately, the leader of his beloved Lifeguard of whom he had said:

'I can afford to try things which they are not expecting, and they will go along with it.' Indeed, at times, they seemed to have an uncanny knack of moving, even thinking, as one.

'Where next, sir?' Crane was as eager as an old war-horse.

A shadow darkened Rupert's face; the war was dangerously extended and he was in demand everywhere, but there was one person whom he wanted very much to see. Maurice had been dispatched to raise the siege when Chester was in danger in the middle of February. It was so valuable as a reception centre for the Irish forces, that the Prince intended to go himself and inspect it.

More travelling—always in the saddle —and no, this time she could not go with him—it would not be worth it—he would be back almost before she had time to notice that he was gone!

TEN

Barney went down on one knee at the feet of Damaris, seized her hand, planted a smacking kiss on the back of it and proceeded to declaim:

' "Tell me not, sweet, I am unkind
That from the nunnery
Of thy chaste breast and quiet mind,
To war and arms I fly." '

She tried to disengage herself. 'Lord, sir, rise do! To begin with I could hardly be called "chaste" and secondly, you are not leaving me—I'm coming with you.'

He leaped up with his broad ingratiating smile, making a grab for her. 'All this I know, Duchess! But you must admit, Richard Lovelace is no mean poet!'

The cavalry had ridden back yesterday with Rupert from Chester where orders had been received for a force to go at once to the relief of Newark. It had been holding out valiantly since early March. Now they

239

were almost starving, and, while the men were willing to try one last desperate sally, it would have meant leaving the women and children to the mercy of the enemy. Stubbornly they sent back answer to the Puritan summons—they would starve, and they would die, but one thing they would not do—and that was to open their gates to rebels!

The Newarkers sent an appeal to King Charles. There was only one person who would attempt the impossible, and this was easier said than done for as yet Rupert had no army to speak of. Will Legge had been dispatched, hot-foot, back to Shrewsbury, for as many musketeers as could be spared. The Prince followed himself, after a couple of hectic days in Chester, spent inspecting the earthworks, giving orders for a new prison to be built, and sequestrating Parliamentarian estates within a five mile radius to pay for the fortifications.

'And that is not all he did,' Barney's pale blue eyes grew unusually serious, and he paused as if he could not decide whether to add more, then said: 'News came that Brereton had already put into practice the Parliament law denouncing all the English troops that come from Ireland—good

Protestants, most of 'em—condemning them as Irish rebel papists! They are to be denied quarter, and those taken prisoner must hang. Brereton had captured thirteen of the Prince's own men, and strung 'em high at Nantwich!'

'And then?' Venetia said on a whisper into the room which had grown suddenly quiet. But there was no need to ask, that waiting stillness held the answer, and the memory of Rupert's face last evening, so stern and terrible, with that black spot of anger of his brow, and the rough way he had taken her as if seeking to smash all thought and feeling in an orgy of sensual indulgence, frighteningly unlike him.

Barney was poking his fingers in and out of the ribbon loops at his waist. 'Why then, sweetheart, there was no rest for any of us till the nearest billets of the enemy were stormed and his murdered soldiers avenged in blood.'

'And that was the end of it?'

Barney shook his head. 'I've never seen him so furious, or so determined. He selected the same number of prisoners as Brereton and hanged 'em from the nearest tree, sending one fellow to Lord Essex with the message that he would hang two Roundheads for every Cavalier who was put to death otherwise than in fair fight.'

Barney's arm came about her bowed shoulders. 'Believe me, he did not want to do it, but he is much in love with his Irish soldiers and will not tolerate their being slaughtered like animals. And an eye for an eye is soldier's law, you know—and no bad law at that!'

The army had changed the character of Shrewsbury, where once nothing more exciting happened than market-days, when the singsong idiom of the Welsh sheep-farmers mingled with the musical dialect of Shropshire. Venetia found it an enchanting place, roaming through the winding streets where the old, timbered houses beetled over the passers-by, and the skyline was jagged with topsyturvy roofs, thatching, crazy pepper-pot turrets and twirling chimneys. The Castle, lowering over all from its prominence, was the finishing touch to this fairy tale setting. It should have been peopled by witches and goblins, dragons, knights and fair ladies, not a motley conglomeration of soldiery and their drabs, the washerwomen, kitchen sluts, and doxies, the usual feminine tribe which pervaded every camp.

Now its antique walls reverberated to the thunder of drums, while trumpets shrilled, men-at-arms cursed, captains barked orders, and Prince Rupert's army moved out, taking the road to Newark. Venetia travelled with Damaris, and Boye jumped into the coach after her at the last moment, insisting on settling himself across their laps. Although the morning had been brilliant with sunshine at the start, cloud quickly settled over the blue Welsh hills and it began to drizzle.

'Oh dear, Rupert will get very wet,' Venetia sighed. 'A state not calculated to improve his humour.'

It continued to rain and, as the days passed, even the irrespressible Damaris grew weary, for how could even the most skilled woman look her best in the damp?

' 'Slife, this is the wettest spring I can ever recall. What a climate! One good thing about France is its weather. Tho', damme, with it all, I'd rather be here. If it had not been for the war, and dear Etienne's interest in it, I should have spent my days incarcerated in that vast chateau of his, among his dreary vassals, bringing up my children in complete boredom, while he had all the fun in Paris!'

Without any doubt, Damaris was in her element, despite the rain. She had all the traditional qualities of a beauty, with her wide-eyed innocence, her superb figure, and her manner which was faintly decadent, mutinous, full of devilry. There was never any lack of escorts riding at the coach window and, as the march progressed, her admirers increased. Rupert drawing off men from every garrison he visited. By the time they arrived at Ashby-de-la-Zouch, the numbers had risen dramatically to three thousand five hundred horse, and more than three thousand foot, all musketeers. It was a patchwork army, but most of the men were experienced, attracted to serve the Palsgrave by the magic of his military repute.

Damaris' coach was roomy and service-able; Rupert borrowed it, and it became dining-hall, council-chamber, headquarters and bedroom as the need arose. Venetia found it fun to ride in, like a small house on wheels, or a dim, padded cave. It had been smart once, but was now travel-stained and battered, the Chevalier's escutcheon on the door scratched by the brushing of bushes. But it was comfortable, with little cabinets in the panelling to store flasks and documents, and seats that could serve as beds, the whole slung on giant leather springs.

Rupert and Venetia spent one night in it. Damaris, high-bosomed and keen-hipped in a suit belonging to one of her pages, had gone off on some mad prank with Barney, so the Prince and his mistress sheltered in its dark intimacy.

Light filtered between the closed leather curtains, green-washed because they parked beneath trees. Venetia lay back against the cushions, watching his silhouetted profile. He turned to her, reaching out and drawing her into the circle of his arm, his free hand sliding up under her skirts, finding the soft flesh of her thigh. They talked and laughed in quiet murmurs while the rain pattered steadily down, penetrating the thick leaves of the wood so that his guards swore and pulled their cloaks more tightly about them.

A kind of bourgeois panic seized Venetia, she struggled to sit up. 'The coach will creak and rock like a boat, Highness!'

'Let it.' She heard the sound of his chuckle as his fingers closed on her wrist and pushed her hand down further through his unfastened clothing, pressing it hard against his skin.

'They will know exactly what we are doing!'

'Who cares!'

She could never have believed such passion possible in such an impossible situation.

Rupert's speed of movement and the complacency of the Roundheads proved their undoing; the besiegers took the news of his approach with light-hearted disbelief, quite unable to imagine that he would have the nerve to attack them. An intercepted letter amused the Cavaliers; in it was mention of "an incredible rumour" of his advance. But a force of cavalry was now dispatched by Essex to tail and, if possible, hinder them.

Ashburnham sent Rupert warning of this in a pithy note, brought by a sweating, blood-daubed galloper; "The strength that followeth your Highness is nine hundred dragoons, and one regiment of horse; which I hope will all be damned!'

'Damned or not, they've been unsuccessful in stopping me,' said the Prince, tweaking Boye's ears, sitting cross-legged on the ground, eating his supper by the camp-fire. They were bivouacking undisturbed not many miles from Meldrum's cohorts, and Rupert had sent out spies to observe them. He rolled himself in his cavalry cloak and lay down to snatch a couple of hours sleep before the action, with the dog curled up against him and the firelight flickering on his face.

Venetia kept watch, unable to rest, nerves taut as bowstrings. She sat with her arms clasped round her knees, her hooded mantle wrapped closely about her, for the night was cold and clear and the moon was rising. God, if she were only a man! Her fingers itched to grasp a sword-hilt and she longed to change her soft, woman's muscles for those of steel, like his. "No need to worry," said a voice within her. "Crane will guard him, and his luck will hold."

What was it that his admirer, Cleveland, had written about him in that long poem, "Rupertismus"? The words came floating into her head.

"Sir, you're enchanted! Sir, you're doubly free
From the great guns, and squibbling poetry."

247

When Holmes woke him, Rupert, fast asleep at one moment, was on his feet the next, grabbing up his sword, taking his helm from the page, and:

'You'll stay with the wagons, Venetia,' he ordered. 'Tonight is man's work. Keep out of it, and no tricks!'

'Have you managed to get in touch with the town?' Venetia knew that he had despatched two messengers already who had not returned.

'I've sent another man with a simple message which I hope that the Governor has the wit to understand.' The Prince was standing with elbows raised while Holmes adjusted the straps of his breast- and back-plate. ' 'Tis this, "Let the old drum be beaten on the morrow morning." He is to sally out against Meldrum at daybreak!'

That cold trembling was beginning within her, she clenched her hands into white-jointed fists to keep them still; familiarity with death had only increased her fears for him. When he was keyed-up for action, he did not like to be touched, nothing must divert him from absolute concentration, but she reached out towards him blindly, her words spilling over. 'Be

248

careful, Highness.'

He hesitated for a split second, his thoughts running ahead to Newark, anxious to maul Meldrum as well as relieve the town, but then he moved, as black and huge as the trees at his back, yanking her up against him, his armour crushing her breasts, gauntleted hand in her hair, his lips finding her face and then sinking on to her mouth.

The trumpets sounded cheerily to horse, and he swung off across the glade, a long shaft of moonlight striking his helmet so that it shone like a white flame. His men were happy, shouting and singing as they got into the saddle and Venetia caught sight of Michael, his foot already in the stirrup, and she ran over to him, forgetting that it was weeks since they had spoken.

'Michael,' she blurted out; 'Keep near the Prince. Have care for him.'

He looked into her face, tip-tilted towards him, silver-blue, her voice tight with terror for her lover. The touch of her hand on his arm seemed to burn through his sleeve, jangling along the nerves, stabbing his loins with raw hopeless desire, reminding him of all that he had lost to the Palsgrave.

'I shall do my duty, Venetia.' Unable to bear her closeness, he mounted his grey gelding, making totally unnecessary adjustment to his wheellock.

Speed was an essential part of the Prince's plan, and with his cavalry on the spur, he outstripped the infantry, leaving the wagons and artillery to struggle along as best they could. They did not reach Beacon Hill till later in the morning when the battle was more than half over, and disjointed accounts were already beginning to come in from scouts, spies and wounded.

At first light the Prince had gained the hill and looked down on the fine old town with its magnificent castle by the river, and the whole beleaguering host in dense array where Meldrum had withdrawn them into the burnt-out ruin of a mansion, just north of Newark, called the Spittal. There were four great bodies of horse awaiting him on the lower slopes of the rise. Rupert decided to attack, knowing the demoralizing effect which this sudden announcement of his presence would have on the Parliamentarians.

He gave the order to charge, leading his men down like an avalanche upon the nearest Roundhead troopers, yelling out

250

the war-cry, "King and Queen!", which was answered by the infuriated rebel roar of, "Religion!"

Astonished, wildly confused, struggling to control their plunging horses and beat off the vicious blows, the besiegers broke their ranks and, at the same moment, the Governor sallied out with his garrison who entrenched themselves doggedly on Meldrum's flank.

Rupert had pierced deeply into the *mêlée*, borne foreward by the impetus of that first charge, and, in the desperate hand to hand fighting, he was set upon by three burly assailants. He laid about him furiously with his sword, running one through, while another fell back with a bullet in the head, fired by one of his Guards. The third had grabbed the Prince by the collar and was trying to drag him from his horse, when a whistling cut from Sir William Neale, who had galloped up behind, sliced off the man's hand at the wrist. Then Crane, and the rest of the Lifeguard, came up like a tidal wave, sweeping the routed cavalry right back to the Spittal.

The Newarkers, Colonel Tillier and Rupert had them hemmed in on all sides. The Royalists seized the bridge across the river which gave access to the only road by which they could retreat, and the guns and infantry of Rupert's army were beginning to arrive. Meldrum had no prospect but to starve on the Spittal, and presently, Charles Gerald, who had been wounded and taken prisoner, came limping across the open ground towards the Prince's standard, with proposals of peace. He was grinning, although the blood was seeping through his breeches, squelching in his boots as he walked, beads of sweat dewing his face.

'We've got the bastards on the hip, Your Highness!' he shouted jubilantly.

Rupert nodded, relaxing against the back of his saddle, 'Good. We'll discuss the terms when you've been to the surgeon, my lad, to get that wound dressed.'

Fatigue parties were getting up tents, unloading wagons, filling water containers, digging latrines. As dusk deepened, fires glowed against the darkness on either side of that waste land between the two armies where the prowlers were stripping the dead, leaving them naked beneath the callous moon which had hung over similar scenes down through the centuries and would blankly survey many more, long after these present antagonists were but dust and memories.

When Holmes put away Rupert's armour, he found a spent shot which had embedded itself in his steel gauntlet. Luck of the Devil!—Venetia kept it as a souvenir.

When the enemy had retired, Rupert made his entry into Newark, not as a triumphant General, but as a blessed deliverer. The populace went mad with delight, packing the streets, cheering wildly. The women fought to get close and touch any part of him that they could reach, kissing his hands, his booted legs, his stirrups, even his horse, strewing his path with flowers. He received this adulation with calm dignity, as became a direct descendant from the Emperor Charlemagne.

By speed, surprise and sheer verve, he had achieved a brilliant, unequalled victory, and Venetia, jogging behind him among the Lifeguard, throat aching with pride and love, knew that this was his finest hour.

' 'Swounds! What the devil do they take me for—a Goddam midwife?' the Prince exploded, and flung the King's latest letter across the table in disgust, before adding the afterthought: 'But thank God, she's

253

abandoned the idea of coming here to have it!'

The Queen was expecting another baby and, in the first flush of the overall enthusiasm about Newark, had considered joining her victorious nephew, but now decided that Exeter would be safer for this event. They wanted Rupert to break off his work in Wales in order to escort her there.

He hardly paused to refresh his men at Newark, and around New Year's Day, March 25th, had hurried them back the way they came; it was unsafe to linger, for the various contingents had to be returned to their garrison, rendered dangerously vulnerable by their removal.

Oxford's reaction to his success was one of unrestrained jubilation. Congratulations flooded into Shrewsbury; King Charles described it as, "no less than the saving of all the North," while Digby, not to be outdone, wrote at great length, praising Rupert's "courage and excellent conduct," which, he was sure, "has made fortune your servant to a degree beyond imagination."

'Which is, no doubt, very fine,' Rupert grumbled, unimpressed. 'But all that was really achieved was the relief of a loyal town, some arms and ammunition, and the surrender of a few scattered outposts which we have not the troops to man properly.'

Will Legge usually managed to coax the Prince out of his pessimistic moods, and Venetia wished that he could have stayed, but he had gone to Oxford which, in spite of its raptures, was not really being very helpful. There were plenty of promises on paper, but few materialized. Will hoped to remedy this.

They had been hard at work recruiting again in Shropshire for less than a fortnight when this new order came from the King. Rupert spent a day, fuming, expending time and energy trying to work out how he could accompany the Queen, and carry on with the enormous task of preparing for the march north. He need not have worried—the next rider brought yet another order countermanding the previous one. Venetia was aroused from sleep by his infuriated shout:

'God! I've wasted a whole day thinking about it! This is Digby's doing! Christ save me from meddling civilians! How am I to effect anything of importance if my plans are to be interrupted by his every whim?'

The usual disputes and jealousies whirled

and eddied in the Court, and Will was doing his best to alleviate some of the troubles.

'He is the kindest man in the world,' Venetia said to Damaris as they strolled down the gravel walks of Mr Jones' pleasant garden, enjoying the April sunshine; everything smelled of fresh leaves, blossoms and moist clods. 'Rupert has asked the King to give Will a place as Gentleman of the Bedchamber. He really deserves it, for he never thinks of his own advancement.'

Damaris produced a hunk of bread, breaking it up and throwing the crumbs to the birds who took time off from the frenzied fervour of nest-building to accept her charity. 'Etienne tells me that there is talk of the Mastership of the Horse being offered to your Prince, now that Hamilton has been dismissed for his disloyalty.'

There were tall yellow daffodils, and heavy-handed purple tulips already in bloom and Venetia began to cut the stems. 'Rupert would accept, but he is anxious that nothing shall be done to make it appear that he had a hand in Hamilton's ruin. He says, let each man carry his own burden.'

'In spite of all their protestations of

admiration towards Newark's saviour, the Courtiers still sink their own personal squabbles to band together against him,' Damaris was smiling under the shady brim of her bongrace, seating herself on a stone garden bench, spreading out her skirts to prevent creases. 'His attitude doesn't help. Jermyn protests that Digby has written several times to our *Pfalzgraf*, and that he has not troubled to reply. He says that Rupert exaggerates the Secretary's dislike of him!'

'Which is arrant nonsense, as well you know!' Venetia's scissors flashed; she wanted to plunge them into the smooth-tongued Digby's throat. What chance did Rupert have against the subtle hints, the sly innuendoes, while up to his eyes in the real work of the King's war?

The flowers were still wet with dew, droplets darkening the taffeta of Ventia's green gown. She gave them a shake, before laying them across her flat basket. 'Digby likes nothing better than giving Rupert orders, provided there are a good many miles betwixt them! He's just sent another, concerning the plight of Lady Derby at Lathom House, and Rupert has taken great exception to his tone.'

He was certainly in an angry frame of mind, scribbling a letter to Will, full of ironical and rather unintelligible complaints against his uncle, and dark threats of his own resignation.

Venetia's spirts sank as she read it before he pressed his seal into the wax, for if he were to leave the country, what would become of her?

The relief of York was now Rupert's principal objective. He rode to Oxford to consult with the King about the impending campaign.

Ella called to see Venetia, not, she was convinced, fired by sisterly concern; a much more likely reason was her avid curiosity to set foot in the Prince's headquarters.

'We shan't have to leave Oxford, shall we?' Her voice was jarringly shrill, Venetia had forgotten just how irritating she could be.

'Would you rather stay here, if the Roundheads take over?' Venetia felt far older than the three years gap between them; living with Rupert was proving a most maturing experience. Ella had been thoroughly ruined by too much attention from cadets, students, the younger sons of peers who were making sure that they kept as far away as possible from disciplinarians like His Highness.

'Oh, 'tis all very fine for you,' Ella tossed her blonde ringlets, madly jealous of the sister who seemed to have won this prize. 'Everyone knows all about you and the Prince! I can't think why Mallory permits it!'

'Be quiet, you silly little bitch!' snapped Damaris, having no patience at all with the vapid beauties who hung about the camps, amateur harlots risking disease and pregnancy without the means of the professionals. Oxford, in common with all garrison towns, was short of nubile population, and overflowing with full-blooded males hell-bent on draining the last dregs of pleasure while life lasted.

There was a change in the atmosphere of the Royalist headquarters; Rupert sensed it and Venetia picked up the general tenor. Some of the best and worthiest of the King's officers had died and the character of his present adherents was gradually lowering.

Rupert found his uncle overwhelmed with grief, now deprived of his adored Queen. He had ridden with her as far as Abingdon and there, amidst tears, they had parted. Charles confided his fears to his nephew, but managed to appear confident when he attended the Council of War.

'I wonder how it is going.' Venetia was sitting on a bank beside a stream which leaped happily over boulders, twisting itself into all manner of colours as if it gloried in the afternoon sunlight.

'Oh, they'll spend hours arguing, making decisions and then revoking them. A tiresome waste of a lovely day.' Damaris kept an eye on Barney, who was fishing further downstream, chewing on an empty pipe, perfectly content to watch the water lazily, refusing to be drawn into idle chatter.

Venetia had met most of the gentlemen who made up the Council, and sympathized with Rupert's distrust of this unreliable body. He usually managed to dominate the gathering, speaking his mind freely and shouting down anyone who disagreed with him. Wilmot and Digby did so on principle; old Lord Forth used his deafness as an excuse for not siding with anyone, while Sir Jacob Astley had the advantage of being able to get along with Rupert. Lord Hopton, honest and brave, was easy game for the vain, dissolute

Wilmot, and the ambitious Digby. The King wavered between them all, usually acting on the advice of whoever was highest in his favour at the moment—or last to speak!

'The level-headed Edward Hyde will try to bring order to the meeting,' Damaris reminded, giving Barney a gay wave. He responded by kissing his fingers and holding up a big fish on the end of his line; he was keeping his hand in for any possible privation on the intended march. Tender light filtered through the young leaves above their heads, midges danced across the surface of the water. 'La, 'tis really quite warm. Soon we shall be able to indulge in the delights of midnight bathing. Stop worrying about the War Council, and dwell on the joys of a communal plunge into some sparkling moonlit stream, everyone playing at being bacchantes and satyrs. Wouldn't Rupert look wonderful, mother-naked, with vine leaves in his hair?'

Sometimes, Damaris, unorthodox notions brought out a prim streak in Venetia. In any case, if that vision became reality, she had no intention of sharing her beautiful Greek God with anyone else! 'Rupert does

261

not believe in heavy drinking. He told me himself, that when in Germany on his way home after being released from Lintz, he upset his hosts by leaving the table early. So they made a hunting party for him instead.'

'Oh, don't be so stuffy,' chided Damaris. 'If Rupert would unbend a little, instead of being so sedately abstemious, maybe even joining Wilmot in his carousals, he might get on better with him.'

'I'm very glad he doesn't!'

'Give him time,' Damaris said thoughtfully. 'There may come a point where he breaks. After all, we none of us thought that he would keep a mistress, but you have proved to us that he is but human after all!'

Rupert came striding down the wooded path, while Boye dived along rabbit-tracks into the brambles, coming back with burrs knotted in his coat. Rupert hooked a finger impatiently under his cravat, tearing open his shirt-band, disposing his long limbs on the grass at her side, shifting across to lay his head in her lap. Venetia leaned above him with brooding tenderness, running her fingers soothingly over his forehead and hair, ignoring Damaris' expression of comic despair at this display of unashamed adoration. Let them laugh, she did not care—ready to admit to all that she genuflected in her heart whenever she thought of him.

'They agreed to everything I suggest,' he volunteered. 'They always do—in the end. My plan is simple—all the King has to do is to keep the surrounding towns well garrisoned, to manoeuvre round Oxford with a body of horse, leave Maurice to finish the affair in the west, and myself free to march north.'

He sat up suddenly, 'Hell! I'm hot! Let's go for a swim in the river. Come along!' And he hauled her up by the hands, then stopped and scowled as they started to laugh, not understanding why. Women! With their maddening feminine allusions to the devil knew what! He turned on his heel, whistling to the more dependable Boye, leaving Venetia to snatch up her skirts and run after him.

ELEVEN

'God go with you, madame.' Pierre filled
Venetia's arms with last-minute parcels.
'Take care, and make sure that those
misbegotten sumpter-masters keep His
Highness's food-boxes out of the sun.
And thanks be to the Lord, that you
are taking that animal with you—I have
had enough of him skittering through my
kitchen—rioting among my sausages!'

Boye was in disgrace. The household cat
normally viewed his hysterical antics with
disdain, from her perch high on the dresser,
contempt for this shaggy clown, exhausting
himself in uncontrolled leaps which fell far
short of her refuge, expressed in every line
of her svelte body. Unruffled, she would
pay meticulous attention to grooming her
whiskers, but lately her spring had lost
a little of its agility, her sleeks sides
bulging and lumpy. That morning early,
while she was absent for a moment only,
Boye had come bouncing in through the
backdoor, poking an inquisitive nose into

her nest of blind, mewling, new-born kittens squirming in their basket under the table.

The lowly tabby was transformed into a fiend of unbridled ferocity. A ball of spitting, clawing venom, she hurled herself upon the astonished poodle, sinking her talons in his back as he leaped away with a shrill yelp of pain and surprise. In his frantic efforts to dislodge this yowling menace, he knocked over a pannikin, and scattered a trug of vegetables. Pierre in pursuit, waving the broom handle, skidded on a squashed onion awash in a sea of cream, landing with a crash which shook the kitchen.

His wrath was forceful but brief, and, as Venetia went out into the yard, he pressed yet another cloth-wrapped package into her hands—bones for Boye.

Having given his advice, visited garrisons who woke up at his appearance, proved to the King that he did not require any more troops but Rupert *did*, and commandeered three hundred barrels of gunpowder, the Prince returned to Shrewsbury. By the 16th of May, his army was ready to march, and not before time. The Earl of Manchester was already on his way northward to

265

join Fairfax and Leven, taking with him the Eastern Association cavalry under his Lieutenant-General, Oliver Cromwell.

There was an electric thrill in the air; everyone sensing that this was the start of a momentous campaign. They forgot the misery of days spent treking through the rain—"pickled with the wet," as Barney put it—now they traversed roads which hardened under the warm breeze, winding into the open countryside with rich rural landscapes of green pastures and fertile fields, unfolding across the valleys.

The soldiers sang as they marched, the women stopped complaining, striding along with a child straddling a beamy hip, or close-wrapped in the fold of a shawl. Some cadged lifts on wagons or gun-carriages, giving the men plenty of backchat. The hedges were heavy with May, a hundred white crowns to garland the brows of the victims to be offered in sacrifice on the altar of political dissensions, religious intolerance, and ambition.

Damaris eased her back against the bole of a gnarled oak, while her servants spread a white cloth on the sward and unpacked hampers. A halt had been called for the night, and in the leaguer there was the usual bustle of settling in; the thumping of mallets as tent-poles were driven into the ground, the whining of tired children, the weary sarcasm of sergeants organizing pickets.

' 'Tis a fine life, if it don't rain,' agreed Barney, expertly sharpening a green stick with his knife, spearing an egg upon it, and holding it in the flames to cook. 'There's nothing like a bit of real service. You may read military manuals till you're blue in the face, but a couple of weeks campaigning will make you a better soldier than a year in quarters—providing you survive!'

He squatted on his hunkers, deftly removing the shell, holding out the snowy contents to Damaris. 'Here you are, Duchess. Try that!' They munched in silence for a moment and then he predicted, cheerily: 'This war, well managed, will last twenty years!'

'Hark to the voice of the true mercenary, who fights only for pillage, giving his allegiance to the side which pays most!' Mallory's lip lifted in a sneer.

There was a feud raging between them over Damaris, who lost no opportunity to stir the embers of their smouldering rivalry. Barney shot him a belligerent glare, even his good nature stung by the slur, and Venetia quickly enlarged on the subject of the expected duration, in order to postpone the duel made inevitable by Damaris' coquetry. They discussed the war in Germany which had already been raging for twenty-five years.

'That is where we get these wild tales of cannibalism,' stated Etienne, who had been watching his wife's games with her lovers with quiet amusement. 'I have seen well-authenticated reports of how Wallenstein and his brother-villains have reduced Europe to such a state that it is necessary to post guards, in some areas where famine is rife, to prevent newly-buried corpses from being dug up, and many cases of children being snatched, slaughtered and eaten!'

Venetia and Damaris shuddered, but Etienne was not trying to frighten them; though generally his brand of teasing humour was not to be trusted, this time his face was perfectly straight. 'I swear 'tis the truth, and the source of the nasty rumours regarding the *Pfalzgraf!*'

Etienne ordered a lackey to carry up another bottle of wine which had been immersed to chill in the emerald gloom where the brook ran deep. He held out a goblet to Barney. 'Try this, my friend. 'Tis a recipe handed down for generations.'

Barney choked on the first mouthful. 'God's blood! What a bite! Does it shift rust? It tastes as if it were brewed from pikemen's feet!'

Damaris' eyes were sparkling at him. 'Lord, you'd be a huge success at dinner with my mother-in-law with such talk! 'Tis one of her best wines, I'd have you know. There is nothing so potent to fuddle the wits and bring instant stupefaction. You should take some to Rupert, Venetia.'

'If you want my opinion,' declared Etienne whose views had not been solicited. 'You'll encourage him to relax, *chérie*. He is much too anxious—like to crack.'

Venetia knew that he spoke the truth, and the sad part about it was that because of his size and talents, Rupert should have been a genial giant, with flesh on his bones, instead of this savage creature flinging himself into every new enterprise.

Certainly, the wine supplied by the Chevalier's mamma was every bit as intoxicating as promised. Against a green and pink sky the dense woods massed and Venetia watched, dizzily, as the birds

269

swirled high before dipping down to nest for the night.

Michael had slipped into the party, taking a cushion beside her, and, somehow he had got hold of her hand and was smoothing her fingers, his fair lashes screening the longing in his glance. Sentimental tears pricked her eyes as she remembered the peace of their relationship, the innocent dreams they had shared of a home and children, before everything had been eclipsed by the meteoric blaze of her passion for the Palsgrave. Almost, she wished that she had never met him, though knowing very well that she would have always been unsatisfied, expecting to find something wonderful around each bend. To be exultantly happy with him, even for an hour, was worth a lifetime of contentment with an ordinary man.

As gently as she could, she detached her hand from Michael's, getting unsteadily to her feet and leaving the glade, Rupert's tent drawing her like a magnet. Above it, his standard was flying, nearly five yards long, blazoned with the arms of his House, the black and gold of the Palatine, the blue and silver of Bavaria. Boye trotted out to greet her, and it was like coming home.

She found Rupert talking with two of his adjutants, and stood aside for some time, waiting till he was done with them. At last he snapped his fingers at Boye who barked sharply in answer, and the three of them started up the wooded slope.

The sinking sun made purple shadows over the velvet green of the vale, throwing the hillocks into sharp relief. From the camp, nestled in the hollow, came a continual hum, and the smell of roasting meat.

Rupert stood looking out over the scene. 'England is the most beautiful country in the world,' he said slowly. 'When first I came here, it seemed like Paradise after flat Holland, and my uncle's Court the very height of luxury and refinement.'

At sixteen, a rootless, landless boy of mixed nationality and cosmopolitan upbringing, he had found at last the country that he loved, birthplace of his mother, this island that, ever after, spelled "home" for him.

'Although they call me a bloody foreigner, I'll warrant I care more for it than many of those born here. Between them, your fellow-countrymen are going to ruin it.'

'What has happened?'

'Only what I half expected,' he said, in that bitter drawling voice which he used sometimes, the words snaking out from his scornful lips. 'A dispatch from the King, sent the day after I left Oxford, revoking the decisions which we had made.'

Filled with distress for him and a woeful sense of inadequacy, Venetia longed for the clear-sightedness of Hyde, the calm counsel of Will, even the solid reassurance of Maurice. All that she could offer was sympathy, which was met with a surly: 'You know nothing of these matters!'

Indeed the convolutions of Court politics would stun a mind even more alert than hers, and Rupert, with his plain language of the barracks, found it baffling, edging his question with an exceedingly forcible oath: 'At times I wonder—do they really want to win this war?'

'At least the Queen is well out the way for a while.'

'Aye, that is one blessing,' Rupert was seated on the ground, his forearms resting on his knees, a long blade of grass between his teeth. 'Although the stupid woman has run herself into trouble, going to Exeter. I advised her against it and I'm sure this only made her more determined!'

Boye was badger-hunting, rooting about in the undergrowth. Rupert glanced over with the same fond indulgence which he reserved for small children, and Maurice. 'Silly old fool, he's making too much noise. With any luck he might chase out an elderly pigeon.'

Venetia, watching Boye clowning, was amazed that anyone could really believe him to be that "devil dog" of the Roundhead pamphlets. He wormed his way into the affections of those who knew him, a valiant, large-hearted companion, as familiar to friend and foe alike, as Rupert's famous red cloak. He had a fondness for Venetia, who could well understand why the King allowed him to sit in his own chair, and romp with the Royal children. Rupert had taught him to leap into the air when he shouted "Charles" and cock his leg at the mention of Pym.

The Prince's mood softened. Boye could usually make him laugh and she sensed that they might enjoy what was left of the evening. She perked up at him, but her smile was arrested by his frown.

'Have you been supping with my officers?' he demanded.

'Yes, Highness—and with my brothers

also.' She wondered if he had guessed that she had been drinking.

He flung aside the grass-stem, his eyes smoking as they slid to where his locket lay on its trail of chain against the deep cleft between her breasts. 'That bodice is cut too low. D'you want to be thought a camp harlot?'

Venetia could feel the blood running into her cheeks. He had turned his back to her, staring off into space.

'Highness—' she reached out tentatively to touch him, then, emboldened by the last remaining whiffs of Madame d'Auvergne senior's brew, slid both arms about him tightly, burying her face against his shoulder-blade. 'Rupert—I only wanted to look well—to please you.'

He turned swiftly, pressing her back on the earth, lithe and furious as a tormented panther. 'I am surrounded by knaves and traitors. You'll not betray me too?'

It was more in the nature of a command than a question, and he kissed her very thoroughly, fingers clenched in her hair.

'Damn the King!' Venetia thought, 'and all those who can hurt him so much more than he could ever hurt them, for all his magnificent strength.'

Charlotte de la Tremouille, Countess of Derby, had been formally summoned to surrender "her Lord's house and its honour," by Fairfax, on the 28th of February. She gained time, by parleys, to plant gabions, raise breastworks, train her domestics, and send her men out to press others to join her little garrison. On March 12th the first shot was fired against her house-fortress. Vainly the Roundhead's artillery hammered the stout walls, and the siege dragged on for eighteen weeks. Lord Derby, miles away from her, again entreated the Prince's aid, reminding him of her courage, and the fact that he was her kinsman.

From almost every quarter came requests for Rupert's help, constant appeals for his presence, the unshaken belief, put forth in many letters "that the Prince alone can do it" and "his very name is half a conquest." Rupert set his course for Lathom House.

Stockport was the first objective. Rupert and his men battered their way in, assisted by Derby thirsting to avenge the insults heaped upon his Lady. The Roundheads drew off their siege and fled to Bolton, which was Puritan to a man, the greatest stronghold for this austere sect in the north.

In the ruined farmhouse which was acting as a base, the women were working with the surgeons, the rain dripping persistently through the gaps in the roof.

'Mother of God! How many more men is he going to send in? They've been hard at it for over two hours now!' Damaris held up a rushlight so that Venetia could see more clearly as she eased Barney's injured arm out of his ripped doublet, trying to staunch the blood running from a jagged gash in his shoulder.

'The first attack had been repulsed, I think he may decide to hold off.' Barney gritted his teeth in pain.

'Not any more he won't!' Etienne was shaken out of his usual equanimity, bloody and bruised. 'Those damned fools got overbold and have hanged one of Rupert's Irish boys over the wall in bravado. *Dieu!* He's gone berserk! Flung himself from his horse, called up more foot and, storming at their head, he's forced his way back among them, pistolling anyone who resists. They don't stand a chance—and he has sworn to give no quarter!'

'I don't believe it!' Venetia looked up quickly from fixing Barney's bandage. Rupert, in a fury, had said this before, but always when he cooled down, the enemy were given the honours of war.

She worked on, trying to dismiss this sense of foreboding. Rupert's spirits had been low that morning, sick with worry about what might be happening at Oxford now that his back was turned.

His regiments rallied to his reckless example, rushing the Roundheads, dealing out bloody vengeance. Lord Derby was amongst the first in, finding himself facing one of his own former servants, now Captain in the rebel army. Derby killed him joyously.

Venetia never forgot the sack of Bolton. In time the impact faded but she was haunted by the booming sheets of flame, the black smoke rolling away before the wind, the screams which reached her, even in the camp. She dreamed of it—everything drenched in scarlet, the colour of fire, the colour of blood, reflected in the blank insane rage in Rupert's eyes when he came to her. He reeked of the Germanic wars in which he had been raised and she trembled, her loyalty jolted. Did she really know him at all, this cruel General deliberately allowing his men to loot, rape and destroy?

She wanted to shriek that these were her people he was letting his men kill. Badly advised though they might be—they were still English! The phrases used by those who hated him rang in her head. He was half foreign! How could he understand the feelings of Englishmen? At that moment he lived up to his reputation as a brutal soldier of fortune.

Reading the disgust in her eyes, he drew his lips back over his teeth in a snarl: 'I'll teach these rebel bastards a lesson they'll not forget in a hurry!'

His accent had become more marked, his face suffused with passion under the tan. His hair was matted with sweat, a red line scored across his brow from the pressure of the helmet he had been wearing for hours. He reached a handful of hay from the floor, wiping his rapier clean before sliding it back into his scabbard.

He looked mad and she was afraid, sensing the undercurrents surging through him, unleashed by bloodlust; the urge to hurt and subjugate, to wreak his will on a woman as a final demonstration

278

of his overpowering masculinity. But his rank stopped him; he could not rampage through the stricken town like a common trooper, destroying and ravishing. Even at this moment of loosened control he would not jeopardize his authority; but the demon whom he had allowed to take over, deliberately blunting all pity and sensibility, was receptive to the wave of revulsion sweeping Venetia and this enflamed him.

'Don't tell me that you are developing scruples, of a sudden?' he said unpleasantly, legs apart to balance his weight, arms hanging at his side. 'How do you think we eat every day, if 'tis not through pillage? What is the matter, *liebchen*? Don't you like me as rough, bloody mercenary? Have I smashed your pretty dreams of a knight in shining armour?'

Venetia was more sharply aware of his body across the space between them, then if she had been in his arms. He wanted her disgust, desired that she refuse him, to give him the excuse to force her. Very well. She would play the game of rape. She glanced at the door, as if measuring the distance, skirts gathered in one hand, ready for instant flight. His mouth curved

279

in a chill smile of enjoyment. He let her wait for a moment and then lunged for her, grabbing a fistful of her hair.

The pain in her scalp was agonizing; she was suddenly angry, wanting this harsh charade to stop. But all thought, all feeling, was being knocked out of her in her impotent struggle against those hard muscles.

The smell of gunpowder and smoke was in her nostrils, the heavy odour of sweat and horse from his clothes. He tasted of blood, his skin wet with the heat of battle. He threw her down, pulling her skirts back over her thighs, his hands taking their toll of her. Normally he was very gentle, knowing his own strength which could so easily snap her brittle bones, wanting to give, as well as take, pleasure. But now he used her brutally, as if he would annihilate all his enemies, smash every woman who had ever teased him, and dominate the one who, all his life, had frustrated and hurt him—the Winter Queen.

Venetia lay limp, every inch of her throbbing with pain, but in deep triumphant exultation as well as discomfort. She would share his bestiality, and burn with his shame, become one with the evil genius which dogged his career, his sins would become hers also. Whatever blame was poured on him for this day's work, let it engulf her too. Without him, she was nothing. And she rejoiced when her body became smeared with the blood of Bolton, transferred from his ruthless hands.

When she thought that he slept, she slid out from under him, and she was crying; angry, despairing tears of pity and indignation at the way in which lesser men were dragging down her noble paladin. Whatever happened she would cleave to him, and words learned long ago at her mother's knee, came ringing back into her tired mind:

"For whither thou goest, I will go; and where thou lodgest, I will lodge; thy people shall be my people, and thy God my God."

A drab twilight darkened the room. Rupert got up, coming over to her where she knelt with her face in her hands, jerking back her head so that she had to look at him, her eyes slanting oddly, dragging up at the corners by the pull of her hair.

'What!' he muttered fiercely. 'Praying for Roundhead Bolton?'

He released her abruptly and she clung to his legs, her face against the leather boots which reached half way up his thighs.

'No, Rupert!' she cried in anguish. 'I pray for you!'

Lady Derby was standing in the hall of Lathom House with her daughters on either side of her, her servants and her garrison drawn proudly to attention to greet their deliverer. But formality could not be maintained by the exuberant Charlotte and, as her husband and Rupert stepped across the threshold, she broke free, running to meet them, kissing Lord Derby warmly full on the mouth, and sweeping Rupert into her motherly arms, laughing, crying and talking all at once.

'Monseigneur! Rupert! My dear, dear cousin—welcome—welcome!'

And they were kissing and he was grinning, suddenly a boy again, as she hung on to him while they jabbered in French, filled with mutual admiration in each other's courage and family pride in their achievements. Venetia, standing forgotten in the background, felt humble and sad, but Charlotte's quick eyes missed nothing, and, when she was calmer, she dropped her voice and asked him:

'Who is this who stares at you with such adoring eyes? Your *inamorata*, eh, Rupert? That is good. A great warrior should have a beautiful lady to love him.' She stretched out a hand to Venetia, a plump, fair, lively woman in her early forties, much kinder than her daunting repute led one to believe. 'Don't blush, *mignonne*, although such modesty is to your credit. I can see that our Prince has shown his usual good taste in choosing you. Come, we will be friends, yes?'

Rupert was watching their faces, smiling faintly, now hardly recognizable from the barbarian of yesterday. He had kept De Faust busy since early morning, and was once more his usual elegant self, his doublet brushed, linen sparkling, boots as soft and unwrinkled as a calf's belly, sword-hilt and spurs glittering. Every evidence of stubble had been scrupulously scraped from his jaw, his hair, freshly washed, shone healthily, the ends coiling into soft curls falling below his shoulders.

'And what am I to do with those twenty Roundhead standards which you have so charmingly presented to me?' Charlotte beamed on Rupert, delighted with his chivalrous gesture.

'Accept them as homage to my fair relative and companion-in-arms,' he said with a deep bow. 'Let them adorn your battlements, madame, and rejoice in thinking of how chagrined Colonel Rigby will be at their loss.'

Then nothing would please her but that they must go on a tour of inspection of her defences. Boye pattering behind them, his nails rattling on the stone flags. Rupert was politely attentive as she told him how a cannon-ball had crashed through one of the casements, during dinner, and how her children had not stirred, and, at a nod from her, had gone on with their meal.

'Take good care of them, madame,' he advised. 'The children of such a father and such a mother will one day do their King such services as their parents have done theirs.'

Venetia marvelled; he was perfectly capable of making pretty speeches as the next man—when he put his mind to it!

Derby and his Lady were very willing for Rupert to use their home as his base from which to continue the subjugation of Lancashire. She welcomed fresh company, happy to accommodate Damaris, Venetia and some of the officers' wives, while the dependents of the soldiers lived under canvas, or billeted themselves in the village. Chaplain Rutter organized a school for the children in one of the barns, keeping them out of mischief, busy with hornbooks and slates.

Venetia took to spending a lot of time on the battlements, her eyes on the north road awaiting the first faint cloud of dust, the distant throb of hooves denoting a galloper carrying news. She breathed in a warm air, redolent of summer, apple-blossom and strawberries, mixed with the rich aroma of the cow-stalls which stretched in a straggly line beyond the fortress walls, and the acrid stench of smoke belching from a near-by chimney-pot.

A choke of loneliness strangled her throat now that he was gone and, to combat it, she dwelt on the stupendous fact that she had known him for almost a year and he showed no signs of tiring. Sometimes, she thought about her home and wondered if anyone was tending her mother's grave in that corner of the country churchyard, or was the moss slowly obliterating the wording on the tombstone so that the world would soon forget that there had once existed Cecilia Denby, who had laughed, danced, cried and loved with all the intensity which Veneita now felt. Had she been as passionately in love with Samuel as she was with Rupert? Somehow, Venetia doubted it. A marriage of convenience—as they would have had her make with Michael, had it not been for the war. Blessed war—which had brought Rupert to her.

She pondered on those who had once been her neighbours, wondering how they faired. Mallory had heard that Giles Fletcher, their erstwhile playmate, had gone into the Eastern Counties, that fastness of Puritanism, where Oliver Cromwell was training his brigades of fiery fanatics who were reputed to spend in prayer the time they did not give in fighting.

Life became an endless vacuum, an eternity of waiting; Venetia dreamed, and, at night, was lost in the enormous four-poster, which itself was dwarfed by the gargantuan stone-walled chamber which Charlotte had prepared for her cousin. She was scared, and ducked under the covers, hugging one of Rupert's shirts which she took to bed for comfort, while the moonlight made eerie shadows over the big bulbous furniture which crouched like beasts waiting to spring.

They kept very busy and cheerful, taking time off for hair-washing and baths, having the maids clean the mud from the hems of gowns, and launder those yards of white, frilly petticoats and voluminous smocks, the collars and lace cuffs. The full-sleeved shirts of their men billowed out, pegged on the clothes-lines, and from the kitchen, the smell of slightly scorched linen mingled pleasantly with that of baking bread, as the maids ironed and goffered.

Lathom House settled back into the life in which it had existed for centuries, the siege no more than a wink of an eye to its aged grey walls, one in a series of many which had been waged times before so that it had been well castellated to withstand the attacks of foemen. Charlotte was always so active, seemingly unconcerned that her Lord had once more departed into danger, superintending every household detail with the same detached efficiency with which, not long before, she had carried on during the siege.

But it was dead—to Venetia they were as ghosts—wandering in her desert of loneliness. Even Boye had gone, perched on the top of the Prince's sumpter-cart; Holmes, De Faust and Trevor had marched out with those brave spirits which left Lathom bereft.

The reports of Rupert's successes seemed almost phenomenal; in ten days almost all Lancashire had been overrun. He should have been pleased with his progress, but his despatches to Charles crossed with a stream of letters in which his uncle announced misfortunes.

The King had had second thoughts as soon as his masterful nephew left Oxford. Contrary to all plans, he had withdrawn his troops from the circle of garrisons. Essex and Waller had closed in, almost trapping him. When in a tight spot, Charles usually did very well, particularly if acting on his own judgement. Now he used ingenuity and daring, leaving most of the cavalry and making a feint towards Abington. Waller fell back, leaving open the road to the west. The King and his men marched through the gap, making for Worcester. It was hoped that Oxford could hold out against siege till Rupert returned.

Everyone shifted the blame for this disastrous state of affairs at headquarters on to one another. Rupert was furious with them all. In a black, sardonic mood he saw knavery everywhere in the King's service.

The way was clear to York, it was mid-June, the weather was good, and Newcastle writing that he could not hold out more than a week. If York were relieved speedily, it would complete the Prince's triumph in the north. He rode back to Lathom House to make his plans.

TWELVE

The hot afternoon was melting into the shadows of evening when the sleepy atmosphere of Lathom was rent by the snorting and trampling of destriers.

Venetia had to force herself not to go flying out to Rupert. Lady Derby must be given precedence and, as always when they had been parted, there was that twinge of fear in case he would not want her again.

He walked into the hall, brushing aside the speeches, the praise of his success, and Charlotte saw at once that he was tired and strained.

'Your Highness, I will have a meal sent to your room. Tomorrow we will talk and you shall tell me all about your magnificent exploits.' She mimed with expressive hands to Venetia, indicating that her job was to go with him and be soothing.

Upstairs, in that vast bedchamber with its wall-tapestries of Grecian scenes depicting buxom goddess and ardent swain, De Faust was directing the disposal of the single valise which contained Rupert's clothes. Still he did not speak, pouring out a goblet of wine and tossing it down in one gulp, staring out across the gardens through the mullioned window. But at last the meal was set, candles lit and De Faust bowed himself out. When the door closed, Rupert was at Venetia's side in a couple of strides, his arms coming about her, burying his face in her hair as if he would blot out the world.

She could feel him shaking. This was no triumphant conqueror. 'What has happened?'

He raised his head and his eyes were those of a damned soul. He cursed and broke from her, striding up and down the room—up and down, as though by walking he could leave his fate behind him.

'They are saying that I want to be King.'

'Who are saying it? You read that tract published in London earlier, and tossed it aside as of no import—'

'This is more deadly.' He no longer looked romantically lean, now positively gaunt, and she had a flash of how he would be in later years, a stern, uncompromising man, when the vicissitudes of life had tanned his youthful fire. 'That was put out by the Roundheads, but now letters come from Court. They say the King grows daily more jealous of me, and of my army. My successes have not pleased those treacherous rats who surround him. Digby, Percy, Culpepper and Wilmot—they say it boldly now, what they have been afraid to voice above a hint before—that it is indifferent whether the Parliament or Prince Rupert prevail—the old King will be deposed.'

'And he believes them?' She shook her head in denial, even as she asked the question, unable to credit that he would not recognize the unfailing loyalty of his most faithful commander.

Rupert stopped prowling and dropped into a chair with so despairing a gesture that Venetia went on her knees at his side.

'If I were there he would not,' he was struggling to be just, to remember his uncle as he had once known him. His fingers flexed as if burning to seize his sword and skewer the whole Council of War on it. 'Damn them all! I'll send the King my Commission and get to France. 'Tis plain I am not wanted here!'

Tears of rage and pain which he was too proud to shed were making his dark eyes brilliant. Venetia put her arms about him, drawing his head against her breasts, her fingers passing gently over his hair.

'Come to bed, my Prince,' she murmured, her lips against his forehead. 'Lie with me, who loves you so deeply, and forget for a while. Let them talk. Truth will out in the end.'

But this wound had gone deep, coming as it did on top of other troubles, paralysing all thought, decision and action in Rupert. By next morning the wild rage had gone, leaving him in a cold, unresponsible trance. He no longer spoke of resigning, of leaving the country—but then, he hardly spoke at all—and the days stretched out in a torpor of inactivity. Lord Newcastle was waiting for him at York. Let him wait. The lethargy which had lain across him for three years in Lintz, dulling his mind, imprisoning his great body, seemed again to hold him in an enforced suspension of energy.

'He is worn out, poor boy.' Charlotte, in the solar, looked up from her accounts when Venetia trailed in miserably, searching for Rupert who had disappeared without a word. 'He has been running the whole war for two years. He takes so much upon himself, convinced that it is his task to ensure that everything and everyone is in the right place at the right time, and if he doesn't have a breakdown doing it, it won't be for want of trying! And now this nonsense about him wanting the Crown!'

Arthur Trevor glanced across from the dispatch which he was drafting. 'There are too many whom it will not at all suit if he returns to Oxford in a blaze of glory.'

'I cannot understand the King.' Charlotte raised shoulders and hands in a wide gesture of puzzlement. 'They were so close, those two!'

They reflected momentarily on the Royal uncle and his impetuous nephew who had had so much in common. Both were transparently honest—Charles did not know how to lie and Rupert had never bothered to learn. They were both mad about hunting, entering into it with hereditary zest, and they shared similar attitudes, decidedly autocratic, sensitive, stubbornly proud.

Venetia could not forgive the King for doubting and hurting Rupert who would never whine, but she could voice it for him, wildly indignant:

'After all that he has done for them! From the very onset breathing life into the King's lukewarm followers! He has given of himself unstintingly, yet he is forever attacked and his authority undermined, by petty, selfish men motivated by spite, envy and dangerous hatred. They are not fit to clean his boots!'

Forced to stop for want of breath, Venetia caught Lady Derby and Trevor staring at her in surprise. Then Charlotte gave a little laugh.

'*Mon Dieu,* what is it about that family which inspires such fanatical devotion? Rupert's great grandmother, the unhappy Mary of Scotland, had the same fatal magnetism. And his mother—look at the noble gentlemen who have devoted their lives and their fortunes, in trying to restore the Palatinate! Rupert has the same magic, people love or hate him! *Sacrément!* These Stuarts!'

Rupert's listlessness was infectious. Discipline became slack, his men loafed with their women in the leaguer while the officers lounged and amused themselves. Lathom House, its parklands and appointments were at their disposal. They could hunt or hawk, and there was plentiful fishing, pursuits which reminded them poignantly of their homes. Given pause to ponder, some wanted to go back to their own counties; it would soon be haymaking time, and the yeomen thought longingly of their untended crops. How good it would be to return to familiar things instead of this continual slog of marching, fighting, falling into bed and starting all over again next day.

And now this old fortified house held them entranced as in some fairy tale. The very air seemed bewitched, languid with the scents of high summer, every movement became an effort, the mind drugged by the heat-shimmer on the turrets, the Roundhead standards hanging limp, as if expiring with exhaustion, along the ramparts. The flat marshy ground enfolded Lathom like the palm of some huge hand.

Inside, it was more than ever like the Palace of Sleeping Beauty. Narrow feudal corridors, tiny rooms shut away, up one stair and down several others, flights of wooden steps which screwed steeply up to the top of any one of the seven towers, impressive halls which stunned both eye and mind, and grand staircases with newels like bedposts supporting handrails fit for giants.

Charlotte opened up remote corners of this imposing structure to accommodate her guests, mazes which led down into darkness and upper storeys which looked as if they needed scaling ladders. Going to bed could be a harrowing experience with smoking candles flickering on the carved balustrading, the thick pillars rearing up to support overhead landings, sprouting tall elaborate finials in the shape of heraldic beasts. This setting gave plenty of scope for such practical jokers as Etienne and Adrian, who exercised much ingenuity with sheets, lengths of clanking chain, and hollow theatrical groans.

Everyone got lost, and, when they met again, it was with something of the sense of an expedition of exploration, and they were merry—most emphatically so—no one wanted to dwell on York where food was strictly rationed, and all the more unpleasant aspects of a closely beleagured city were being keenly felt.

'The falconry is better lit than the apartment which I have been given,' complained Damaris, annoyed because the servants' quarters were at an inconvenient distance from their masters, most difficult for the performance of their duties, especially after dark. But this disorder had its compensations, permitting, by its very confusion, a relaxing of the etiquette which Lady Derby might otherwise have expected. Most of them retired after dinner, during the full blaze of afternoon, either alone or with some congenial companion. Rupert was one of the stalwarts who did not indulge in a siesta. He could usually be found by the beck where a mill-wheel churned, his long limbs in unwonted laxity on the grass, contemplating the water without seeing it; an inert, chained giant, sulky and uncommunicative. Boye would lie with him, whining now and again, thoroughly uneasy with his gloomy master.

Venetia learned painfully that he was best left alone, and would drift away to find Damaris, chatting with her in her bedchamber while she took off her dress, brushed out her hair and annointed her breasts with perfume, in anticipation of delights to come.

'Oh, do be more cheerful, Venetia,' she glanced at her in the mirror, irritated by the sight of her drooping shoulders. ''Slife, I should have thought you would have been overjoyed to have the Palsgrave with you constantly, and so idle too. It must give him plenty of energy for the boudoir.'

'He is so unhappy.'

'Out of temper, more like,' Damaris studied her image critically. 'One good thing comes out of this rushing about after the armies—it gives one little opportunity to put on weight.'

'I wish I could help him,' Venetia was following her own train of thought.

'I'm quite sure you *do*, my dear. He walks all over you—though I have yet to be convinced that it is a good thing to swell his head even more.'

Venetia had, long ago, accepted the fact that Rupert was not in love with her, trying to be content with the casual affection and physical need which he expressed, yet, sometimes, she became angry. 'You should hear the change in his voice when he speaks of Suzanne Kuffstein or Mary Lennox,' she burst out irrelevantly.

'Men always have this sentimental hankering after the wenches they did not quite succeed in laying.' Damaris was always so down to earth, her worldly wisdom dashing aside self-pity.

'I cannot imagine Rupert ever being a rejected lover,' Venetia gnawed her thumb despondently.

'Well, in these instances he was.' Damaris deliberated between two equally ravishing lounging robes.

Venetia was determined to labour the point, almost enjoying the hurt; 'It was his fine sense of honour which stopped him.'

'Fine sense of fiddlesticks!' Damaris' head appeared through the neck of a rose-pink diaphanous creation cunningly designed to reveal more than it concealed. 'You find him devastatingly attractive, I know, but his unpolished roughness may not appeal to all.'

Venetia envied Damaris' capacity for amours in which she remained emotionally excited, mentally stimulated, but heart-whole. She never fell in love, though constantly with some affair either being carefully nurtured, or already in full bloom. When Venetia left her after these conversations, she invariably greeted in the winding stone passageway either Barney, already unfastening the ribbon lacing of his breeches or Mallory, more restrained, knowing that he might bump into her. Occasionally it was neither of these, but an unfamiliar officer, or even a ranker; Damaris was not a snob.

Ten days of suspended animation, and, in the oppression of a thundery evening, the men were playing billiards. Venetia paused in the rounded arch of the Norman doorway seeing, in the lurid sunset glow, Adrian's narrow backside, and his heels lifted from the floor as he reached across the table for a difficult shot, while Etienne made encouraging noises. On the opposite side of the room Michael stood, balancing his cue like a rapier. He saw her and fixed her with a long look which she could not meet. Rupert was not there.

'Of course, his Majesty's action outside Oxford is keeping Waller busy, and Essex is trying to break up Maurice's siege of

Lyme,' Trevor was saying from deep in a cloud of tobacco smoke, nodding, pleased, as Adrian sent the ball bowling smoothly across.

'Prince Maurice has not the craft of war at his finger-tips, like his brother.' Michael took aim, and Venetia knew that he had to be always bringing Rupert into the conversation when she was present to test her reactions and add to his torture.

Once she had done the same, making seemingly casual reference to the Duchess of Richmond, every sense alert to catch any nuance in Rupert's replies, or even in his very silence! But lately it had not been necessary; Mary wrote seldom, and then purely formal communications; sometimes a rider might be added to a letter from Oxford to the effect that she had found the cash to pay the messenger.

'Even the Roundheads admire His Highness's Generalship.' Trevor never attempted to conceal his pride in working for Rupert. 'They've no one to touch him—though reports are coming in about this fellow Cromwell. If these are to be believed, he thinks of the welfare of his men in a similar way to our Prince—concerned about clothing and equipment.'

'*Sacré nom!* Any competent quarter-master can do that!' Etienne was aristo-cratically scornful. 'I have often considered that His Highness demeans himself with these cares, bothering about such things as boots and horse-fodder—like a tradesman, *mon ami!* He is the great Generalissimo! He has no need to worry about such trifles.'

'Pay and provisions are the common soldier's reward for the danger and hardship,' Mallory regarded the frivolous Chevalier as if he were some peculiar species and not too wholesome at that!

'The war is dragging on too long,' Michael had been saying this often of late. 'It should have finished after Edgehill—I shall never forget that battle—no one, I am sure, was more grieved than King Charles, forced to wage war on the people whom God had placed in his care.'

Venetia noticed how thin Michael was getting, now his temples seemed almost transparent under the thin sheen of sweat, eyelids half lowered over his strained eyes, fine pale hair lank on his forehead. He reminded her of a young girl she had once known who had been jilted by the man she loved; as the months passed, so she had sickened, with this same pallor, till she became consumptive and died. A pang of guilt shot through her, but no, surely it was the conflict which was upsetting him so much—not herself?

'The King had no choice! It was rebellion—what we did was right!' Mallory had no patience with such talk.

'Was it?' Michael's gaze was turned within, seeing horrors. 'When the drums beat to arms in the dark of that first, frosty morning, how many must have wondered what the devil had induced them to fall thus upon their own countrymen?'

'But the exhilaration of that charge!' Mallory's eyes were shining. 'They'd never seen anything like it. None of the old-fashioned sedate trotting, stopping to fire—no, we set spur to our horses and swept down, gathering speed with every stride—a slashing, pounding onslaught—straight through their ranks.'

'When the slaughter was over we settled down to endure that bitter night.' Michael's voice was low. 'We built watch-fires and huddled round them and thought about our dead. We could hear the groans of the wounded, and English voices screaming out for help. It was so cold that the wounds froze—congealing the blood—!'

Was this part of that lethal spell which had held them over the past awful days—this brooding on scenes best forgotten? The atmosphere was thick and heavy—soon it would thunder.

Then, abruptly, Rupert came in through the door, a sheaf of papers in his hands. The yawning stopped.

As if he had never spent an idle moment in his life or this had been no more than a pause in which to fix their arms, he gave his orders:

'Get your men mustered. We march at daybreak.'

'George Goring, by all that's Satanic!' Barney was leaning far out of the upper casement window, attracted by the uproar in the yard.

The Prince had rushed his army over the Pennines and now he and his staff were supping at Skipton Castle.

'I was expecting him.' Rupert looked up sharply.

'The Kings wants you to send him to his aid, doesn't he, sir?' Trevor reminded gently.

304

The black brows winged together. 'I have the greater need of him,' said the Prince.

He did not add that he much preferred to keep Goring under his eye, knowing that intrigues were boiling in the wandering Court, unprincipled enough to cause untold damage without the addition of an officer such as Goring who had no morals, knew no qualms and was not troubled with a conscience.

Venetia had not yet met this General, her curiosity aroused, looking expectantly towards the door when noisy shouts and laughter heralded his arrival.

Almost before Rupert had called to enter at his knock, Goring was in their midst, flourishing his hat in an elaborate bow, a tall, attractive swashbuckler, disarming those who had been prepared to dislike him, with his gay, affable camaraderie. A ripple went round the table.

'Goring! You old ruffian!'

'Couldn't the Roundheads stand your presence any longer? Glad to kick you out of their prisons, were they? Tired of your debauching their women, eh?'

'Kept you snugly out of the war for a bit though, didn't it?'

He stood there grinning at them mockingly, almost imperceptibly insolent as he bent over Rupert's hand. 'Greetings, my Prince!'

Venetia wondered how Rupert managed to refrain from striking that impertinent face. Boye was barking hostilities from behind Rupert's chair, baring his teeth as if longing to fasten them in the seat of those fashionable breeches.

His wayward glance roved to Venetia, reading volumes in the Prince's icy manner, guessing the cause and finding the situation highly entertaining.

'You are to be congratulated, Your Highness, on having this lovely creature grace your camp,' he was murmuring, undressing her with his eyes. 'Rare solace for us poor soldiers, in our bleak, lonely wanderings, to have life made sweeter by such a delightful votary of Venus.'

'What have you to report, General?' Rupert said, as curtly as if he was speaking to an orderly.

Goring bowed again, hand on his heart. 'My horse have wrought wonders in the way of forage. We've been playing the cowherds to any number of "borrowed" cattle, which will be mighty useful when converted into slabs of beef! Since receiving your latest summons, I have neither rested, supped, nor even drank, till I could be instantly in the glory of your esteemed presence, to fling myself at those illustrious feet!'

'My dear fellow, you must be exhausted.' Etienne murmured. 'I am sure that His Highness will wish you to share our meal.'

'I am hardly fit company,' said Goring modestly. In fact he was very beautifully turned out and knew it; a little dust, a hint of dishevelment seemed to enhance his velvets and gold lace. In his spurred boots with the red heels and welts, he stood in a spread-legged stance with all the audacity of an Alsatian bravado. He was a King's man—a Cavalier, and proud of it! He flaunted it defiantly to damn and mock and fly in the face of the Puritans. If the Roundheads wanted copy for their news-sheets, he was only too happy to supply it in its most exaggerated form. They would have no need to invent lies about his doings.

Rupert wiped his slender brown fingers on a napkin, pushed back his chair and stood up. 'Have your men on parade at five of the clock tomorrow morning. I will review them before we march. Now, I leave you, Your Lordship. I have work to do.'

Everyone rose while the Prince made his exit and Goring was loudly and insincerely devastated at Rupert's dedication to toil. 'Ah, my dear Palsgrave, always so conscientious. And you, madam—' he was reluctant that Venetia should depart—'are you too equally dutiful? Or may I dare hope that you will sample a bottle of Rhenish with me?'

Rupert did not express his fury, but the room fell silent as he outfaced him, forcing him to look away at last, unable to meet the scornful stare from under the Prince's heavy eyelids.

'Have you really work to do, Highness?' Venetia watched while Rupert lay back in an armchair in their chamber, bracing himself as De Faust straddled his boot in a tugging position. One came off and then the other, and the valet bore them away for cleaning. And Venetia forgot her question, lost in admiration and that glow of happiness because he resented Goring for even daring to look at her.

Rupert threw off his doublet and shirt. 'I

308

left because I should have challenged that Goddamed rakehell if I'd stayed a moment longer. And there would have been a ripe piece of news—two of the King's Generals fighting, and over a woman too. That should please you, you vain little minx.'

He padded across to grip her under each elbow, drawing up to him, re-establishing possession. Her hands were against the smooth brown flesh of his chest, fingers tracing the line of dark hair which ran plumb down to his navel. She caressed his throat and neck where the skin was soft to the touch, like a girl's.

'Why do you look at me so intently?' he asked, smiling.

'I was thinking—it is the way you carry your head which makes you regal—proud and haughty. You are so beautiful, Rupert.'

He laughed, embarrassed by her compliments. 'I should not carry it for long if the Roundheads caught me. It would be the block and a traitor's end. Maurice and I top their list.'

She shuddered, her too lively imagination filling in the details. 'Don't talk about it! It will never happen! You are invincible— everyone says so!'

'I can never imagine myself dead,' he shook his head. 'I see so much slaughter, yet cannot believe it could happen to me. It is so strange to think that though I now stand here, holding you, by this time tomorrow a bullet, or a blade more skilled than my own, could put an end to it all.'

He had changed—tendrils of that spell which had held him in thrall at Lathom still clung to his mind. This was dangerous talk; part of the charm against defeat was that he should have an unshakable faith in himself...

There was an odd expression in his eyes, as if he saw into the future and did not like what it held. 'And beyond death, *liebchen*, is there anything more?'

'Of course! There must be!' Venetia felt as if she were tottering on the brink of an abyss, one fact only standing out with blinding clarity—a personality as strong as Rupert's must continue—and she had again that conviction that she had known him before in some other life, and would ever wander, searching for him, until united with him in existences yet to come. These ideas frightened her; Meriel was the only one to whom she dared speak them—she understood. 'Do you believe in God, Highness? You have prayers said for your men.'

He gave his short, ironical laugh. 'And doesn't this infuriate the rebels! Red-hot off their presses come complaints that, "The Devil Prince pretends piety to his tongue! Rupert, that Bloody Plunderer, would forsooth to seem religious!" ' His amusement gave way to irritation; ' 'Swounds, don't they understand that I as well as their own Generals, know the worth of a hymn or two for the men to sing to keep up heart when they are tired of waiting for action.'

'You don't really believe in an after-life, do you, darling?' Venetia was sad, needing his strong conviction to strengthen hers, an entrenchment against separation—an eternity of blackness without Rupert would be the worst kind of purgatory.

'Goddam, I was reared to be a good Calvinist! As children we had a most strict training—taught to know the Heidelberg Cathechism by heart—without understanding a word of it!'

'Pierre told me that Bethlem Gabor, one of the sponsors at your christening, is reputed to be half a Turk, and more

311

Moslem than anything.'

He was laughing again, with that wild mirthless gaiety which she distrusted deeply. 'You seem to spend a deal of time gossiping with my cook! Aye, it is true and my family never let me forget it. They said that my temper proved me to be a heathen.'

He rarely mentioned those at the Hague, though she knew that he had been made happy at the rumour that a cache of mail from his mother had been intercepted by the enemy and, because of its contents, words of praise for her soldier son, Parliament had stopped her pension.

But other letters did not please him so well. He was still pursued by contradictory, worrying messages from the King, half-apologetic for having jettisoned his nephew's orders, full of such phrases as: "I confess, the best had been to have followed your advice."

Even the usually calm Richmond had written gloomily: "We want money, men, conduct, diligence, provisions, time and good counsel."

Now Venetia found herself reading yet another despatch which Rupert had received at Liverpool and brooded over at Lathom.

It was written in Charles' usual complicated style, full of congratulations on Rupert's successes, regrets at not being able to supply him with powder and then arriving at the real point of the communiqué: "Wherefore I *command and conjure you*, by the duty and affection which I know you bear me, that all new enterprises laid aside, you immediately march, according to your first intention, with all your force to the relief of York."

The Prince had bowed to the direct orders of his King; gathering everyone up and plunging them across the border. All he could do was hope that he might be able to complete the operation without having to suddenly fly to the rescue of Charles.

Venetia continued to look at the King's letter long after she had ceased to read it. A draught from the open window made the candle flame waver. Darkness crouched thick outside the circle of light. Rupert stood leaning against the bedpost, lost in thought. Boye was curled up on the quilt, and he stirred and whimpered in his sleep, in the toils of a nightmare.

THIRTEEN

'Why do we have to spend the night in this damned wood when we could have ridden triumphantly into the city and found a comfortable bed?' Damaris vented her complaints on Barney, who, instead of consoling, teased her, but then Barney never took anything seriously. He was seated on a tree-stump by the camp-fire, whistling to himself, polishing his weapons.

'You should have stayed in your coach!' Venetia was short-tempered; it had been raining again and the ground was soggy. Rupert had pushed them hard, still gathering recruits as he advanced.

Three armies beleaguered York—the Scots under Leven, the Northern army under Fairfax, and the Eastern Association commanded by Manchester. They had cause to be confident, for they far outnumbered the Royalists, but, as usual, the very fact that the Prince was in the vicinity was enough to cause elaborate marching and countermarching. When he reached Knaresborough, just twelve miles away, it was to find the Puritans reporting; "Their Goliath himself is advancing, with men not to be numbered."

'Holy God!' said the Prince, casting an eye over his very mixed regiments. 'I would that they were right!'

Morning showed to the apprehensive rebel commanders, that a formidable body of Royalist cavalry was moving out of Knaresborough in their direction. For days the air had been alive with alarmist rumours and now it was a natural reaction of draw off from their siege-works and marshal the armies into battle array. Hours passed, while Rupert's horsemen curvetted on the skyline, making a spectacular show, but no infantry came to join them and night closed in on all.

The Roundheads were puzzled. Where was Rupert? What devil's scheme was afoot?

They had underestimated his speed and skill in manoeuvre. While the horse kept the Allies amused by their pretty display, he had struck rapidly northward with the infantry and the rest of the cavalry, crossing the river, then marching briskly down the left bank making for the North Gate of York. As dawn bronzed the sky, the Parliamentarians watching in impotent rage as Rupert's victorious brigades bore down on the city from the side least expected. His men had marched twenty-two miles in a day, but York had been relieved. Now they quartered in the Forest of Galtres, which did not suit Damaris at all.

'We have to sit here in this miserable place, while, I wager, they are having a fine time in there.' She pulled the hood of her cloak up round her ears. 'I wish I'd gone with Goring—he wanted me to!'

Barney took no notice, sauntering off to join a picket posted to keep the main road clear. There was little rest for anyone as Rupert's regiments passed across the bridge. The Prince had already been over, eager for battle, anxious to do his own scouting and select the terrain on which he would engage the enemy.

'It might have been more diplomatic if he had presented himself to the Marquis,' Etienne was keeping out the cold with a bottle of cognac. 'I hear that he is a very proud grandee, much inclined to send in his resignation every time he fancies himself slighted!'

'Why, surely he will be so pleased that his city has been freed that no petty considerations will enter his head?' Venetia rejoined, busy looking after her pony, giving him an extra feed of oats. He had carried her well that day, and another hard one was anticipated on the morrow.

'Mayby, *chérie,* but don't forget that he is something of a poet, and only an amateur soldier. I have heard him described as one of Apollo's whirligigs, who, when he should be fighting, is toying with the Muses—or the Dean of York's daughters; a silken General made out of perfume and compliments.'

'He sounds quite delicious!' Adrian was combing the tangles out of the windswept curls. 'Just think, my dear, we shall meet William Davenant, the playwright, now Newcastle's Lieutenant-General!' He was atwitter with excitement for, although he had left the players and joined Etienne's troop, rigged out by the fond Chevalier in a fine leather coat, with handsome arms and accoutrements, his first love was the theatre.

'Venetia, my sweet, did you not hear that poem which he wrote to celebrate your Prince's glorious saving of Newark?'

317

Without waiting for her reply, he began to recite:

' "As he entered the old gates, one cry of
  triumph rose,
To bless and welcome him who had saved
  them from their foes;
The women kiss his charger, and the little
  children sing:
"Prince Rupert's brought us bread to eat,
  from God and from the King".'

While applauding the sentiments, Venetia thought Davenant's verse excruciating. Lord! Was Rupert to be bedevilled by yet another crowd of dilettantes? This would not be calculated to improve a temper already raw through almost two days and nights without sleep.

She found him by the bivouac-fire, drinking a mug of hot soup and talking with a group of musketeers. He laughed when she repeated Etienne's remarks.

'He'll not give trouble.' Rupert sounded confident. He was not really concentrating on the Marquis, his mind already leaping ahead to the impending confrontation. 'I've sent Goring to tell him to be ready to march with us against the enemy at four

318

o'clock tomorrow morning.'

'Wouldn't it have been more tactful to have gone yourself, Highness?' she suggested—really, he had a blind spot sometimes where relationships were concerned. 'After all, he is a commander twice your age who has exercised unquestioned authority here for a long time. And what about his men? Don't you think they will be looking forward to a rest after such an exacting siege? They may not take kindly to peremptory orders from a stranger who has not even bothered to show himself in the town, or offer his praise and encouragement!'

At times her temerity astounded her. She would not have dared to speak thus to him a few short weeks ago. He stared angrily at her down his aquiline nose, and she knew him well enough by now to hazard a guess that she had put a finger on his own misgivings.

'I'm a fighting man!' he said in a sort of snarl. 'Not a pampered Court witling! D'you think I have time to waste bandying compliments with the Marquis?'

She plucked at his sleeve. 'Won't you rest for a while, Highness? You were up all last night.'

'Rest? No time for that—too much to be done.'

A quick bear-hug, his cheek resting briefly against her head and then blackness swallowed him up. Venetia dozed in a corner of Damaris' coach, Boye a restless companion; every so often she was disturbed by his rough tongue licking her face and his dreams appeared to be as hagridden as her own. At last she surfaced into the reality of an overcast summer morning not yet light.

The stream was icy, the shock waking her fully as she splashed her face and scrubbed round her mouth with her bone-handled tooth-brush. She would have given anything for a hot bath and clean linen. The leaves of the trees hung heavily, occasionally dripping; there was a good deal of mist about. Then the early bird-calls were drowned by the noise of trumpets, and Damaris was reeling out, yawning and complaining.

Rupert's army was already in position and the sun climbing high when some of the coaches lumbered across the moor to join them. By that time he had stopped fuming and impatiently riding down the ranks, despatching messengers back to York

320

to hurry Newcastle who had not yet turned up. He forced himself to check his every instinct that was urging him to launch one of his charge on the rear-guard of the enemy infantry. They were straggling along the lanes to Tadcaster, sent to secure the bridges to prevent the Cavaliers moving south, should that be their intention.

So the Prince chafed, chewing his nails till the blood ran, and his caution surprised those closest to him—this new, controlled Rupert, waiting for belated allies, letting the chance of a lightning attack slip away. His men eyed him anxiously, voicing their own disapproval at this delay, making unflattering comments about that languid, lackadaisical fellow, Newcastle. They eased their horses, watered and fed them and kept up their own spirits by singing rude ditties about the urges of the Puritan women and the inability of the Roundheads to satisfy them.

Rupert was drawing up a battle plan, using the top of a drum as a table. He grunted without looking up as Venetia put down the blackjack of ale, the coarse wheaten bread and cold beef, and there were dark crescents beneath his eyes, tight lines around his mouth, and a kind of sag to his shoulders which was frighteningly unlike him. When he did meet her gaze, she saw, with a kind of sick horror, that the dead dream-state of Lathom still haunted him.

There was constant coming and going, the hurrying feet and churning hooves sending up a stagnant smell from the trampled grass. Around nine o'clock an ostentatious coach and six, with a glittering troop of outriders, drew up near the Palatine standard which marked Rupert's command post. Newcastle had arrived.

He made his entrance with all the pomp of an actor pretending to be a great General in a play. His gentlemen posed in their beautiful armour, elaborately courteous, full of effusive flattery. They were taken aback to be greeted by this powerfully-built, suntanned foreigner with his clipped speech and abrupt manner, silencing their carefully rehearsed words with a brusque:

'My Lord, I wish you had come sooner with your forces but I hope we shall yet have a glorious day.'

Newcastle raised a supercilious eyebrow, and there was a split-second pause; 'You intend to fight, Your Highness?'

Rupert's face hardened, instantly guarded. 'Of course, my Lord. And pray explain why you have been so tardy in arriving?'

A flush spread across the Marquis' thin cheeks, and he replied stiffly. 'Two reasons, sir. Firstly, our men have been plundering the deserted camp of the enemy—'

'What did you get?' The Prince cut across Newcastle's smoothly modulated voice.

It took a moment for the Marquis to adjust to this rude interruption, then: 'A large amount of ammunition and four thousand pairs of boots,' he said.

'Splendid!' For the first time Rupert smiled at him. 'You'll give us half!'

Newcastle chose to ignore this mercenary demand. 'The second reason, Your Highness, is because a great many of our soldiers have refused to march until they have received their arrears in pay. I have left General King to bring them back to their obedience.'

'God's blood! And how long will that take him?' Rupert shouted. 'The enemy are weak at present. I think we should attack at once before they get wind of our intention and draw their foot back from Tadcaster.'

Newcastle risked his spotless boots across the stretch of muddy ground between them. 'Would it not be more prudent to wait patiently? My spies report much dissension among their Generals. I would swear they will break up their camps and depart, ere long.'

'Nothing venture, nothing have!' Rupert replied; some of the Marquis' theatricality seemed to have rubbed off on him. 'I have a positive and absolute command to fight the enemy, which in obedience, and according to my duty, I am bound to perform!'

Newcastle had already spent a wretched night soul-searching, tempted to resign, bitterly offended by the Palsgrave's offhand message, delivered by Goring in a way calculated to cause problems. He felt that he was justified in his indignation; after all, he had raised and maintained the whole Northern army at enormous cost, had sacrificed his love of peaceful, artistic pursuits to become a very passable soldier. And now, how was he received? By this haughty upstart, Royal though he might be, tousled, unwashed, wearing a dirty shirt, as lean and gaunt as a marauding wolf, telling him what to do! Just as if the Marquis were no more than some member of staff come to get his orders for the day!

'You have had a direct command from His Majesty?' Newcastle managed to mould his lips round the words.

Rupert did not look at him, slinging his baldrick across his wide shoulders. 'I have, my Lord.'

'May I see it?'

'No, sir, you may not. You'll take my word for it.'

The air was crisp with animosity. Rupert's officers had come up to attention at his back; there was some surreptitious easing of swords in scabards, and Newcastle's Yorkist gentry eyed these bearded, flint-faced henchmen apprehensively.

The Marquis managed to cling to the rather splendid image of himself which filled his imagination and his genuine feeling for the Sovereign whom he had sworn to serve. What would happen to King Charles if all true noblemen of superlative breeding left him to the mercies of such uncultured ruffians as his nephew?

'Very well, Your Highness, I am ready and willing, for my part, to obey you in all things, no otherwise than if His Majesty was here in person himself—I will never shun a fight, for I have no other ambition but to live and die a loyal subject.'

Rupert calmed down, ready to be more reasonable at Newcastle's compliance with his wishes, and he had already abandoned the idea of falling upon the Allies rear without waiting for the York foot to arrive. The morning was wearing on anyhow and not only would he be blamed for rashness if such an attack failed, but really the opportunity had slipped away.

As the day advanced, the atmosphere became increasingly humid, the leaden sky lowering over the activity on both sides. There was some skirmishing and sporadic firing. A prisoner was brought to Rupert who asked him:

'Is Cromwell there? And will he fight?'

The man nodded, and, to his astonishment, was sent back to his own lines with the message that they should have "fighting enough!"

To which Cromwell retorted: 'If it please God, so shall he!'

Damaris' carriage was parked near Lord Newcastle's, close against Wilstop Wood. 'Heavens, how I wish they would get on with it, if they are going to fight at all today.' She fanned herself with her hand, little beads of sweat breaking through her rouge.

'It will start—all too soon.' Meriel had insisted on coming with them, though most of the other camp-followers had gone into York.

Mallory pulled in beside them and Damaris handed him a wineskin. He took a long swig, wiping his mouth on the back of his glove.

'I think the Prince was right when he wanted to go after them earlier,' he was shading his eyes with one hand, peering across at the enemy ranks. 'Then we should have had naught but horse and dragoons to fight.'

Rupert's horsemen fidgeted, watching uneasily as more and more men swelled the Allies regiments, and both armies engaged in the elaborate process of drawing into battaglia, with the cavalry on either flank, the hedgehogs of pikemen between rows of musketeers in the centre.

The Royalist infantry sat themselves down in their ranks, opened their snapsacks, ate their rations, talked, smoked and cleaned their arms.

'Man, are they never going to begin?'

muttered a young Welsh boy, one of the new levies who had not yet taken part in a pitched battle, though pleased enough with the action at Bolton, Stockport and Liverpool which had put money into their pockets.

A more experienced musketeer scratched about under the broad-brimmed grey hat which covered his greasy locks, hoisted his bandolier, heavy with the made-up cartridges, the leather bag containing spare bullets, and a powder flask, and squinted at the lines of men who formed the opposition among the trampled rye.

'If I know anything about it, that ain't all their lads, not by a long shot. I think there's going to be a tough bout ahead.' A ripple passed down their ranks. 'Ah—there's General King come at last. See, he's brought the Marquis' foot with 'im. That's them, in those undyed wool jackets. They call 'em, "Newcastle's Whitecoats." '

It was midafternoon, and all day the Prince had been forced to wait and see his chances of victory ticking away. The enemy infantry back from their vain trek, were taking up their positions; across the humid heat of the July day came the sound of metrical psalms. Rupert and James King

328

faced each other for the first time in six years and the Palsgrave's eyes were frosty as he looked down on the Scottish commander, now elevated to the peerage and entitled Lord Eythin. They had fought together at Vlotho, that battle which had led to Rupert being captured. King had been blamed for letting him down badly, there had been hints of treachery, he did not forgive the imputation and had borne a grudge ever since. The Prince could place little faith in him, though he was a professional and knew his trade. He was too sharp a reminder of the past, that first defeat, those dreary years at Lintz. His appearance on the field brought with it an odour of calamity.

King stumped up to him, having spent an irritating day calling his surly troopers every name in the book, now finding himself quite incapable of the courtesy with which Newcastle cloaked his frustrating objections. After a curt exchange of greetings, he immediately started to criticize the way in which the Prince had placed his forces, saying that they were too close to the enemy.

Rupert kept his temper. 'Very well, my Lord. I can withdraw them a little.'

'No, sir,' said King truculently, seeming deliberately to forget that he was not still addressing the very young colonel whom he had known at Vlotho. 'It's too late.'

The Prince refrained from making the obvious remark that if it was "too late" it was due to King's dilatory appearance. He showed him the sketch map he had made, explaining how he meant to conduct the operation. King studied it, pulling at his grizzled moustache while Newcastle hovered at his shoulder. He had made him his right-hand man, glad to let him take over the disagreeable aspects of the York defence which left him free to lose himself in his luxurious library. Now he had a pang of unwonted doubt in his own judgement in giving him so much power, especially when King unceremoniously tossed back the chart with a snort.

'By God, sir, it is very fine on paper, but there is no such thing in the field.' The small, sharp eyes ran over the imposing figure of the youngster who was now his superior in every way and he added, tauntingly: 'Sir, your forwardness lost us the day in Germany, where yourself was taken prisoner!'

There was stunned silence save for the

colonies of rooks rising in noisy complaint, alarmed by the gun-fire which burst forth occasionally from either side to keep everyone on their toes. Venetia could feel the effort which Rupert was making to check his temper and give King no chance to speak of him again as a hot-headed young fool! But his adjutants were bristling on his behalf. Was it to meet such carping inaction, coupled with Newcastle's tepidity, that they had marched and fought from Shrewsbury to York? And yesterday's twenty mile slog when they had bullied their grumbling soldiers to keep up speed so that the whole manoeuvre had been carried out with unlooked for rapidity, was this done to see the fire drain out of their beloved chief?

Newcastle was most embarrassed by his Commander's lack of manners. He might not like Rupert much, but was shocked to the core at the way the fellow dared to address a grandson of King James!

The muscles tightened about Rupert's mouth. 'I think we should take the initiative and attack.'

Newcastle and King, banding together, began to argue. The Prince looked from one to the other, asked one or two questions, made a few points, but for the most part listened in silence. At last he glanced up at the coppery, thunder-heavy sky, shrugged wearily and gave in.

A hush fell on the two armies, staring across the ditch at each other, nearly fifty thousand men, mostly of the same nationality. For hours they had endured the gruelling test of being without cover and at a range close enough to see every detail, with intermittent showers adding to the discomfort.

The evening set in with ominous gloom, and distant thunder made the horses toss their manes and sidle nervously. The unearthly light when a struggling sun admits defeat and dies behind a blanket of dense cloud, played over the array of men poised rank on rank, arms sparking sullenly, flags limp on the staves, the pikes as dense as stalks of wheat before it falls to the sickle. That gleaming display of destruction with its colour, its magnificence and its foolhardy gallantry, moved the heart in breathless excitement, stirred the spirit like a fanfaronade of war trumpets, and touched the soul with dread.

'Nothing will happen tonight,' Rupert swung out of his saddle, put up his hands and removed his helmet. He turned to Newcastle and spoke in a tone void of all expression. 'We will charge them tomorrow morning.'

His chaplain, William Lacy, was still mounted, and Rupert added: 'Have prayers said for the men before they are dismissed.'

'I have been thinking about the text, Your Highness,' Lacy replied. 'These words came to me—"The Lord God of gods, the Lord God of gods, he knoweth, and Israel shall know; if it be rebellion, or if in transgression against the Lord, save us not this day!" '

' 'Sdeath! Let us hope we win,' muttered Goring in Venetia's ear. 'For if not, those damned rebel rinse-pitchers over yonder are going to say we brought a curse upon ourselves which was accordingly answered by the Lord—*their* Lord, of course!'

When the sound of praying rose from each regiment along the Royalist lines, a loud, answering hymn of denunciation swelled from the throats of the Round-heads; the gloomy psalms rolling, dirge-like, above that dark mass of iron-clad troopers who watched for Cromwell's battle-word.

Boye loped over to greet the Prince, tail

swishing joyously, sharing the meat which servants had unpacked from straw-lined boxes. Newcastle had retired to his coach and was already enjoying a pipe of tobacco, and Venetia shared his relief that matters had been postponed—for one more night at least Rupert would not be at risk.

'God, my head aches!' he ran a hand through his hair, scanning the banked-up clouds. 'I hope the men are able to sup before it starts to pour.'

On the edge of the moorland which rose black to meet the sepia sky, the Royalist army was dismounting, grounding their pikes, resting their muskets, while, in the rear, the smoke from camp-fires spiralled towards the storm rushing in.

Suddenly the sky was rent by a blinding fork of lightning followed by a crash of thunder which broke overhead. Boye started to bark and the rain fell in great heavy drops. Venetia was snatching up the provisions, ready to dash for shelter when she stopped, head lifted. Above the clamour of the heavens, there was another much more alarming noise—cannon-fire and the steady pounding of hooves. The Allies had attacked.

With an oath Rupert was up and had

seized the bridle of the nearest horse, vaulting into the saddle, standing in the stirrups to see what was happening. From several points at once, officers pelted, sent by their generals to the command post. The Prince's crisp orders penetrated the din and, within minutes, he was at the head of his reserves, leading the cavalry to the aid of Lord Byron on his right wing, shouting: 'For God and for the King!'

Above the pealing tumult of the skies, the smarting sting of hailstones, the salvos, the yells and clash of steel, Rupert's voice rang in anger and incitement as he met his own regiment already in disorder and turning their backs on the enemy.

' 'Swounds, do you run?' he roared. 'Follow me!'

Byron's front line was being crushed back against his second by that indomitable wall of armoured horsemen who had splashed heavily across the intervening ditch. There was a great heave, then a counter-effort which restored the position, then another heave and Cromwell's well-timed fanatics were locked in sword to sword struggle with the best of the Prince's horse. Rupert fought like a madman, his blade an entrenchment which none passed, something more than human about him, while the long rapiers of his Lifeguard did terrible execution.

After the first immobilizing shock, Venetia pelted for cover, her shirt and breeches already soaked before she reached the coach. She slammed the door shut and looked from the window, but it was too far away to make any sense of the maelstrom of fighting glimpsed through the sulphurous glow of storm, smoke and fast enveloping night. She managed to get hold of Holmes, making him pause as he rushed past, the rain coursing like tears across his upturned face.

'Where is Boye?' she demanded.

'I don't know, madam. I thought he was with you.'

Usually the poodle was tied to one of the wagons when Rupert went into action, but this had all happened so quickly. She leaned further out, careless of the wet which poured onto her head and trickled down the back of her collar, calling his name repeatedly, hoping to hear an answering bark above the clamour.

Time became disjointed; tiny, fragmented vignettes imprinted themselves on Venetia's mind. A musketeer cursing because the lit end of his match-cord had gone out, a Catholic crossing himself, a pikeman spitting on his hands, amid the hellish racket of throbbing drums, trumpets blaring to the standard, and nature's cannonade dwarfing the human cacophony.

The Royalist musketeers still reeled from the shock of looking up from their suppers to see the enemy brigades rolling down the slope on top of them. The rain ruined their matches and powder and they stood no chance, armed with nothing but a musket-end, against a formed push of pikes. Goring had recovered quickly and was acquitting himself rather well against the Scots, so said the rumours, along with tales of Cromwell and Fairfax wounded. Some said that Byron had made a premature charge, but no one really knew anything, concerned only in straining every sinew to rally to their colours, to keep on their feet, to stay alive.

It was getting ever darker. Usually night called a halt to battles, but not to this one. From the direction of the greatest noise, the most fierce confusion, came the melancholy procession; two pikes and three swords with a cloak flung over all to make

337

an improvised stretcher, and on it a limp form, dyed darkly with blood and rain. A shot had smashed Jonathan's leg, severing an artery, and life was pumping out of him with every beat of his heart.

Kneeling in the mud, they tried to apply a scarf as a tourniquet, but nothing they could do stopped that relentless flow.

Meriel kept repeating in a hopeless monotone: 'Help him—help him.'

'Get him into the carriage,' Damaris recovered her wits. 'We'll drive to York and find a surgeon. You'll come, Venetia?'

'No—' Even now, with her brother dying, there was that overwhelming other. 'Where is the Prince?'

'In the thick of it—where else?' one of Jonathan's comrades replied. 'He has just led a counter-attack. Cromwell has retired to have his injury dressed.'

Cromwell—that name had reached Rupert's ears. He had wanted to fight Cromwell. Her brother was bleeding to death and all that she could think of was her lover. She was like a being split in two; one half holding Jonathan's head, her tears falling onto his waxen face, the other, in that press of hacking, sweating men, with Rupert.

If only it would stop raining. The thunder had rumbled away, but still water sluiced from on high as if the gods wept for the massacre below. It washed over Jonathan till the puddles on either side of the stretcher were red.

They settled him across one of the seats in the vehicle, and he no longer knew them, his breath rasping, eyes rolled up with only the whites showing between half-closed lids. Venetia stood outside in the deluge while the driver whipped up the horses and Damaris lurched at the window, yelling:

'Find Etienne! Tell him where I am. We'll see you in York!'

Strange and terrible were the things Venetia saw as she wandered on the battle's fringe, ever and again returning to the guards round Rupert's standard, dying a little each time a horse was led to the rear with its rider slumped on its neck, or dangling cross-ways over the saddle. But it was not the body of a tall, dark man of unearthly beauty. The legend held good; his life was charmed indeed.

The fighting was still hot, every pike thrust home, every musket levelled low, and the noise was deafening, the thundering hooves, the ringing armour, the maddened shouts, and the roar of artillery. Venetia traversed the broken ground, among the dismounted guns and shattered carriages, where the dead lay heaped. The distinctions which had separated them in life, these sons of a common country, seemed trifling now. Plumed helmet, plain steel cap, rolled in the mire together; the flowing lovelocks of the Cavalier drenched in the dark blood of the enthusiastic republican.

At one point, she found Arthur Trevor. He had ridden from Skipton with dispatches for the Prince and reined in his sweating bay when he saw her.

'Where is he?'

'I don't know.' She wanted to cling to that familiar figure, but could only stand at his stirrup and read her own dread mirrored in his eyes.

'I've coasted the country around,' he said. 'But not a man has been able to give me the least hope of where he is to be found. And the runaways from either sides which I have fallen into, so breathless, so speechless, so full of fears. Yet, some say that we have won, that Goring has carried the day. But you, madam? You should not be here. Let me bear you to a place of safety. Get up behind me.'

She shook her head. 'I cannot leave till I find the Prince. While the fighting continues, he is bound to remain—and where he is, there I must be.'

Trevor looked at her for an instant as if he thought she was mad, then dug the bloody rowels into his horse's scarred ribs and was gone into the gloom. Perhaps, in that sad hour of despair, she was indeed unhinged. Who could survive such carnage and remain totally sane? Oh, they might be ringing a premature carillon for victory in York Cathedral, but she had seen the irrecoverable disorder and Rupert's jaded cavalry fleeing along past Wilstrop Wood.

The rain had stopped and the moon came up, illuminating the field where those stubborn Yorkshire men, Newcastle's Whitecoats, refused to break. They were penned in White Sike Close, attacked in flank and rear by Cromwell's and Leslie's cavalry, but remaining unmoved as a rock amid the surges of the horse and foot hurled against them. So solid did their pikemen stand that dragoons were called in to force a gap for the troopers to enter. And when their square was broken, they still fought on, those who fell goring the bellies of the horses with sword or broken pike, before dying beneath the thrashing hooves. They refused to cry for quarter, cut down in their ranks until Fairfax crashed in among his troops, his face streaming with blood from a sword cut, beating up their weapons and shouting:

'Spare your countrymen!'

It was late—very late—no longer came any rallying cries. The Cavalier commanders who were able had withdrawn their shattered forces. Every soldier who could move had crept away to shelter, the weary to rest, the wounded to die. The constant rattle of fire had sputtered out to an occasional isolated shot. A hush shrouded the moor, broken only by the sound of men crying out in their agony.

Venetia roamed the stricken field, seeking one face only among the heaped up dead, sprawled as grotesquely as puppets whose strings had been abruptly severed. She came upon something which at first sight appeard to be a dead sheep. Why, her fogged mind argued, was the poor beast there? Had it strayed from its pasture? Certainly, under that cold, searching finger of moonlight, it was white and woolly like fleece, except where the blood was clotting blackly. Withdrawn, wondering, she contemplated this phenomenon, refusing to accept that it was Boye, already stiffening, lips retracted over his fangs in a silent, frozen snarl, blank eyes wide as if still searching for his master.

She looked down at her hands, seeing them wringing in woe in the blunt blades of moonshine, hearing a woman sobbing like a lost thing, and turning to trail after the sound—it was herself.

Michael found her at last, sitting on the tail-board of the Prince's sumpter-wagon, from which every guard had disappeared. He fell from his trembling horse, his voice cracking with relief:

'Venetia! Thank God I've found you! Come away—all is lost!'

'The Prince—where is the Prince?' was all that she would say, and he could not get her to move.

Thus they were captured by victorious Roundhead troopers galloping up to plunder the Prince's baggage, when the last of the Cavaliers had fled, leaving the bloodily contested moor to the Puritan fanatics and Cromwell.

FOURTEEN

As the Parliamentary cavalry jogged back to the field, they were raising hymns of praise to the Lord, after ruthlessly slaughtering fugitive Royalists. Predominant among them were those well-armoured troopers whom Oliver Cromwell had made his special unit. They gave thanks to God for his referential treatment of their side, never doubting that it was Divine intervention which had won the day, rather than superiority of numbers, regular pay, strict discipline and the astuteness of their commander who had turned to his own advantage the lessons learned from his adversary—Prince Rupert.

Venetia and Michael watched mutely as their captors hauled down Rupert's standard, the most important among the hundred or so taken. Anger burned through the numbness which blanketed feeling as she heard them calling him, "The greatest of Malignants, the Prince of Blood and Lies!" and saw them scrabbling in and out of his wagons. The money which had been intended to pay his troops now went to swell Roundhead coffers, and she and Michael were taken for interrogation to a farmhouse situated close to the wrecked rye fields.

Wet cloaks were steaming before the fire in the kitchen where some of the Allied commanders sat at the table, candles glowing on tankards and used platters, a muddle of papers, ink-horns and quills, all very similar to the paraphernalia which surrounded the Royalist officers. In fact, Venetia decided, it could very well have been a meeting of members of her own side. Most of them wore their hair long, but their doublets were unadorned, their collars plain, and when they talked the difference became more marked, for they seemed obsessed with the war-like phrases and names of the Israelite tribes of the Bible, firmly convinced that they were God's elect and that He was their General.

The sergeant escorting them saluted smartly, addressing the elderly man who appeared to be in command. 'Sir, we have captured Prince Rupert's sumpter-carts. These prisoners were close at hand.'

Lord Manchester turned kindly eyes to

them, but the gaze of everyone else was hard and unfriendly. Venetia wished that she made a more brave figure to do Rupert credit, but she was soaked to the skin, her teeth chattering with cold. Before anyone could speak, a figure stepped from the darkness beyond the candlelight. Venetia's flash of hope at recognizing him as Giles Fletcher, was dashed by his first words.

'I know them, sir. The man is Michael Haywood, one of the Prince's Lifeguard, and the woman is Venetia Denby, His Highness's concubine.'

Fletcher's revelation sparked off an immediate reaction. She felt the full blast of their outraged Puritan disgust and shrank closer to Michael, while Giles watched her like a cat who has had the unbelievable good fortune to come across an injured bird.

'I see God's hand in everything this day. The wicked are being delivered up unto us,' said the ugly, moon-faced man in his middle forties, seated by Manchester, staring at her from deep-set eyes under beetling brows. His forehead bore marks of severity, his mouth a touch of pride, and instinct told her that this was the owner of that new name, cropping up

346

with ever increasing frequency among those of Waller, Fairfax and Essex—Oliver Cromwell.

Fear was making a bad taste in her mouth—deep in his trust, Rupert had given her the key to the cyphers for the Royalist's correspondence. If they tortured her, she might tell all that she knew. But Giles had other ideas.

'Think what this means, sir. He will want her back, his Babylonian whore, that they may continue their iniquities together. We can use her as bait with which to trap him.'

'Fletcher, verily thou hast the cunning of Machiavelli.' The harsh flat voice of Cromwell held a grudging admiration.

'He won't do it!' Venetia flared up. 'You'll never catch Rupert like that!'

Cromwell ignored her. 'What have you in mind, Fletcher? Speak, man. If we could but take the Prince, the war would be as good as won.'

Giles' face was working with excitement. 'We'll send a trumpet into York. I hear that he has already reached there with the remains of his army. We can tell him that we hold her and suggest that he come to treat, then we can ambush him!'

Was this the same person who had enjoyed her father's hospitality for years? Once there had been a humane streak, though the rigidity had been apparent, but, none the less, they had all grown up together back home. A picture flashed through Venetia's memory, an embarrassing incident when Giles had shown that his interest in her had been more than neighbourly. It had been a night of harvest celebrations—she saw again the laden tables in her father's barn, the laughing faces of his farm-workers, the cider and ale flowing in abundance, and herself going out into the garden to cool down after the hectic dancing. Giles had followed her, begging her to be kind, pouring out the story of his unhappy, childless marriage—and she had been sorry for him, but had warned herself against any show of pity. She had been frightened by his insistence, running back to the merry-makers and Michael.

Now she experienced the same fear mingled with contempt as she spat out: 'D'you think Rupert is a fool? He'll guess your intent. For a start, you'll have to give him proof!'

Giles came close to her, pleased to see

her humiliated, her Prince beaten and her cause threatened. He was the type who would never forget an injury, prepared to use any means, religion, party or country, to gain power. Cromwell was a man after his own heart; Manchester was too gentle, well-mannered and aristocratic. Giles had offered his allegiance to the blunt, verbose Lieutenant-General, that efficient mixture of Welsh and English ancestry, who was already merging his spiritual scruples with his political aspirations.

His hand shot out and snatched at the thin chain around her throat. It snapped and he held aloft her locket, side-stepping as she grabbed for it.

'Look, sir. 'Tis his picture. My spies were right when they reported that she wore it always as a keepsake of her demon lover. She should be burned as a witch who has lain with the Devil!'

He flung her into the arms of a grinning soldier who held her fast while Giles chopped off a lock of her hair. 'We'll send Prince Robber those mementoes of his mistress, and she shall put her signature to the letter. That will be proof enough!'

'My Lord Manchester! This is monstrous!' Michael protested, struggling with the guards. 'Mistress Denby is a gentle-woman, not a camp whore!'

Manchester ordered the man to release her. 'There is no call for such hard usage, Fletcher. But your idea is sound. I shall leave the details in your capable hands.'

'I'll not sign it!' Hysteria was threatening to swamp her reason, the sights, sounds and horrors of the day crowding in on her like a nightmare from which she had no hope of waking. Cromwell's face, marred with tight lines of repression, seemed to swim in space above her.

'It will do little good to be unhelpful, madam.'

His voice held neither animosity nor threat; his only desire to act in the most speedy, profitable manner. A big man, with heavy features, filled with the conviction that he was God's mouth-piece, for whom the Civil War had become something of a Holy Crusade.

Venetia wanted to smash her fist into that dedicated face. She remembered the slaughter of the Whitecoats; they had died out of sheer Yorkshire stubbornness, not particularly driven by any sense of love or loyalty. She was blessed with both, therefore she could surely yield up her life as bravely.

'Kill me,' she demanded.

Cromwell's eyes were cold. 'Madam, mock heroics will avail you naught.' He turned to Manchester, barely able to conceal his irritation with his superior; already they disagreed on many issues and Cromwell was fast gathering a party for himself which was likely to split the Roundheads into hostile factions, not unlike the troubles in the Royalist camp. 'I suggest, my Lord, that if the lady persists in this obstinate attitude, Mr Haywood pays the price. At dawn, we will draw up a firing party. He will be shot with his back against the farm-house wall.'

'No!' Her lips framed the denial.

'I think it may cause difficulties for our own prisoners in the hands of the Delinquents,' Manchester demurred.

Giles shared Cromwell's impatience with these niceties. 'My Lord, we all know that the Prince is the most evil of the King's counsellors. Can we but take him, their forces will collapse.'

'I am prepared to die,' Michael said quietly.

'Don't listen to him. I will sign.' Venetia

heard her own voice speaking as if it were someone else.

Satisfied, Cromwell stood, begging Manchester's permission to withdraw. 'I must go away alone to perform a painful duty, my Lord.'

'Ah, yes, my dear fellow—I had heard that your nephew died today. A brave young man, and now you must send word to his mother.' Manchester sighed for all of equal courage, on both sides, who had stained the turf with their blood. He was glad that this slender girl standing defiantly before him had relieved him of the necessity of ordering yet another death. They would have him believe that she was a whore and a witch, denying the sincerity and a kind of purity which transformed her white, tear-streaked face.

There was a corporal at the door, carrying something. He came across and dumped his burden on the table.

'Sir, 'tis that accursed cur, the Prince's dog, who was valued by him more than honest creature of more worth!'

Giles leaped forward eagerly to peer at the carcass. 'Give Glory, all Glory to God! The Prince's wicked familiar is slain!'

The soldier was appealing to Manchester.

'Why, look'ee, sir, the lads want to know if they can use it for target practice, seeing as how 'twas no mortal beast. They have already cut off his ears to make him crop-headed, like us, instead of a shag-polled Cavalier.' With a grin, he raised the bloody, mutilated head, displaying their handiwork.

Cromwell gave a shout of laughter, but Manchester rose to his feet in disgust. 'For the love of Christ, man! 'Twas only a poor dumb brute, following his master into battle! You'll give it decent burial at once, d'you hear?'

The fellow backed away awkwardly, his jest fallen flat, and Venetia could not tear her eyes from the bundle in his arms. Boye, bereft of those soft silken ears which had pricked at the sound of Rupert's voice, so often caressed by his strong, sensitive fingers.

The farmer's wife, Mistress Hazeldean, lit a rush and conducted Venetia to an upper room. A thin sad woman, not really a bad one, owing fealty to none, her only concern to keep her children fed in the holocaust which had hit the land, first Royalist, now Roundhead troops unceremoniously billeted upon her. It was small wonder that there was a dash of vinegar about her speech.

In the dormer bedroom which smelt faintly of herbs, she fixed the rush holder, glancing at the sentry who had taken up his post, leaning against the door. Venetia was shivering violently, and looked ill enough to drop.

'I'll get you some clothes,' offered the woman, and ransacked the linen-press. A woollen skirt, laced bodice and plain blouse came out of one drawer. Thick knitted hose, a shift and black shoes from another. 'There now, get into those, and I'll dry your things.' The guard was watching in sly anticipation but she soon had him out of the room. 'And you, sirrah, can wait in the passage while the young lady changes.'

'Lady!' He spat to show his contempt. 'Captain Fletcher says we shall burn her after we've caught the Devil Prince!'

Mistress Hazeldean made no comment, holding wide the door, jerking her head in the direction of the corridor and closing it firmly after him, then:

'Damned soldiers!' she said. 'Coming into folk's houses, as if they owned them!'

Venetia wondered if the woman might

354

be bribed, then remembered that she had nothing to offer. She prayed that Rupert would ignore the letter, stifling the small voice which whispered that if he loved her, he would at least attempt a rescue. There was no time to sound her out, for Giles was hammering at the door, demanding admittance, ordering away both the sentry and the reluctant goodwife.

Helplessly Venetia sought an avenue of escape, but the only window was almost at floor level, letting in a thin strip of moonlight which flashed across Giles' boots as he came towards her. He was well armed, with pistols slung on a belt across his shoulder, and a sword which knocked against his left leg as he walked.

It was difficult to believe that he really meant to harm her. They shared a common birthplace and she wanted to suggest that they stop this masquerade, find Michael and ride home to the Cotswolds together.

For a moment it seemed as if he had the same thought. 'Well, Venetia, how fortunate that we should meet again.'

She watched his lean face with its high forehead and fleshy nose, his piercing eyes used to probing in his role as a Roundhead agent.

'Fortunate for you, perhaps.'

Under the faintly shadowed moustache, his smile deepened, that cold lift of the lips which never reached his eyes. 'I need your signature, my dear.'

'You know that it is useless.'

'D'you mean that your famous Prince will not bother to aid his harlot?' His mockery cut her. 'That he may consider the risk too great for such as you, and that there will be other trollops who will take your place within a week?'

She could not begin to explain the Prince's probable reasons; his instinct for treachery and his duty which would dictate that he retreat, not for his own safety, but for that of the King's army. Only when this was done might he make a bid to save her.

The insidious voice was going on: 'We have told him that you will be tried on the charge of witchcraft. I expect he has a strong imagination—he will know exactly what the punishment will be.'

He moved swiftly, locking a hold on her impossible to break. Her arm was bare from wrist to elbow and he forced it close to the rush flame, his pupils retracting, twin points of light, boring into hers as pain made her gasp. He let her go and she stumbled back, pressing her palm to her blistered skin.

He was smiling still. 'Fire is agonizing, is it not? Have you ever seen a witch burn, Venetia?'

She would call his bluff; this cruel law was no longer put into operation. 'Witches are hanged, these days.'

'Not always,' he said with unconcealed relish. 'In the Eastern Counties the authorities are bringing back the stake. And you will be a very special case.'

Giles was enjoying himself; still the spiteful boy who had allowed his ferret to savage her rabbits and fed her song-bird to the cat, always the first to come up with ingenious ideas for destructive games.

'How is your wife?' Venetia asked suddenly.

His eyes narrowed in anger. That sickly girl with her wealth, her repugnance of his embraces, her inability to produce a live heir. Prudence—his wife—always bearing, always burying. In Venetia's face he read her awareness of this, the scornful curl of her lip showing that she was comparing the sad situation with her own passion for Rupert. Months before he had received reports about the Prince's mistress, crushing back his envy when he realized who it was, forcing himself to be patient, certain that, with careful manipulation of circumstances, his time would come.

Lately, visions had arisen to torment him whenever he thought of her with the Prince. He could almost believe the accusations of sorcery which he would level against her, so disturbed was he by his own inflamed imagination which dwelt on her while he embraced Prudence. Prudence—that skinny, shrinking jade who always lay like a block of wood in his arms, her silent protests letting him know that it was only her sense of wifely duty which allowed him the use of her body. Dreams of Venetia pursued him still, when he slept at last, sated but unsatisfied.

Now she was here, helpless under his hands, and he asked, huskily: 'Do you love the Prince, Venetia? Tell me what you do when you lie with him—talk to me about it.'

Venetia could feel her psyche shrivelling away in horror from the unclean rims of his mind, just as her flesh had cringed from the flame. 'You are disgusting.' Her voice rang with loathing. 'No wonder Prudence hates you.'

Confident that this time she could not escape him, he pressed closer to her, still talking, in a kind of chant: 'He is very tall, isn't he, this demon lover of yours? Very strong. I have heard it said of him, that he has the face of an angel, and the temper of a devil—such a powerful, handsome man. Does he please you, Venetia? Does he rouse your body to ecstasy when he fondles your naked skin?'

'Stop it!' Venetia wanted to gag, feeling as if she had swallowed a mouthful of dirt. 'Let me sign the paper and take yourself off!'

He relaxed his hold, watching her keenly. 'I could help you to get back to him.'

'What do you mean?'

'An escape could be arranged.'

'How can you do that?' Her intellect warned her to beware, yet hope flared up.

'I am in charge here for the rest of the night. It would not be too difficult to engineer.' His self-satisfaction was nauseating, there was no doubt that he had wangled himself into a position of some importance.

'How much?' she snapped.

'How much?' he repeated, puzzled.

'Your price, Captain Fletcher. I cannot believe that you would aid me for nothing.'

His harsh laughter rang under the low beams. 'Oh, you are right, my dear Venetia.' He was so sure of himself. 'I am no gentleman of noble lineage fired by chivalrous motives, as your father once told me in no uncertain terms. Naturally, a low fellow, such as I, will always be on the watch for his own interests. My price is this—your body in exchange for a dismissed sentry and a pass through the pickets.'

'How will you explain my disappearance to your commanding officers?' She knew that this conversation had been fated to take place between them always, in the same way in which she had been certain of one day meeting Rupert. It did not seem strange to be here, playing for time, on the edge of Marston Moor where the unburied dead lay in their thousands, under the pitiless moon. How would Rupert feel when he read the letter? What desolation would strike into him, already crucified by defeat and humiliation? Rupert, her soul's star.

She was bargaining sordidly with this

man who wanted her body—and she shuddered with abhorrence, committed to the Prince to whom she surrendered with sublime happiness, his embrace a blissful seal of love, and yet with Giles the very same act would be a loathsome test of endurance.

'I can't do it,' she said.

'A witch—' he reminded softly. 'They will try you as a witch. I have known you for many years and will not hesitate to testify against you. When you have been proven guilty, they will conduct you back to your cell and shave off your hair, then take pincers and tear out your finger and toe nails and drag you to the stake, pile faggots around you and burn you alive. In your agony you will pray for death, and, by that time, your Prince's head will be adorning a pike on Tower Bridge.'

He took her hands, pulling them down from her face. 'Don't cry, Venetia. Lie with me, and you shall return to Rupert. Save yourself, and him. Come, let me look for witch-marks on the secret places of your body.'

She twisted away from his grasp. 'How do I know that you will not cheat me?'

'I'll give you back your locket and your

361

hair—you can take the letter too. I am well trusted here.'

'And Michael will be free too?' She was trying desperately to think of every eventuality. He nodded, and she added: 'I have no guarantee that you will not go back on your word.'

'That is very true.' This cat-and-mouse game appealed to him. 'But you have no alternative, have you?'

'You had this planned from the moment I stepped into the kitchen, didn't you?' she accused.

He shrugged, wanting to boast to this woman who so openly despised him. 'The war has been good to me. I hope to do much better out of it as time passes. There will be parcels of land and titles to be shared out among the friends of Oliver Cromwell.'

'Your side have not won yet!'

'This is the beginning of the end. Can you doubt it, after today?'

Doom thundered like a roll of drums —the sense of defeat as strong as her conviction that Giles intended to betray her. He would take her, and then revoke his promise. She would protest to both Manchester and Cromwell, telling them what he had done; and he would stoutly deny her charges, while they pretended to believe him.

She was so tired that she could not think clearly, her very bones seemed to be crumbling with fatigue and her eyes smarted as if there was grit under the lids.

'Lie down on the bed, sweeting,' Giles was purring. 'I will write a safe-conduct pass.'

He scribbled away busily, using the shelf of the press as a table. Because he was a methodical person, he carefully laid his pistol, sword and dagger beside the bed, before stretching out at her side.

'Venetia—you are so warm, so beautiful—' His hand was passing over her hair. 'Why can you not love me as you do the Bloody Prince? You deceived Haywood for his sake, did you not? What madness is it which runs in your veins?'

He muttered in a crazy fashion as he struggled with her clothing, his mouth coming down painfully on hers, jarring her lips with his teeth. She shoved against him as hard as she could, her resolve melting into disgust.

'That's right, leaguer-bitch! Fight me!'

he jeered and fetched her a blow across the face which half stunned her. 'When the Prince is a prisoner, I shall enjoy telling him that you put up some resistance before I took you!'

His laughter roared in her ears, the cruel mockery of the taunting bully, and he was still laughing when she reached over, seized his knife and plunged it into his back. He gave a grunt and slumped heavily on her.

Escape. There was no room for other thought. So much horror had washed over her since that fateful morning that her emotions were in a state of suspension. She rolled Giles over and searched through his pockets, unmoved by the blood which was spreading out in an ever widening circle on his shirt. Systematically, she took the things which belonged to her, as well as money and weapons. Michael must be found and then they would get away.

Giles had planned his night of pleasure with characteristic thoroughness. A keg of ale, secretly appropriated, had ensured that the guard would absent himself. Venetia could hear him singing happily and drunkenly somewhere downstairs, as she opened the bedroom door.

It was all so effortless, like a dream.

She moved lightly, feeling disembodied, almost sure that she was invisible and could float right past the soldiers without being noticed. But to Michael she was solid enough, and he sprang up with a start when she turned the key in the lock.

She thrust the pistol into his hand, giving him no time to argue, her only concern to put as much distance as was humanly possible between themselves and the farm before daylight.

They stood at the head of the stairs, looking down into the black well. Deep in the bowels of the house, a clock boomed the hour—it was two in the morning and quiet as the grave. Even the sentry was asleep, his head in a puddle of ale on the kitchen table.

A door behind them opened abruptly and Mistress Hazeldean was framed against the candlelight. Michael jabbed the pistol into her ribs.

'Lord save us, sir, don't shoot!' She understood the situation at a glance. 'I'll not raise the alarm!'

In her bedchamber, Michael kept her covered while Venetia negotiated, using Giles' money as a further incentive.

'You'll not get through tonight,' the

goodwife shook her head. 'There is still much activity out there. I'll hide you, and later you can mingle with the country folk.'

There was a cupboard built at the back of the room and she led them there, pushing her way among the musty clothing.

Michael held the candle, shielding it from the garments so that they did not catch alight. Mistress Hazeldean fumbled with the panelling, seeking a vital knot-hole. A narrow door opened, a draught of cold damp air rushed from the black aperture beyond.

'You'll not be the first runaways to hide here. This secret has been handed down through the Hazeldean women—the men were never told it—they blab too freely. I'll bring you food and drink when I can—you'll find a bucket for the relief of nature.'

While she talked, she gathered up blankets, thrusting them into Venetia's arms, and they stepped into the priest-hole. The panel slid into place behind them and both had the sobering thought that perhaps she had gone to betray them.

'We'll fight,' said Michael grimly. 'I'll

take a couple of the bastards with me before I die!' He settled down to keep guard, pistol cocked.

'Michael, d'you think she means to leave us here to die of starvation?' The full terror of the day's happenings were swamping reason in this claustrophobic situation, making her tremble violently. Michael held her firmly, drawing her head onto his shoulder, as he sat with his back pressed against the wall. His voice was soothing as in the old days when they had played hide-and-seek, secreting themselves away from the others, waiting in the same dry-mouthed suspense. He reassured her, making his tone confident, rocking her gently like a frightened infant, so that she slept at last, drugged with exhaustion.

With the dawn, Fletcher's murder was discovered. Michael and Venetia clung to one another, listening to the shouts, the bumps and crashes as the house was searched. She had the wild urge to jump up, hammer on the panelling and scream out their presence, ending the nerve-racking tension. But she did not do so, burying her face against Michael's chest and praying instead.

Tiny dots of light from air-vents high above their heads, made it possible to judge the passing of time. The day passed and it grew dark again. True to her word the goodwife pushed in food. They dozed, woke to speak in whispers, and slept again. Venetia found herself glad that it was Michael with her and not Rupert. With his height and size such a cramped compartment would have been torture, and she could not bear to think of him uncomfortable or cold, hungry or unhappy.

Michael told her something of the battle, of how Rupert, separated from his Lifeguard, had striven to rally a few deserted followers, but in vain. Wherever a group was gathered, the Roundhead horse were upon them in force, and eventually the Prince was left alone. Michael's last sight of him was when he broke from his assailants and roused his destrier to one final effort, clearing a high fence into a bean-field.

Early next morning Mistress Hazeldean came again, saying that it was safe to leave. They stumbled from their nook, blinking like owls in daylight, and she fed them and found Michael rough clothing as a disguise. 'I can't let you have horses.' She was apologetic. 'They've taken all but a couple of spavined nags which I must keep for the ploughing if we are not to starve. I'll put you on the right road and you'll have to make your own way.'

It was a sobering experience, to walk calmly away from shelter and into the open ground bordering the moor. No one heeded them, taking them to be either spectators drawn by ghoulish curiosity, or else some of the villagers who had helped dig the shallow pits into which the dead had been tumbled, soon to become no more than a melancholy legend of the bleak, windswept heath.

Venetia was eager to push on to York, strength pouring into her at the thought of reaching Rupert. It was afternoon when they entered by Micklebar Gate, to find the streets filled with wounded, most of them in a sorry state, helped as much as possible by the citizens who were panicking, some already packing up and leaving. The Prince had departed at dawn, and the Roundheads would be back to besiege them again.

Venetia wanted to sit down and cry, but Michael would not allow this, insisting that they search until they found someone who could give them news. And, after a deal of enquiry and false trails, they came upon Thomas Carter. He was able to tell them what had happened, details which he omitted filled in by the players who were still dazed by the shock under which all were reeling.

'Ah, my dear, our Prince did not give in readily. When he had hidden for a while, he rounded up such fellows as he could find unparalysed with panic and led them to where narrow lanes afforded the only approach to York. He lined the hedges, and fired so fiercely upon the pursuers, that even Cromwell stopped and called them off. He was one of the last to get back here, dropping in with his weary officers about eleven at night.'

Venetia was hunched up, rocking in misery. 'Oh, if we'd only left sooner, I should not have missed him.'

'Sometime during the turmoil of that night, Rupert, King and Newcastle came face to face and warm words were exchanged.' Carter continued, and Venetia could well picture the scene. Warm words! Surely this must be the understatement of the year!

'General King asked him what he

370

intended to do, and the Prince made answer: "I will rally my men." '

The tired faces lit up, they nodded their approval of this stout reply, and Carter's voice strengthened as he went on:

'Then the General says, "Know you what Lord Newcastle will do?", and the Marquis himself replies, "I will go to Holland," looking upon all as lost. The Prince would have him endeavour to recruit his forces, but, "No," says he, "I will not endure the laughter of the Court." King was determined to go with him, though Rupert tried vainly to detain them and, in the end, he let them depart, wasting no more time, but he was very angry.'

'As he had every right to be!' blazed Venetia. How unfair of the Marquis to run away, leaving all the onus of failure on Rupert, as well as the heavy work of reorganizing his shattered forces for their dangerous march south.

She jumped to her feet. 'I must go to him.'

Carter reached out a hand to clasp one of hers. 'My dear, wait for us. We but delayed to arrange your brother's funeral.

371

As soon as Meriel is fit to travel, we shall follow the army.'

Jonathan had died in the coach before they reached York, and now Venetia mounted the wooden staircase to find his mistress and try to bring consolation. But it was Meriel who comforted her when grief surged up in an uncontrollable torrent and she cried until it seemed that there could be no more tears left within her.

At last utterly spent, the two women huddled together for a long time and then Meriel stirred. 'I must go and help father. He gets into such a wax if I'm not there to sort things out. We'll be away from here by nightfall. Will you come with me and see Jonathan's grave before we leave?'

They managed to find a few flowers and took them to that new mound of earth in a secluded corner of the churchyard.

'We buried his sword with him,' said Meriel softly. 'Laying it on top of his coffin.'

'We won't forget you, Jonathan,' whispered Venetia, kneeling on the turf, the soil fine and warm under her hand. 'When the war is over, we'll come back and fix a headstone, I promise.'

Meriel's touch was gentle on her bowed shoulder. 'He is not there, Venetia. 'Tis but a husk which lies rotting beneath the earth. It was selfish of me to grieve for him, this only made him sad and held him fast to those poor remains, but now he is free to come and go at will, like that bird there.'

She pointed to where a skylark was soaring, high in the blue vault above, its joyous notes barely discernible to their ears. But Michael's eyes were still on his friend's last resting-place and he said quietly:

' "Oh, blessed Peace!
to thy soft arms through death
itself we flee;
Battles and camps and fields
and victory
are but the rugged steps
that lead to thee!" '

And they turned their backs on York and its unhappy memories, setting out in search of the Prince.

The story of Venetia and Rupert continues in the sequel, CAVALIER.

373

BIBLIOGRAPHY

Ashley, Maurice: *Life in Stuart England* (1964)

Bund, J.W.W.: *The Civil War in Worcestershire* (1905)

Burton, Elizabeth: *The Jacobeans at Home* (1962)

Burne, A.H. and Young, P.: *The Great Civil War, 1642-1646* (1959)

Cattermole, R.: *The Great Civil War of Charles I and the Parliament* (1841)

Chapman, Hester, W.: *The Tragedy of Charles II* (1964)

Clarendon, Earl of: *The History of the Great Rebellion* (1819)

Coate, Mary: *Cornwall in the Great Civil War and Interregnum 1642-1660* (1930)

Edgar, F.T.R.: *Sir Ralph Hopton. The King's Man in the West* (1968)

Farrow, W.J.: *The Great Civil War in Shropshire* (1926)

Ferguson, B.: *Rupert of the Rhine* (1952)

Firth, C.H.: *The Journal of Prince Rupert's Marches, September 1642-July 1646* (1898)

Granville, R.: *The King's General in the West. The Life of Sir Richard Granville* (1908)

Hibbert, Christopher: *Charles I* (1968)

Hole, Christine: *The English Housewife of the 17th Century* (1953)

Lattimer, J.: *Annals of Bristol* (1908)

McChesney, Dora Greenwell: *Rupert, by the Grace of God—* (1899)

Nagel, Lawson C.: *Prince Rupert's Blue-coats. The Story of a Civil War Regiment* (1973)

Oman, Carola: *Elizabeth of Bohemia* (1938)

Robinson, Derek: *The Shocking History of Bristol* (1973)

Howsell, M.C.: *The Life-story of Charlotte de la Tremoille, Countess of Derby* (1905)

Scott, Eva: *Rupert, Prince Palatine* (1900)

Shelmerdine, J.M.: *Introduction to Woodstock* (1971)

Smith, G.R.: *Without Touch of Dishonour. Life of Sir Henry Slingsby* (1968)

Toynbee, Margaret and Young, P.: *Cropredy Bridge. The Campaign and Battle* (1970)

Tucker, John and Winstock, L.S.: *The English Civil War. A Military Handbook* (1972)

Varley, F.J.: *The Siege of Oxford, 1642-1646* (1932)

Warburton, E.: *Memoirs of Prince Rupert and the Cavaliers* (1849)

Watson, D.R.: *The Life and Times of Charles I* (1972)

Web, J.: *Memorials of the Civil War in Herefordshire* (1879)

Wedgewood, C.V.: *The King's War, 1641-1647* (1958)

Wenham, P.: *The Great and Close Siege of York* (1970)

Wilkinson, Clennel: *Prince Rupert the Cavalier* (1934)

Winstock, L.S.: *Songs and Marches of the Roundheads and Cavaliers* (1971)

Woolrych, Austin: *Battles of the English Civil War* (1961)

Wroughton, John: *The Civil War in Bath and North Somerset* (1973)

Young, P. and Tucker, N.: *The Civil War. Richard Atkyns and John Gwyn* (1967)

Young, P.: *Edgehill 1642. The Campaign and the Battle* (1967)

Young, P.: *Marston Moor 1644. The Campaign and the Battle* (1970)

Young, P.: *The English Civil War Armies* (1973)

Other DALES Romance Titles
In Large Print

RUTH ABBEY
House By The Tarn

MARGARET BAUMANN
Firefly

NANCY BUCKINGHAM
Romantic Journey

HILDA PERRY
A Tower Of Strength

IRENE LAWRENCE
Love Rides The Skies

HILDA DURMAN
Under The Apple Blossom

DEE SUTHERLAND
The Snow Maiden